THRAXAS
and the
SORCERERS

By Martin Scott

THRAXAS
and the
SORCERERS

Martin Scott

Sign up for the free Orbit Newsletter at
www.orbitbooks.co.uk

An *Orbit* Book

First published in Great Britain by Orbit 2001

Copyright © 2001 by Martin Scott

The moral right of the author has been asserted.

A CIP catalogue record for this book
is available from the British Library.

ISBN 1 84149 077 6

Typeset by Palimpsest Book Production Ltd
Polmont, Stirlingshire
Printed and bound in Great Britain by
Mackays of Chatham plc, Chatham, Kent

Orbit
A Division of
Little, Brown and Company (UK)
Brettenham House
Lancaster Place
London WC2E 7EN

0216534 0

CHAPTER
ONE

Turai is in the grip of one of the fiercest winters in memory. Ice lies in thick sheets over the frozen streets. Snow falls incessantly from the grey sky. The vicious north wind whips it through the alleyways, where it comes to rest in huge banks deep enough to bury a man. The citizens groan in frozen misery and the church sends up prayers for relief. The poor huddle miserably in their slums while the wealthy hide behind the walls of their mansions. In the taverns, great log fires struggle to keep the cruel weather at bay. Deep inside the imperial palace, the King's Sorcerers expend their powers in keeping the Royal family warm. Winter in Turai is hell.

Three hours before dawn, the snow is falling heavily and the wind is howling. No creature dares show its face. The beggars, whores, dogs, dwa addicts, thieves and drunks that normally infest the streets have vanished. Even the lunatics have better sense than to invite death in the appalling cold. No one is outside. No one would be so foolish. Except for me. I'm Thraxas the Investigator. In the course of my work, I often do foolish things.

I'm down at the docks, looking for a man the Transport Guild suspects of stealing shipments of dragon scales. Dragon scales are valuable items but the rare cargoes that arrive in Turai have been going missing almost as soon as they arrive. The Guild has hired me because it believes that one of its officials has been stealing from their harbour-front warehouses. The idea is that I catch him in the act. It never seemed like that great an idea to me, but I needed the money.

I'm hiding behind a low wall in the freezing darkness. I can feel the frost gathering on my face. I'm tired, hungry and I need a beer. My legs have gone numb. I'm as cold as the ice queen's grave and that's a lot colder than I want to be. I'm in a very bad mood. There's no sign of the suspect, who goes by the name of Rezox. No sign of anyone. Why would there be? Only a crazy person would be out on a night like this. I've been shivering for two hours and I figure if he doesn't show up in the next few minutes I'm giving up and going home. Dragon scales may be valuable, but they're not worth freezing to death for. The only thing that's keeping me alive is the spell that warms my cloak, but the warming spell is wearing thin.

I think I hear something. I'm no more than ten yards from the warehouse but it's difficult to make out anything through the driving snow. The door of the warehouse is opening. A large man wrapped in furs emerges, carrying a box. That's good enough for me. I've no intention of hanging round any longer than I have to, so I struggle to my feet and clamber over the low wall. Unsheathing my sword, I walk up behind him. The howling wind prevents Rezox from hearing my approach, and when I bark out his name he spins round in alarm.

'What—?'

'Rezox. I'm arresting you for stealing dragon scales. Let's go.'

Rezox stares at me while the snow settles on the furs that shroud his face and body.

'Thraxas the Investigator,' he mutters finally, low down so it's difficult to catch.

'Let's go,' I repeat.

'And why would I go with you?'

'Because I'm freezing to death out here and if you don't start walking I'm going to slug you and carry you off. Easy or difficult, I don't mind, just so long as it's quick.'

Despite the interruption to his criminal activities, Rezox doesn't seem perturbed. He lays down the box carefully then stares at me again.

'So what do you want?'

'A warm bed. Let's go.'

'You want money?'

He's trying to bribe me. Of course. The cold has made me slow-witted. I shake my head. I don't want money.

'Gold?'

I shake my head again.

'Women?'

I stare at him blankly. I just want to get home.

Wrapped in his furs, Rezox doesn't look cold, but he's puzzled.

'Are you saying you can't be bribed?'

'Just get in the cart, Rezox. I'm cold and I want to go home.'

The wind intensifies and Rezox has to raise his voice to make himself heard.

'Everyone in Turai can be bribed. I've paid off Senators.

I'm damned if I'm going to be arrested by a cheap Private Investigator from Twelve Seas. What is it you want?'

I don't seem to want anything.

Rezox claps his hands. The snow muffles the sound, but it's enough to bring two men out from the warehouse, each one carrying a sword and neither looking like he'll mind using it.

'Let's be reasonable, Thraxas. Just take a little money and walk away. Hell, it's not like the Transport Guild can't spare a few dragon scales.'

I raise my sword a couple of inches. Rezox has one final attempt at talking me out of making the arrest.

'You'll die for nothing, Thraxas. Take the money. No one will ever know. What are the Guild paying you? Thirty gurans? I'll give you three hundred.'

I remain silent. The two thugs advance. Normally on a case I'd be carrying some spell for dealing with emergencies, but right now I'm using all of my very limited supply of sorcery just to keep warm. The snow flies into my eyes, making me blink.

As the man on my left lunges in, I step nimbly to one side, bring my blade down on his wrist then kick his legs so he crashes to the ground. The second man leaps at me. I parry his blow, twisting my own blade in such a manner that his flies from his hand, spinning through the air to land in the snowdrift behind us. I punch him in the face. He loses his footing on the icy ground, and lands with a dull thud.

I stare at Rezox.

'Were these the best you could find?'

Rezox screams at the men to get up and attack me again. I look down at them.

'Better get going. You just used up the last of my patience. Attack me again and I'll kill you.'

They're petty thugs. Not good for much but just smart enough to know when they're about to die. They scramble to their feet and without so much as glancing at Rezox stumble off into the darkness. I place the point of my sword at Rezox's throat.

'Let's go.'

I lead him off to the next warehouse, where I've left a small wagon and a horse. The horse is none too pleased about being left in the cold space, and snorts angrily as we arrive.

'I'll split the dragon scales with you,' says Rezox as I load him into the cart. I don't reply. We set off. Technically it's illegal to ride horses or wagons in the city at night, but on a night like this there won't be any civil guards around, and I've no intention of struggling on foot to the Transport Guild's headquarters.

'You're a fool,' he sneers. 'You're too stupid to know what you're doing. What does the Guild mean to you? They're just as corrupt as everyone else.'

'Maybe. But they hired me to arrest the thief. And you're the thief. So here we are.'

Rezox can't understand why I care. Neither can I.

'I'll hire a lawyer and beat the charge in court.'

I shrug. He probably will. Turai is a corrupt city. There are plenty of clever lawyers always ready to represent men like Rezox.

The warming spell has completely worn off and my cloak offers me no protection from the elements. I'm numb with cold. Rezox still looks comfortable in his luxurious fur. He should have tried to bribe me with that.

CHAPTER

TWO

Next morning I sleep late. I'd sleep later if Makri didn't barge into my room complaining about the weather.

'Is this stupid winter ever going to end?' she demands.

Makri is young and she hasn't been in the city that long. She isn't used to our climate yet. The seasons in Turai may be grim, but they're very regular.

'Sure it'll end. In two or three weeks. And how many times have I told you not to barge into my room in the morning?'

Makri shrugs

'I don't know. Ninety, a hundred, something like that. Will it get hot in two weeks?'

'No. After winter we get the cold, rainy season. Which is also terrible.'

'I hate this place,' declares Makri, with feeling. 'The summer's too hot, the autumn's too wet and the winter's too cold. Who'd build a city here? It just goes to show that Humans are foolish.'

Makri is actually half Human herself, along with one quarter Orc and one quarter Elf. Which race she chooses to criticise depends on the circumstances.

By this time I've dragged myself out of bed and opened my first beer of the day. My rooms are freezing and I throw some wood on the fire, which is still smouldering from the night before.

'At least the Elves have the good sense to live in the Southern Isles where it's hot. And I still don't see why we had to come back so quick.'

I'm in agreement with Makri about this. Just six weeks ago we were far south on Avula, one of the largest Elvish islands. After some initial unpleasantness – the Elves panicking about Makri's Orcish blood, me being slung into prison, the usual sort of thing – life smoothed itself out and we were settling down for a pleasant vacation, more or less welcomed by all. Unfortunately Deputy Consul Cicerius and Prince Dees Akan, also members of the Turanian visiting delegation, wouldn't let us stay, claiming that they were needed back in Turai for important official business. This led to all Turanians being obliged to board ship and set off homewards in some of the worst weather I've ever voyaged in, and I've sailed through a lot of bad weather. Makri, a very poor sailor, set some kind of record for sea sickness. She swore on more than one occasion she was going to kill Cicerius for making her endure such a journey. When we put in at Turai and found ourselves deep in the middle of such a fierce winter, I was tempted to agree with her.

I tell Makri to stop prowling around.

'If you have to infest my rooms at this time in the morning, at least sit down.'

'I can't sit down. I've got too much energy. I want to go to college. Why do they shut it in winter?'

'Because most students wouldn't want to fight their way through snowdrifts to get there. And neither would the professors.'

The twenty-one-year-old ex-gladiator is a very keen student and finds this interruption to her studies extremely frustrating. Yesterday she struggled all the way up town to the Imperial Library, only to find that it too was closed.

'I was furious. Don't librarians have some sort of duty to the public?'

'It'll be open again soon, when the Sorcerers arrive in town.'

'I can't wait. I can't stand doing nothing. Are you tracking anyone violent just now? Do you need me to kill them?'

'I'm afraid not.'

Makri continues to pace up and down. She's been in an odd mood since we got back from Avula and I'm not sure why. I wouldn't care, if it wasn't for the fact that she keeps waking me up in the mornings, and I'm finding it wearing. Fifteen years ago I could march all night and fight all day. These days I need my sleep. She asks me how I got on last night and I tell her that everything went fine.

'Just hung around outside the warehouse till Rezox showed up. Nothing to it really, he had two thugs along but they weren't what you'd call fighters. I chased them off, Rezox tried to bribe me, I refused and now he's in the custody of the civil guards, charged with stealing dragon scales.'

'Who wants dragon scales?'

'Elegant women.'

'What for?'

'Jewellery.'

'Aren't dragon scales too big for jewellery?'

'The jewellers cut them to size. Then they sell them to rich women who want to sparkle. Costs a lot for a pair of dragon-scale earrings.'

'Did the Transport Guild pay you well?'

'Standard thirty gurans a day. I thought I wouldn't have to work all winter with the money we won on Avula.'

Whilst there, Makri trained a young Elf to fight. She did this so effectively that the young Elf won the junior tournament. As this Elf was previously the weakest, most pathetic Elf on the island, I was able to pick up a bundle by shrewdly backing her at long odds. It was a gambling triumph, one which was rather marred by a run of bad luck at the card table on the journey home.

'It was dumb to lose your money.'

'What else was I meant to do on the ship? At least I enjoyed my share. What did you do with yours?'

Makri doesn't answer. In all probability she gave it to the Association of Gentlewomen. More fool her. There are plenty of rich women in the Association, but Makri says she has to do her bit. She gets back to complaining about the weather.

'I hate the cold. I have to wear too many clothes. It doesn't feel right. Why won't they open the library? How am I meant to practise with my axe when it's too cold to go outside? You know Gurd warned me for taking some thazis from behind the bar? As if he can't spare it. I hate working here. I hate Turai. I hate Twelve Seas worse. Why is it so cold? At least in the gladiator slave pits no one froze to death. What's the point of living in a place like this? Nothing ever happens. I loathe it. I need a new nose stud, I'm bored with this one. You know that young guy that comes in the tavern, he works at the tannery? He had the nerve to ask me out, and only last month I heard him saying how anyone with Orcish blood should be run out the city. I was going to punch him but Gurd always complains if I hit the customers. It gets me down. Don't you ever tidy your room?'

'Makri, would you get the hell out of here? It's bad enough you wake me up without standing around complaining about everything and generally being as miserable as a Niojan whore. Here. Take this thazis stick. Maybe smoking it will improve your mood. Now leave me alone. You know I like to enjoy my first beer of the day in peace.'

'Are you still annoyed about the Sorcerers Assemblage?' asks Makri.

'Of course I'm still annoyed. All the world's top Sorcerers are arriving in Turai and there's nothing I like better than being reminded that I'm a washout when it comes to sorcery.'

I studied magic when I was young but I never completed my apprenticeship. I only ever learned the basics and I was never good enough to join the Sorcerers Guild. Since when, I've struggled my way round the world as a soldier, a mercenary and finally an Investigator. Which has been tough, and since I passed forty, somewhat tougher. There are a lot cushier ways of growing old than pursuing criminals round Twelve Seas, the rough part of a rough city.

'You wouldn't have been happy as a Sorcerer,' says Makri. 'I can't see you sitting round the Palace casting horoscopes.'

I shrug. It doesn't sound too bad. It's very comfortable

at the Palace. I know, I used to be a Senior Investigator for Palace Security. They got rid of me some time ago. I drank too much. Now I drink more but I'm my own man.

Makri and I both live in rooms above the Avenging Axe, one of Twelve Seas' more convivial taverns. Makri earns her living working as a barmaid, which she doesn't particularly enjoy, but it pays for her studies and the occasional new weapon. She glances out of the window.

'Still snowing. Well, I'm not hanging round in here. I'm going out to see Samanatius.'

'Samanatius? The quack philosopher?'

'He's not a quack. Samanatius is sharp as an Elf's ear and the most brilliant thinker in the west.'

I snort in derision.

'All he does is sit around talking about the mysteries of the universe.'

'He does not. He talks about ethics, morals, all sorts of things.'

'Great. See if he can teach you anything useful. Like how to earn money, for instance.'

'Samanatius is not interested in money,' says Makri, defensively.

'Everyone is interested in money.'

'Well, he isn't. He doesn't even charge for his classes.'

'So the man is an idiot,' I say. 'How good can a philosopher be if he doesn't charge anything? If he had any talent he'd be raking it in. Anyone who does anything for free in this city has to have something wrong with them.'

Makri shakes her head.

'Sometimes your stupidity baffles me, Thraxas.'

'Thanks for waking me up to tell me that.'

Makri asks if she can borrow the magic warm cloak.

'Okay. I'm not planning on going anywhere.'

I hand it over.

'Don't give it to that cheap philosopher.'

'Samanatius is indifferent to the climactic conditions.'

'He would be.'

Makri wraps herself in the cloak.

'This feels better. I hate this city. Who would live here?'

She departs, still cursing the weather. I shake my head. Her moods are definitely getting worse.

I finish my first beer and move on swiftly to a second. The Sorcerers Assemblage is depressing me. It's many years since it's been held in Turai and it's quite a big deal for the city, with so many powerful Sorcerers from all over the west heading our way. They're due to elect a new head of the Guild, and that's always a major event. Despite the predilection of Sorcerers for sitting around palaces having an easy time of it, they are of great importance to every state because without them we'd be doomed in the event of war with the Orcs. The Orcs outnumber us, and last time they marched over from the east it was only the power of our Human Sorcerers which held them off long enough for the Elves to come to our rescue.

Downstairs in the tavern, Tanrose is making food, ready for the lunchtime drinkers. Despite the fierceness of the winter, trade here is not too bad. Even the biting snow can't keep the population of Twelve Seas away from Gurd's ale. Gurd, a northern Barbarian, knows how to serve his ale. Tanrose greets me jovially. We get on well, partly because of my frank admiration for her excellent cooking. Even in the depths of winter, when fresh meat is impossible to come by, Tanrose manages to make salted venison into an admirable pie. I take a large portion and sit at the bar with another tankard.

'Have you seen Makri today?' asks Tanrose.

I nod.

'She woke me up. Felt the need to complain about a few things.'

'Have you noticed that she's been in an odd mood since coming back from Avula?'

'Yes. But Makri's often in funny moods, I try to ignore them.'

To my surprise this brings a hostile response from the cook.

'What do you mean, you try to ignore them? That's not very nice.'

'Nice? What do you expect? I'm an Investigator. I track down criminals. If the criminals protest too much I kill them. I like Makri well enough, but I'm not the sort of man to help her with her problems.'

Tanrose looks annoyed.

'Don't you realise how much Makri relies on you?'

'No.'

'Well you should.'

Not liking the way this conversation is going, I try concentrating on my venison pie. Tanrose won't let it drop.

'Makri grew up in a gladiator slave pit. Since she arrived in Turai she's had a hard time. You're probably her best friend. You should listen to her more.'

I choke back my angry response. As always, Tanrose, as the maker of the best venison pies in the city, has me at a disadvantage. I can't afford to offend her.

'Come on, Tanrose. You know I'm a wash-out when it comes to personal problems. Why do you think my wife left me? Makri's twenty-two years younger than me. I don't know what the hell her worries are.'

'Yes you do. She tells you. You just refuse to listen. Do you know she had her first romantic experiences on Avula?'

I down my beer and ask for another. This is really too much for me at this time of day.

'Yeah, I had some idea . . .'

'So now she's confused.'

'Can't you sort her out?'

Tanrose smiles, fairly grimly.

'Not as well as you, Thraxas. She trusts you. God knows why. Probably because you're good with a sword. It always impresses her.'

I'm starting to feel trapped. There's nothing I want to discuss less than Makri's first romantic involvements. Tanrose dangles another slice of venison pie in front of me.

'Well, all right, goddammit. I'll listen if she brings up the subject. But only under extreme protest. I haven't had a romance for fifteen years. Longer maybe. I've forgotten what it's like. When it comes to love I'm about as much use as a one-legged gladiator. I don't want to hear about her encounters with a young Elf.'

'I think it left her rather depressed.'

'She's always depressed.'

'No she isn't.'

'Well, there's always something wrong. She's a quarter Orc and a quarter Elf. That's bound to lead to problems. What makes you think I can help?'

'Have another slice of pie,' says Tanrose.

I take the venison pie and another beer back upstairs to my rooms. I look out of the window and all I can see is snow. My fire has gone out. I try lighting it with a simple spell. It doesn't work. It's a poor start to the day. I curse. Life in Turai is bad enough without having to act as nursemaid to Makri.

CHAPTER
THREE

Despite the ice, snow and general misery, many Turanians are still working hard. The Transport Guild rides wagons over almost impassable roads, distributing food and supplies around the city. The blacksmiths in their forges hammer out iron wheel rims to keep the wagons going. Whores wrap up as warmly as they can and walk the streets gamely. The Civil Guard still patrol, or at least the lower ranks do, while their officers remain comfortable in their stations. And the Messengers Guild count it as a point of honour to always make it to their destination.

The young messenger who climbs the stairs to my outside door looks as though he's had a difficult journey. His cloak is caked with snow and his face is blue with the cold. I rip open the scroll and read the message. It's from Cicerius, Turai's Deputy Consul. That's a bad start. Cicerius wants me to visit him immediately. That's worse.

I can't work up any enthusiasm for visiting Cicerius. I've had a lot of dealings with the Deputy Consul recently. On the whole these have worked out well enough, but he's never an easy man to work for. He's Turai's most honest politician – possibly Turai's only honest politician – and the city's most brilliant lawyer, but he's also cold, austere and utterly unsympathetic to any Private Investigator who feels the need to interrupt his work to take in the occasional beer. On more than one occasion Cicerius, on finding me drunk in pursuit of a criminal, has delivered the sort of stinging reprimand that makes him such a feared opponent in the law courts or the Senate. I can only take so much of this. Furthermore, while there's no denying he is a fair man, he's never found it necessary to bump up my fee, even when I've done him sterling service. He comes from the traditional line of aristocrats who think that the lower classes should be satisfied with a reasonable rate of pay for a fair day's work. In view of some of the dangers I've faced on his behalf, I'd be inclined to interpret 'reasonable' a good deal more generously than Cicerius.

I can't ignore the summons. I'm desperate to make it out of Twelve Seas and back into the wealthier parts of town. I'm never going to do that unless I make some inroads into Turai's aristocracy. Since I was thrown out of my job at the Palace I've hardly had a client who wasn't a lowlife. It's never going to earn me enough to pay the rent in Thamlin, home of the upper classes. And home of a few rather select and expensive Investigators, I reflect, as I make ready to leave. You wouldn't catch anyone from the Venarius Investigation Agency freezing to death on the docks in mid-winter.

I suddenly remember that Makri has borrowed my magic warm cloak.

'Damn the woman!' I roar. I can't believe I have to venture out in these freezing temperatures without the warm cloak. How could I be so foolish? Now Makri gets to stay nice and comfy while listening to that fraud of a philosopher Samanatius. Meanwhile Thraxas, on his way to do a proper man's job, has to freeze to death. Damn it.

I rummage around in the chest in the corner of my bedroom and drag out a couple of old cloaks and tunics. I try putting on an extra layer of clothes but it's difficult, because my waistline has expanded dramatically in the past few years and nothing seems to fit. Finally I just have to wrap an ancient cloak over my normal attire, cram on a fur hat I once took from a deceased Orc and venture out. The wind goes straight through me. By the time I'm halfway along Quintessence Street I'm as cold as the ice queen's grave, and getting colder.

The city's Prefects have been doing their best to keep the main roads passable. If I can make it to Moon and Stars Boulevard I should be able to catch a landus up town, but getting there through the side roads is almost impossible. The streets are already treacherous with ice, and fresh snow is falling all the time. I haven't been out in weather like this since my regiment fought in the far north, and that was a long time ago, when I was a lot lighter and nimbler of foot. By the time I make it to the Boulevard I'm wet, shivering and cursing Makri for tricking me into giving her the warm cloak.

I have a stroke of good fortune when a one-horse cab drops a merchant off right in front of me. I climb in and tell the driver to take me to the Thamlin. The landus crawls up the Boulevard, through Pashish and over the river. Here the streets are a little clearer, but the large gardens are all snow-bound and the fountains are frozen over. The summons was to Cicerius's home rather than the Imperial Palace, and the driver, on hearing the address, gives me his opinions on Cicerius, which aren't very high.

'Okay, the guy is famous for his honesty,' says the driver. 'But so what? He commissions a new statue of himself every year. That's vanity on a big scale. Anyway, he's a Traditional and they're as corrupt as they come. I tell you, the way the rich are bleeding this city I'll be pleased if Lodius and the Populares party throw them all out. How's a landus driver meant to make a living the way they keep piling on the taxes? You know how much horse feed has gone up in the last year?'

The King and his administration are not universally popular. Plenty of people would like to see some changes. I sympathise, more or less, but I prefer to stay out of politics.

The landus deposits me outside Cicerius's large town house. There's a Securitus Guildsman huddled over a small fire in a hut at the gate who checks my invitation before ushering me in. I hurry up the path past the frozen bushes and beat on the door, meanwhile thinking that this job had better be worth the journey.

A servant answers the door. I show her my invitation. She looks at me like I'm probably a man who forges invitations, then withdraws to consult with someone inside. I'm left freezing on the step. I struggle to keep my temper under control. It takes a long time for the door to open again. This time the servant motions me inside.

'What took you so long? A man could die out there. You looking to have your nice garden cluttered up with dead Investigators?'

I'm ushered into a guest room. I remove my outer cloak and start to thaw myself out in front of the fire.

Whilst I'm in the process of this, a young girl, nine or ten, arrives and stares at me. The daughter of one of the servants, I presume, from her rather unkempt appearance.

'You're fat,' she says.

'And you're ugly,' I reply, seeing no reason to be insulted by the children of the domestic help.

The kid immediately bursts into tears and retreats from the room, which cheers me a little. She should have known better than to cross swords with Thraxas. Thirty seconds later Cicerius appears. Clutching the hem of his toga is the same young girl, sobbing hysterically and denouncing me as the man who insulted her.

'What have you been saying to my daughter?' demands Cicerius, fixing me with his piercing eyes.

'Your daughter? I didn't know you had a daughter.'

'Do you normally insult the children you encounter in your clients' houses?'

'Hey, she started it,' I protest.

Cicerius does his best to calm his daughter before sending her off to find her mother. The little brat is still in tears and Cicerius is pained. This has got our interview off to a bad start. With Cicerius, that usually seems to happen.

'Have you been drinking?'

'I've always been drinking. But don't let it stop you from offering me some wine. You know the landus drivers in Turai are turning against the Traditionals?'

'For what reason?'

'Too many taxes.'

Cicerius dismisses this with the slightest movement of his head. He's not about to discuss government policy with the likes of me. On the wall of the guest room is a large painting of Cicerius addressing the Senate, and there's a bust of him in a niche in the corner. The landus driver was right about his vanity.

'I need your help,' he says. 'Though, as always when we meet, I wonder why.'

'Presumably you've got a job which is unsuitable for the better class of Investigator.'

'Not exactly. I hired the better class of Investigator but he fell sick. As did the second.'

'Okay, so I'm third choice.'

'Fourth.'

'You're really selling me the job, Cicerius. Maybe you'd better just describe it.'

'I want you to act as an observer at the Sorcerers Assemblage.'

'Sorry,' I say. 'Can't do it. Thanks for the offer, I'll see myself out.'

'What?' Cicerius is startled by my abrupt refusal. 'Why can't you do it?'

'Personal reasons,' I reply, and head for the door. I'm not about to tell the Deputy Consul that attending the Sorcerers Assemblage would make me feel small, powerless, insignificant and a general failure in life.

Cicerius plants himself in front of me.

'Personal reasons? That is not an acceptable reason for refusing the commission. I am not offering you this job for fun. I'm offering you it because it is a service that Turai needs from you. When the city needs you, personal reasons have no significance. Now kindly sit down and listen.'

The Deputy Consul could easily make my life in Turai

very awkward. He wouldn't have to pull too many strings to have my licence revoked. So I sit down and listen, and drink his wine, but I don't make any pretence I'm enjoying it.

'You are aware that the Sorcerers are to elect a new head of their Guild?'

I am. The Deputy Consul doesn't have to tell me that this is an important matter for Turai, as well as every other Human nation. The Sorcerers Guild in each land has its own organisation and its own officials, but unlike many of the other Guilds, the Sorcerers have an international dimension. While a member of the Turanian Bakers Guild would probably not be too interested in the Simnian Bakers Guild, every magic user in the west looks up to the leader of the Sorcerers Guild. The post carries a lot of weight and brings a great deal of prestige to the home city and state.

'Our King and our Consul are most keen that a Turanian is elected new head of the Guild.'

I'm not surprised. Turai has been slipping in political importance for a long time now. We used to be a big voice in the League of Independent City States, but that organisation has now almost fallen apart, riven by internal rivalries, leaving the small state of Turai dangerously exposed. We're in the front line against the Orcs to the east. To make things worse, Nioj, our northern neighbour and historical enemy, has spent the last decade making threatening noises. King Lamachus would like nothing better than to swallow us up, and if he decides to do it there doesn't seem much prospect of anyone else coming to our aid. Turai is still a great friend of the Elves, but the Elves are a long way away. It would make a lot of sense to cement the Sorcerers Guild to our city state.

I can see problems ahead.

'Are we seriously going to try for this? Who have we got for the post? There are a lot of powerful Sorcerers in the world, and the way Turanian Sorcerers have been dying in the past few years, I don't see who we could nominate.'

Cicerius nods, and sips some wine from a silver goblet.

'We had hopes for Tas of the Eastern Lightning. Very powerful.'

'But not very loyal. It's probably just as well he got killed, he'd have sold us out in the end. I guess Mirius Eagle Rider would have been the next best choice till he handed in his toga. But who else is there? Old Hasius the Brilliant is too old, and Harmon Half Elf doesn't qualify for head of the Human Sorcerers Guild.'

'We considered Melus the Fair,' says Cicerius. 'She is strong. But she's already employed as Stadium Sorcerer and the people like her. Removing her from that post would be very unpopular. However, we do have another very excellent Sorcerer. Lisutaris, Mistress of the Sky.'

I raise my eyebrows.

'You're not serious.'

'And why not? Lisutaris is very, very powerful. It was she who overcame the eight-mile terror which almost destroyed the city last year. She has a good reputation at home and abroad because she fought valiantly in the last Orc War. Even now people still talk about the way she brought a flight of war dragons crashing from the sky.'

'I was there. I remember the incident. And very

impressive it was. But that was more than fifteen years ago. Before Lisutaris developed into the city's most enthusiastic thazis user.'

Cicerius pretends not to understand me.

'Does she use thazis?'

'Does she? Come on, Cicerius, Lisutaris, Mistress of the Sky, might be a heavy-duty Sorcerer, but she lives for the weed.'

Cicerius is untroubled.

'In these decadent times, Thraxas, we cannot set our standards as high as we once might have. You know as well as I do that a great deal of degeneracy has taken root in the Sorcerers Guild as well as elsewhere. Dwa abuse is common, and the drinking habits of many of our Sorcerers leave a great deal to be desired. For some reason Sorcerers seem very prone to this. Compared to dwa and alcohol, thazis is a very mild substance. I do not approve of it but I do not see it as a serious impediment. You, for instance, use thazis quite openly, despite it still being illegal.'

I doubt that Cicerius fully appreciates the nature of Lisutaris's habit. Many people use the occasional stick to calm them down. On a busy night, the Avenging Axe is thick with thazis smoke. But Lisutaris's liking for thazis is on a different level. She actually invented a complicated new kind of water pipe to enable her to ingest more. She spends half her life in a world of dreams. Last time I was at her villa I found her comatose on the floor after successfully developing a spell for making the plants grow faster. Still, none of this is really my concern. Lisutaris is not a bad sort as Sorcerers go, and I'd be happy enough to see her as head of the Guild.

'So why do you need me?'

'Because we have good reason to fear that the election will not be as fair as we would wish,' replies Cicerius. 'Your job would be to ensure that it is.'

Cicerius's daughter appears behind him. She makes a face at me. I let it pass. Cicerius carries on.

'There are other candidates for the job and their nations are equally keen to succeed. We fear that some of these lands may not be averse to using underhand tactics.'

'Unlike Turai?'

'Unlike Turai.'

'So you're not wanting me to do anything illegal?'

'If you are caught doing anything illegal, the government will disown you.'

'That's not quite the same thing.'

Cicerius shrugs.

'Am I being hired to make sure the election is fair or to make sure Lisutaris is elected?'

'We are confident that if the election is fair, then Lisutaris will be elected,' replies the Deputy Consul.

'In other words, I'm to stop at nothing to get her the post?'

Cicerius's lips twitch, which is as close as he ever comes to smiling.

'It is very important to Turai that Lisutaris secures the position. However, I repeat, if you are implicated in anything illegal, the government will disown you.'

'I don't really understand why I'm the man for the job, Cicerius. Wouldn't it be better to send someone from Palace Security?'

'I have selected you.'

It's possible that the Deputy Consul is having problems with Palace Security. It's headed by Rittius, a bitter rival of his. Cicerius doesn't elaborate, but he points out that I am fairly well qualified for the mission.

'You have good investigating skills. You have some knowledge of sorcery, albeit slight. And your uncouth manners will not offend the Sorcerers as much as they might offend others.'

'I guess not. Sorcerers can be pretty uncouth themselves when they get some wine inside them.'

The Deputy Consul acknowledges that this is true.

'Turai will not, of course, be relying solely on you. We will have many representatives catering to the needs of the Sorcerers. Every effort will be made to make them look favourably on Turai. However, many other nations are keen to win the post. I feel that you might well be able to alert us to any underhand dealing that may occur.'

I finish off my wine.

'Possibly. But the fact remains that I don't want to go to the Sorcerers Assemblage. And I don't need the work. I won a lot of money on our trip to Avula.'

'You lost it all before you returned to Turai and you are now sorely in need.'

'How do you know that?'

'I have my own sources of information. You will go to the Assemblage.'

Every time I end up working for the Deputy Consul, it's something I'd rather not be doing. It never seems to bother him.

'You know the Sorcerers don't allow civilians at the Assemblage? It's Guild members and their staff only, and they're strict about it. So unless you can get me a position as Lisutaris's secretary, they're not going to let me in.'

'I doubt that you would be an acceptable secretary for Lisutaris,' replies Cicerius. 'But I have already dealt with the problem. The Sorcerers Guild does allow several observers from the government of the host city to attend, as a matter of courtesy. I will be there for much of the time.'

'You're the Deputy Consul. If I walk into the Assemblage claiming to be a government official they'll be down on me like a bad spell.'

Cicerius makes an impatient gesture.

'As I said, I have dealt with the problem. You will be there as a representative of the people of Turai. I am nominating you as a Tribune of the People.'

'A what?'

'A Tribune of the People. Are you not familiar with this post?'

I shake my head.

'It used to be a famous position in Turai. There were six Tribunes of the People, and they played an important role in the governance of the city. They were, as the name implies, responsible for representing the interests of the general population in city affairs. Three were elected by the population and three were nominated by the King and his administration.'

'When was this?'

'The institution fell into disuse about one hundred and fifty years ago. But it is still within my power to nominate Tribunes. I have already appointed Sulinius and Visus, both Senators' sons, to assist at the Assemblage. You will be the third.'

I drink more wine. It's a fine vintage. Though not given to excessive drinking, Cicerius keeps his cellars well stocked. An aristocrat has to, or he loses status.

'How come the post of Tribune was abandoned?'

'They fell out of favour with the King when they became too keen on supporting radical policies. After some civil unrest it was felt that they were no longer necessary, which was wise. It is far better to leave the administration of a city to the King and his officials. But none of this need concern you. You are not expected to do anything as Tribune. It is merely a convenient way of gaining access to the Assemblage.'

I'm dubious.

'Are you sure I don't have to do anything? If there are any official duties involved, I'm not interested.'

Cicerius assures me there are no duties involved.

'Look on it as a temporary honorary post.'

'Is there a salary?'

'No. But we will be paying you for your time. Now listen carefully. We are facing some formidable opposition. The Simnians have nominated one of their own Sorcerers, and the Simnians are enemies of Turai. It is vital that their candidate is not elected. Unfortunately, Lasat, Axe of Gold, acting head of the Sorcerers Guild, is believed to favour them, which makes our task more difficult. Our city will have to make a great effort to ensure that Lisutaris gathers sufficient votes to at least make it into the final stages of the process. Are you familiar with Tilupasis, widow of Senator Gerinius?'

'I've heard of her. Runs some sort of salon.'

'Indeed. She is commonly described as Turai's most influential woman.'

'Didn't she publicly criticise you a while back? Something to do with wasting money on a statue?'

Cicerius brushes this away.

'We have had our disagreements. Tilupasis has an unfortunate habit of speaking out of turn. Nonetheless, she is a woman of considerable influence. She has proved herself to be a highly efficient organiser, and the King himself was pleased at the reception she gave for our Elvish visitors last year. Consul Kalius feels that she can play an important role in the vote-winning process.'

Cicerius, great speaker that he is, doesn't give away too much in the way of unguarded emotions, but I get the feeling he's not entirely convinced about this. Women are forbidden to enter politics in Turai, and an aristocratic Traditional like the Deputy Consul never feels wholly comfortable with any sign of female influence in the city. However, Cicerius can't disregard the views of the Consul, his superior.

'Kalius trusts Tilupasis . . .' continues Cicerius.

I bet he does. They're strongly rumoured to be having an affair.

'. . . and indeed, there is every reason to believe that she will perform her duties of hospitality well. I have already instructed Visus and Sulinius to listen to her views respectfully, and I now tell you the same. With Tilupasis to organise our hospitality, Visus and Sulinius to cater to the Sorcerers' needs, and you to make sure there is nothing untoward going on, I am confident that Turai can succeed.'

Cicerius carries on in this manner for some time. My spirits sink lower. Arrogant Sorcerers, wealthy young senators' sons and Turai's most influential matron.

What a collection. I'll be the only ignobly born person in the whole place and probably as welcome as an Orc at an Elvish wedding. Thraxas, Tribune of the People. That's going to cause a few laughs when word gets around Twelve Seas.

CHAPTER
FOUR

The journey home is grim. I never figured I'd come so close to death just riding in a landus along Quintessence Street. Not for the first time I bitterly regret not saving enough of my winnings from Avula to buy some furs. I burst into the Avenging Axe and beg Tanrose to provide me with some hot food, before positioning myself as close to the fire as I can get without actually stepping over the grate.

Makri is wiping tables and collecting tankards.

'Have a good time with the philosopher?' I say, cuttingly. 'Nice and warm in my cloak?'

'Yes thank you,' responds Makri. 'The magic cloak is a great creation.'

'Well, it's the last time you get your hands on it. I nearly died out there. Damn that Cicerius, he's not human. You know he wants me to go to the Sorcerers Assemblage?'

I'm feeling angry about all things sorcerous. It's ridiculous to hold their convention in the depths of winter.

'They're only doing it to show off. No one else can move because of the snow, but the Sorcerers will all come rolling into the city boasting about how easy it was for them to manipulate the weather and what pleasant journeys they had. Braggarts, all of them. This job is a waste of time. Who cares who gets the post as leader of the Guild?'

'Samanatius says it's a very important position,' says Makri.

'He would. Shouldn't you be bringing me a beer instead of talking about philosophy all the time?'

'There's nothing wrong with philosophy.'

'It's a waste of time.'

'It's enriching,' says Makri.

I find this very annoying.

'If you were enriched you wouldn't have to wear that ridiculous chainmail bikini.'

'Samanatius says that women who are obliged to exhibit themselves to make a living are not degraded by the experience,' says Makri stiffly. 'The audience are.'

'Samanatius is an idiot. Bring me a beer.'

'Get your own beer,' says Makri, which is hardly the way for any barmaid to talk to a customer. She should learn some manners.

I get my own beer and return to the fire to think gloomy thoughts. I know most of the Sorcerers in Turai and plenty others from around the world. It's no secret that I failed my apprenticeship all those years ago, but I don't like my nose being rubbed in it. I still advertise myself as a sorcerous Investigator to bring in business, though the spells I can work are pathetic, child's play compared to their powers.

'If any Sorcerer laughs at me, I'm going to punch him right in the face.'

I finger my necklace. It's a spell protection charm, and a good one. I might need it if things get rough.

Gurd had the excellent sense to provide the tavern with a plentiful supply of logs for the winter, and the Avenging Axe is warm enough to comfort the coldest guest. It's warm enough to allow Makri to wear the tiny chainmail bikini. I shouldn't have mocked her for it. It's not like she's crazy about it herself. She relies on it to earn tips, a stratagem which has proved successful over the past year, which is not really surprising, given Makri's figure. Mercenaries who've been all round the world and seen everything there is to see can still be struck dumb when she appears. Tanrose says that Makri's beauty will one day get her married to a Senator or a prince, but given that Makri has Orc blood, pointed ears and plenty of attitude, I reckon she's more likely to end up dead in a gutter, probably not long after me. I never figure she's that beautiful anyway, but I gave up thinking about women a long time ago, so I'm a poor judge.

I finish my beer. Makri ignores my request for another. I swear at her. She swears back at me. Other drinkers laugh. Her moods are really getting me down. I retreat upstairs.

My magic warm cloak is on the bed. I'll have to charge it up again before I go out tonight. I've a small piece of business to attend to – checking up on a woman for a jealous husband – but after that my diary is empty. Cicerius was right, I do need the work.

Makri strides into my room.

'Thraxas, can I—'

'Will you stop marching into my room uninvited?'

A tear trickles from Makri's eye. I've never seen Makri cry before, at least not in misery. A few tears of joy after massacring some opponents, maybe. She hurries from the room. It's strange behaviour.

Outside it's snowing again. I wish I didn't have to go out. I've been watching the activities of the wife of a wealthy merchant for two weeks now. He's suspicious of her and is paying me for reports of her movements. Normally I'd be glad of the work – no danger and not too strenuous – but it's been tough in the cold weather. So far I haven't found the wife doing anything particularly odd. The only visitors that ever call are representatives from high-class clothing concerns, make-up artists, hairdressers and the like. There's one beautician who looks in every day, but this is standard behaviour for any rich Turanian woman. The merchant has no objections to his wife beautifying herself. He now thinks he may have misjudged her.

I wrap myself in the warm cloak, fit on my sword and depart before Makri can bother me again with her moody behaviour. As expected, the assignment turns out to be a waste of time. If the merchant's wife has any thoughts of being unfaithful, she's probably waiting till the summer months, when her husband is away trading in foreign lands, which would be the smart thing to do.

I'm relieved when midnight rolls around. It's another foul night and my magic warm cloak is starting to lose potency. I hurry off through the snow to the house of Astrath Triple Moon. Astrath is an old friend. He's a powerful Sorcerer and might have expected to be a candidate for head of the Guild himself had it not been for some irregularities in the chariot races when he was employed as resident Sorcerer at the Stadium Superbius.

The Stadium pays a Sorcerer to ensure that no magic is used to interfere with the races. When a rumour spread that Astrath Triple Moon had been taking bribes to look the other way while a certain powerful Senator hired a Sorcerer to help his chariots romp home easy winners, there was a lot of bad feeling in the city and Astrath faced a lengthy period in prison.

Fortunately for him, I managed to gather – and when I say gather, I mean fake – enough evidence in his favour to make prosecution impossible. Astrath was allowed to resign quietly provided he never showed his face in the stadium again. Thanks to me, he also escaped expulsion from the Sorcerers Guild, so he's entitled to attend the convention, although whether he's planning to, I don't know. It might be a touchy subject. Astrath isn't welcome in polite circles these days and I'm not certain how he stands with the other Sorcerers.

Astrath's house is reasonably comfortable but not really the sort of place a powerful Sorcerer would expect to live in. Up in Thamlin, Harmon Half Elf has a villa with grounds so large he holds a horse race every year for all the Sorcerer's apprentices, but here in more modest Pashish you'd be hard pushed to fit a horse into Astrath's back yard.

He greets me warmly, as always. It's a relief to him to see a friendly face from the old days.

'Thraxas, I've been expecting you. Some wine?'

'Beer would be better. And let me get myself in front of your fire, my warm cloak is starting to cool off.'

Astrath makes a living casting horoscopes, selling healing potions and such like, but there's not much money around in Pashish. There's not much money

anywhere south of the river in Turai, unless you count
the Brotherhood, who control the local criminal activity. They always do well, but you couldn't say anyone
else was prospering. Astrath only has one servant and
she's finished for the day, so he leads me inside himself,
and takes my cloak.

'I'll charge it up for you before you leave. What are
you doing out on the streets in this weather?'

I tell him about my fruitless tailing of the merchant's
wife.

'The woman is completely blameless as far as I can
see. Obsessed with beauty treatments, but having met
the husband I can understand why she'd want a hobby.'

We sit and chat about this and that. I let Astrath get
some wine inside him before raising the subject of the
Assemblage.

'Are you planning on attending?'

The Sorcerer strokes his beard. Most Sorcerers in
Turai are bearded, and they wear rainbow cloaks, the
badge of their Guild.

'I'm not certain. I'm still a member, but—'

He shrugs. I tell him he should go.

'Be a shame to miss seeing your old friends.'

'There's a lot of old friends not too keen to see me
these days, Thraxas.'

'People in the Palace maybe. And round the race
track. But your fellow Sorcerers? Do they care about a
little trouble with the law? It's not like you broke the
Guild rules or anything. Hell, if the Assemblage banned
every Sorcerer who'd had a run-in with their city
authorities, the place would be empty. I'm forever getting Gorsius Starfinder out of trouble.'

Astrath smiles. Gorsius Starfinder, who holds a respectable post at the Palace these days, does have an unfortunate tendency to get drunk in brothels and cause a scene.

'Maybe you're right. It's a long time since they've held the Assemblage here, be a shame to miss it.'

Astrath knows that the Turanians are nominating Lisutaris for head of the Guild. He doesn't give much for her chances.

'I still hear all the gossip, and Sunstorm Ramius from Simnia is the favourite. He's sharp as an Elf's ear and he has a lot of friends. And if he doesn't win it, there's a few others not far behind. Rokim the Bright from Samsarina, for instance. The Samsarinans control a lot of votes. Or Darius Cloud Walker. He impressed a lot of people when he brought down that stray war dragon right in the middle of the Abelasian Sorcerers' drinking contest. Just pointed his finger, down it came, and he carried on drinking and won the contest. A man like that carries a lot of weight with Sorcerers.'

'True. It takes a good man to win the drinking contest in Abelasi. But Lisutaris is powerful too.'

'Maybe. But everyone in the Guild knows she's not always in a fit state to take care of business. Or even put on her own shoes.'

He looks at me knowingly.

'Are the authorities sending you to fix the election?'

'Absolutely not. Just to see it's fair.'

'The Sorcerers have plenty of ways of their own to make things fair. Lasat, Axe of Gold, and Charius the Wise are running things till the new chief is elected, and no one's going to slip anything by that pair.'

'Then I'll have an easy time of it.'

Astrath lets it go. Like all Sorcerers, he's a man of powerful intuition and he guesses there is probably more to my mission than I'm admitting, but he doesn't press the point.

'So you're reckoning on Sunstorm Ramius, Rokim the Bright and Darius Cloud Walker as the main rivals? Abelasi is small and far away, so Darius wouldn't affect Turai much one way or another. Rokim the Bright wouldn't be too bad, but Samsarina is a long way off. No chance of help arriving quickly if Turai is in trouble. The worst choice would be Sunstorm Ramius. It's a long time since Turai has been friends with Simnia.'

Astrath brings me more beer. After discussing the convention for a while, we get to reminiscing about old times, and eventually I doze off on the couch. Astrath shakes me awake and points me towards the guest room. I sleep well under the Sorcerer's roof and leave next day without waking him. My cloak has been fully recharged and keeps me warm as I tread carefully over the icy streets back to Twelve Seas.

There are few people around, though I notice several youths that I know to be dwa dealers scurrying along about their business. Nothing interferes with the dwa trade. I'm planning to stop at Minarixa's bakery to buy some pastries for breakfast, but I'm surprised to find a small crowd outside her shop, standing and staring in spite of the cold.

A few Civil Guards are holding back the onlookers. This is worrying. I depend on Minarixa's bakery almost as much as Tanrose's pies. If they've been robbed and the ovens aren't fired up yet it's really going to spoil my day. I arrive just as Captain Rallee, wrapped in a black government cloak, emerges from the premises. He's scowling.

'Trouble?'

'Trouble. Minarixa's dead.'

I gasp. Not my favourite baker.

The crowd moan as the body is brought out wrapped in a shroud. The baker is one of Twelve Seas' most popular characters.

'What happened?'

'Overdose,' says the Captain.

I stare at him like he's crazy.

'An overdose? Minarixa?'

He nods.

'It can't be. Not Minarixa. She didn't take dwa.'

'Well, she certainly took enough last night,' says Captain Rallee.

It's some time since I've seen him looking so depressed. The Civil Guards loved that baker's shop.

I stare dumbly as Minarixa's body is loaded on to a wagon and driven away through the falling snow, then I walk home, cursing. Word has already reached the Avenging Axe. Gurd, Tanrose and Makri are as miserable as three Niojan whores. No one can believe that our cherished baker has gone and died of an overdose.

'Such a respectable woman,' says Gurd, shaking his head. Gurd, sturdy Barbarian that he is, finds it impossible to understand why the city has been gripped by the plague of dwa.

'Why did she do it? Surely she was a happy woman?'

'She kept that bakery going through the worst times,' says Tanrose, sadly. 'Orc wars, riots, even the famine.

She kept it going when the True Church tried to have it made illegal for women to own businesses. I can't believe she's finally gone because of this.'

The event casts further gloom over Twelve Seas. Citizens already struggling with the weather, beset by poverty and surrounded by corruption curse the powdered plant that has brought so much misery in the past few years.

Makri is madder than a mad dragon at Minarixa's death. Not because of the bakery – Makri has little enthusiasm for food – but because Minarixa was the local organiser for the Association of Gentlewomen. The Association dedicates itself to raising the status of women in Turai, and Makri supports it to the extent of helping to collect money, a thankless task in Twelve Seas. She spends a long time expressing her outrage that such a fine woman as Minarixa should succumb to a drug overdose.

'Are you going to investigate?' she demands.

I shrug.

'What's to investigate? She took too much dwa. So did about thirty other people in Twelve Seas this week. You've seen the bodies.'

Makri is furious. When Captain Rallee calls in late in the evening for a beer to unwind after a hard day, she demands to know what he's going to do about the death.

'Nothing,' replies the Captain, gloomily.

'Why not? Shouldn't you be arresting whoever sold her the dwa?'

'How? You think we could find a witness? Or make anything stick in court? No chance. All the dwa trade is controlled by the Brotherhood and no one's going to give evidence against them. Anyway, you arrest one dwa dealer and another appears on the street before the day is out.'

'I've never seen you arresting even one,' says Makri.

Captain Rallee shifts uncomfortably. Makri's right, but it's not the Captain's fault. He's as honest as they come but his superiors aren't. The Brotherhood have far too much influence for a captain of the Civil Guards to tangle with them.

'I'm as outraged as you about Minarixa. But no one is going to pay for her death. That's just the way it is.'

'If I meet her dealer I'm going to gut him,' says Makri.

'Fine with me,' says Captain Rallee. 'I'll be happy to look the other way.'

'I hate this place,' says Makri, and goes upstairs to read some mathematics treatise and curse the weather, the Brotherhood and everything else in Turai. Makri escaped from the Orcish gladiator slave pits a couple of years ago, an event involving such incredible carnage that the Orcs still talk of it with awe. She made her way over to Turai on hearing tales of its fine cultural tradition, but while she admits that Turai does contain a great amount of art and learning, she refuses to admit that our level of civilisation is much better than the Orcs. Sometimes I'm inclined to agree with her, though in the Orc-hating city of Turai, it's not an opinion I'd voice in public.

Dwa is now plaguing all the Human lands. A few months ago on Avula I discovered that it was starting to make inroads into Elvish society. It's said the Orcs encourage the trade, to weaken us. If that's true, it's a good plan. It's working.

Captain Rallee buys me a beer, not a common event, though the Captain and I go back a long way. We don't get on as well as we used to but we've still got some kind of connection. We drink to the baker.

'Congratulations on finding the dragon-scale thief,' says Rallee.

He must be emotional. The last time the Captain complimented me on anything, I'd just killed an Orc and tossed him from the city walls, which was sixteen years ago at least.

'What's this I hear about you being some sort of government official?'

I explain to him that Cicerius is making me a Tribune of the People.

'What the hell is that?'

'Some old post that used to exist a hundred and fifty years ago.'

'I've never heard of it. Does it involve staying sober?'

'Not as far as I know. I'm not planning on staying that sober at the Assemblage.'

The Captain grins. The fire illuminates his long yellow hair, picking out his handsome features.

'Better take care you don't offend someone.'

'I'd be more likely to offend the Sorcerers if I was sober.'

'True enough. When I heard our government were putting up Lisutaris for head of the Guild, I thought they were crazy. Everyone knows she's stoned every day. But who knows? It might be in her favour. Sorcerers, they never could control themselves.'

'You remember the time we were camped up in the north and Harmon Half Elf was meant to be keeping watch?' asks Gurd, bringing up an old war memory.

'Sure,' replies the Captain. 'He got so drunk he thought our pack mule was a troll and blasted it with a fire spell.'

'And he burned all our supplies so we ended up eating the mule!'

We all laugh, and call for more beer, and we spend the night telling war stories and drinking.

'It was different in those days,' says Gurd, some time after midnight. 'The Orcs were always attacking us. We had to fight to stay alive. But there wasn't any dwa. I liked it better then.'

CHAPTER
FIVE

The Assemblage is due to start in three days' time. Already Sorcerers are arriving in the city, though there's little sign of them in Twelve Seas. They're either staying as guests of Turanian Sorcerers in Truth is Beauty Lane or else living in villas rented by the Guild in Thamlin. Some of the more adventurous among them may be visiting the Kushni quarter in the centre of town, where there's a lot of diversion in the way of whores, gambling, drinking and dwa, but none ventures as far as Twelve Seas. This doesn't mean we're not interested in them. The local citizens read news of each new arrival in the *Renowned and Truthful Chronicle of All the World's Events*, the cheap and poorly produced news sheet that brings the population of Turai its regular dose of gossip and scandal. Faced as we are with so many enemies, it's comforting for Turanians to have powerful Sorcerers within our walls. When it's learned that I'm to attend the Assemblage, most people are impressed, although fairly amused at the thought of me being some sort of government official.

'Of course,' as Chiaraxi, the local healer, points out, 'it's not as if our officials are all sober, responsible citizens. From what I've seen of these degenerates in the Senate, Thraxas would fit right in.'

'Only if they could make a special outsize toga,' replies Rox, who should stick to selling fish.

Bolstered by such support, I'm wrapping up all other business. The Transport Guild has paid me for the apprehension of Rezox and I've been to visit the suspicious merchant with regard to his wife. He's a timber dealer by the name of Rixad. While I can't say he's the friendliest client I've ever had, he does seem to take my opinions seriously and he doesn't quibble over payment. Rixad is around fifty, overweight and not the handsomest man in the city. I can see he might be suspicious of his glamorous young wife, but if he wants to use his wealth to scoop up a beauty in need of money, it's almost bound to happen. His wife started off on the stage and might have thought it a wise move to swap the uncertain life of an actress for the luxury of an important merchant's household, but she's probably bored by now.

I report that as far as I can see she has no external interests save in beautifying herself.

'I checked out her visitors but there's nothing suspicious. Standard crowd, cater for all the richest women in the city. I expect it's costing you a bundle, but apart from that you've nothing to worry about.'

Rixad nods.

'The last bill from Copro was for more than a shipload of timber. I don't mind. It keeps her happy.'

Copro is quite a well-known man in Turai. One of our finest beauticians. Since arriving in Turai he's attained such a reputation that the female aristocracy fight for his services. Princess Du Akan swears by him, I believe. He's been a frequent visitor to Rixad's wife, but as Copro is rumoured to have a close relationship with his young male assistant, he's not a man you have to worry about your wife misbehaving with.

Business completed, I make my way home, reasonably satisfied. I'm still in a bad mood about having to attend the Assemblage, but at least it will be warm. The temperature has dropped even further and the streets are quieter than I've ever seen them. Only the most vital services are still in operation and many of the population are obliged to chip blocks of ice from frozen aqueducts and thaw it out for drinking water.

I arrive at the Avenging Axe just as Makri is climbing the outside stairs to my office.

'I just had an argument with the dealer who sold dwa to Minarixa,' she says. 'Do you think there might be any trouble?'

'How bad was the argument?'

'He's dead.'

I mutter the minor incantation to open my door and hurry inside.

'Of course there will be trouble. Did anyone see you?'

Makri doesn't think so.

'The alley was dark and it was snowing.'

'Did you have to kill him?'

Makri shrugs.

'I wasn't planning to. I was just going to beat him. He pulled a knife so I ran him through.'

I swear it was only last week that Makri was telling me in glowing terms about some lecture she'd attended concerning the importance of moral behaviour at all times.

'You think this was moral?'

'He deserved it.'

'I'm sure Samanatius would be highly impressed. If

the Brotherhood find out they'll be down on us like a bad spell. I don't fancy trying to escape the city when the gates are frozen shut. Do you always have to do things which lead to trouble?'

Makri opens her mouth to reply but instead she starts to cry. I stare at her in complete astonishment. She's never reacted like this before. When I shout at her she normally just shouts back louder, and maybe reaches for her axe.

Faced with a tearful Makri, I have no idea what to do. I'm worried it might be some sort of menstruation problem, a subject I had successfully avoided for forty-three years until Makri insisted on breaking one of Turai's strongest taboos by bringing it up in public a few months ago, thereby throwing the whole neighbour-hood into panic. The local priest swears he'll never visit the Avenging Axe again. Makri slumps down heavily on the couch and continues to cry. I wonder if I could escape downstairs for a beer.

'Um . . . well, it might not turn out so bad . . . dwa dealers get killed all the time. Maybe the Brotherhood won't care too much . . .'

Tears trickle down Makri's face. I'm trapped.

'What's going on? Is it something, er . . . personal . . .?'

Makri seems reluctant to talk.

'Okay, maybe you could tell me later, I've got some important . . .'

'Are you trying to get rid of me?' she demands.

'What do you mean? I was trying to be sympathetic. If you're just going to sit there all day being as miserable as a Niojan whore, what the hell do you expect me to do? I'm a busy man.'

'Well, that's fine, I wouldn't want to bother you,' says Makri angrily. 'I won't bother saving you next time you get in trouble.'

'Makri, the last thing in the world I want to do is discuss your private life, but Tanrose says I have to, so spill it.'

'You expect me to tell you about my private life? No chance.'

'That's fine with me, I don't want to hear it anyway.'

'All right, I'll tell you,' says Makri. She sniffs, and drinks some of my klee.

'I slept with an Elf on Avula. And I've been miserable ever since.'

I silently curse Tanrose. She should be dealing with this sort of thing.

'Right . . . well . . . you know . . . I'm sure it will work out fine.'

Makri dabs her eyes and looks at me.

'Is that it? Is that the best you can do?'

I spread my arms wide and contrive to look hopeless.

'Makri, I might be number one chariot when it comes to investigating and sharp as an Elf's ear at the race track, but I never claimed to be any good on emotional problems. I assume this is an emotional problem?'

'What did you think it was?'

'With you it's hard to tell. If it turns out you stabbed the Elf I wouldn't be surprised.'

Makri starts crying again. I wish the Brotherhood would attack. A good sword fight would take her mind off it. Makri never had a lover before and now appears to be suffering some sort of crisis.

'Wasn't that what you wanted? I mean, an Elf, leafy

glades and such like? Better than some lowlife in Twelve Seas anyway. The first time I was with a woman I was fourteen, drunk, and her pimp came in halfway through to check I had enough money.'

'Why hasn't See-ath been in touch?' wails Makri. 'He's ignoring me. Wasn't it important?'

'He's thousands of miles away on an Elvish island. How's he going to get in touch?'

'He could send a message.'

I point out that in the middle of winter even the Elves can't make the voyage to Turai. Makri is unconvinced and seems to think that he should have tried harder.

'I'm sure he could have sent a message.'

'How?'

'He could've used a Sorcerer.'

'Makri, Sorcerers can sometimes communicate over long distances but it's not easy. Only a very powerful Sorcerer could contact Turai from Avula, and he'd need plenty of help from the right conjunctions of the moon, not to mention calm weather and a certain amount of good fortune. It's a difficult business. I really don't think your young lover could persuade the local Sorcerer to send a message to his girlfriend, no matter how much he wanted to.'

'Fine,' says Makri, angrily. 'Be on his side then.' She stands up and storms out the room.

I take a hefty slug of klee. I'm unnerved. I resolve to have a strong word with Tanrose. She should be dealing with this, I'm far too busy investigating. I take another drink and realise I'm feeling angry about the whole thing, though I'm not sure why.

There's a knock on my outside door. I answer it warily,

fearing that the Brotherhood may be here to ask questions about their sudden loss of a dwa dealer. It turns out to be Lisutaris, Mistress of the Sky. I'm moderately pleased to see her and welcome her in. It's probably a good idea to talk to her before the Assemblage, though I'm surprised she's travelled to Twelve Seas. If I was a powerful Sorcerer living in the pleasant environs of Truth is Beauty Lane, nothing would get me south of the river.

Lisutaris has high cheekbones, a lot of fair hair and carries herself elegantly. We're about the same age but you wouldn't know it. She's attractive, and rather glamorous when she takes the notion, though when she arrives she's wrapped in a sensible amount of fur and her rainbow cloak is a practical winter model rather than the fancy thing she normally wears.

My rooms are extremely untidy. Lisutaris isn't overly concerned about the niceties, however, and sweeps some junk off a chair before sitting down and enquiring if I can provide her with some wine to keep her circulation moving while she prepares some thazis for consumption.

'No wine. Beer?'

Lisutaris nods, and concentrates on her thazis. Most people smoke thazis in small sticks, but Lisutaris, when separated from her water pipe, constructs far larger versions, and she proceeds to do this while I bring her ale. In no time the room reeks of thazis and Lisutaris is looking more comfortable.

'It's cold as the ice queen's grave out there,' she mutters. 'I've got a warming spell on my cloak, my hat, my boots and my carriage, and I'm still shivering.'

I ask her what brings her to Twelve Seas.

'I hear you're going to the Assemblage as Cicerius's representative.'

'I am.'

'Did he ask you to fix the election for me?'

'Not exactly. Just to make sure it wasn't fixed against you. Do you care?'

Lisutaris shrugs.

'Not particularly. It will be bad for Turai if the Simnian gets the post, but what the hell, the Orcs will destroy the city soon enough, either that or Nioj will.'

'The King thinks that having you as head of the Guild will give us protection.'

'It might. Who knows?'

Lisutaris inhales another vast amount of thazis smoke.

'What I mainly want to happen at the Assemblage,' she continues, 'is for me not to get killed.'

'You think that's likely?'

She does.

'I received an anonymous message saying an Assassin was on his way.'

Lisutaris is short on details. She's brought the message with her and hands it over. A small piece of paper with neat handwriting.

You may be in danger from an Assassin at the Assemblage. Covinius is coming.

There's nothing else. Nothing else to see, that is, though a piece of paper can often yield a lot to sorcerous investigation. I tell Lisutaris I'll get to work on it.

'Did you inform the Civil Guard?'

'Yes. But the Guards won't be allowed into the Assemblage. That's why I want to hire you.'

I tell Lisutaris that strictly she doesn't have to. Cicerius has already hired me to work on her behalf. Lisutaris insists she'd be happier if she hired me directly, and there's some sense in this so I take a retainer fee from her.

'It's very hard to get any information about the Assassins. But I'll do my best. Most probably it's just some crank.'

'Who is Covinius?' asks Lisutaris.

'A member of the Simnian Assassins Guild. He has an evil reputation. People say he's never failed on a mission.'

'I'm not feeling any better,' says Lisutaris, frowning. 'I don't want this job enough to get killed for it.'

Lisutaris is strong enough to carry a powerful protection spell at all times. This will turn a blade, but there's no saying how many ways a murderous expert like Covinius could find to get around it. I repeat that there's probably nothing in it, but in truth I'm worried.

A freezing draught from under the door is badly affecting my feet. I kick an old cushion over to cover the gap. Lisutaris smiles. There are plenty of Sorcerers I wouldn't welcome here, but Lisutaris isn't the snobbish type. Back in the war she slept in a tent by the walls like everyone else. I realise I rather like her. I'll be sorry if she ends up with an Assassin's dart in her heart.

'I need someone to watch my back,' says the Sorcerer.

'Didn't you just hire me for that?'

'Yes. But you're going to be busy with other things at the Assemblage. I want to recruit Makri as a bodyguard.'

This doesn't seem like a bad idea. If you want a bodyguard, Makri is a good choice, providing you don't mind her killing a few extra people every now and then. And with the Guild College being closed for the winter, she's got time on her hands.

'I think she'll be pleased to do it. Cheer her up, probably.'

'Has Makri been unhappy?'

In other circumstances it would be strange that the well-bred Mistress of the Sky would even know Makri, but they've met through the Association of Gentlewomen. So I believe anyway, though the Association keeps its business secret.

'Fairly unhappy. A few personal problems. I sorted most of it out.'

Lisutaris's attention is already starting to wander. When I ask her about the Assemblage it takes a few moments for her to reply.

'How exactly is the new head of the Guild chosen? Is it a straight election or is there some sort of test?'

'Both. The Sorcerers vote on the candidates and the top two go on to a final elimination.'

'Which involves?'

'A test inside the magic space.'

'What test?'

The Mistress of the Sky doesn't know. Charius the Wise will set the test, and he's keeping the details close to his chest.

'With any luck we'll be looking for thazis plants,' says Lisutaris, who's fairly single-minded about her pleasures these days. I show her along the corridor to Makri's room and leave her at the door before heading downstairs for a beer. I get myself round a Happy Guildsman jumbo tankard of ale and inform Gurd that his barmaid will be missing for a few days as she is about to perform the duties of bodyguard for Turai's leading Sorcerer. Gurd looks relieved. He's been suffering at the hands of Makri's moods, and ever since Tanrose told him it was due to some emotional difficulties, the Barbarian has been terrified that Makri might broach the subject with him. Gurd has more than enough emotional problems of his own. He's attracted to Tanrose and never quite knows what to do about it.

'It will take her mind off things,' says Gurd. 'Why did she want to get involved with an Elf anyway?'

'I don't know. Probably thinks they're handsome.'

'Why would she care about that? A good fighter and a good provider, that's what a man should be.'

Sensing that Gurd is now worrying that Tanrose might not think he's handsome enough, I change the subject.

'I'm about to look after an election. Not a job I ever thought I'd end up doing.'

'You think it will be fair?'

'I'll make sure it is. Turai is depending on me, and I'm depending on the hefty fee Cicerius has offered me.'

'But what about all the magic they'll be using?' asks Gurd. As a northern Barbarian, he's never been too comfortable with magic.

'It won't matter. If there's anything irregular going on I'll pick it up. Easy as bribing a Senator for a man of my experience.'

The tavern fills up as the evening draws on. The fierce winter is not harming Gurd's business. People would rather be drinking in the warmth of the Avenging Axe than huddling miserably at home. I load up with several bowls of stew, then depart upstairs with beer. I look in on Makri to see if she's taken the job as bodyguard. Lisutaris is still here. She's lying unconscious on the floor surrounded by the remains of numerous enormous thazis sticks. Makri is comatose beside her. The room is so thick with smoke I can barely see the far wall. I shake my head.

'You'll be a fine new head of the Sorcerers Guild,' I mutter, and leave them to it. If Cicerius could see her now, I figure he'd be regretting his choice.

CHAPTER
SIX

I take the paper to Astrath Triple Moon and ask him to work on it for me.

'Do you have any more details?'

A good Sorcerer can often glean information from an object but only if he has something to go on, something to anchor the enquiry. Left to his own devices, Astrath might scan the city for days and not link the paper to anything.

'It might not even have originated in Turai.'

'It did. I checked the watermark. The paper was made and sold right here in Turai. And it's a woman's handwriting.'

'How do you know?'

'I know. I'm an Investigator. The message was handed in at the Messengers Guild post in the middle of Royal Boulevard, which doesn't narrow it down much. That's a busy station, and the man on duty doesn't remember who brought it in. But I have a hunch. Not that many people in Turai would ever have heard of Covinius. A few people at Palace Security maybe, but they don't employ women. But there is one woman who'd know all about him. And she's based in Kushni, not far from that messenger post. Hanama.'

'Hanama?'

'One of our own Assassins. She might send a warning to Lisutaris.'

'Wouldn't that be against the Assassins' rules?'

'Hanama seems to be playing by her own set these days.'

Astrath Triple Moon agrees to check her out, and I carry on with my preparations for the Assemblage. Cicerius is providing me with expenses money so I'll be okay for beer. Makri complains continually about the weather and is even more irritating than usual.

'Maybe she should sail back to Elf land,' suggests Gurd, after clearing up the tavern following a fight between Makri and three dock workers who she claimed had insulted her. 'A barmaid has to expect a few insults, it's part of the job.'

Two days later I'm standing outside a large hall at the edge of Thamlin, just outside the grounds of the Imperial Palace. The grounds are white, covered by snow. The trees are frosted and the ponds and fountains frozen over. Snow is falling heavily and the assembled soldiery and Civil Guards stand miserably in shivering ranks. They're gathered here because the King himself has been making a speech to the Sorcerers, welcoming them to the Assemblage and wishing them a pleasant time in the city state of Turai.

I'm stuck outside because I wasn't invited to this part of the ceremony, which demonstrates that Tribune of the People is not that great a thing to be. While I'm waiting to be let in, I reflect sadly that a few years ago, when I was Senior Investigator at Palace Security, I'd see the King regularly. I doubt he'd recognise me these days. If he did he wouldn't acknowledge me. A man who's been bounced out of his job for drunkenness at the Palace no longer has enough status to be noticed by the King. I wonder if Rittius will show up at the Assemblage. He's the current head of Palace Security and a bitter enemy of mine. I've done him plenty of bad turns and he's paid them all back. Last year he took me to court and damn near bankrupted me. I shiver. Maybe I can persuade one of the Sorcerers here to show me a more effective spell for warming my cloak.

It's a relief when the King and his retinue emerge from the building and ride off through the blizzard. I trudge forward to the huge portico that leads into the Royal Hall. This is one of the largest buildings in Turai, almost as big as the Senate. It dates from a few hundred years ago but, as with Turai's other public buildings, it's kept in excellent repair by the King. He likes his public works to look impressive and he's not short of money since the trade route from the south opened up a few years back, and the gold mines in the north ran into some very productive veins of ore.

'Sorcerers and their staff only,' says a young woman at the door. Her blue cloak signifies that she is an apprentice.

I bring out my letter bearing Cicerius's seal and flash it in her direction.

'Official Turanian government representative,' I say. She studies the paper.

'Tribune of the People? What's that?'

'A very important position,' I reply, and march past. After standing outside in the cold for what seems like hours I'm not about to explain my business to the hired help.

Once inside, my first task is to find beer. Sorcerers
need a plentiful supply and so do I. After making some
enquiries I find that refreshments are served in the Room
of Saints at the back of the hall. It's already crowded
and no one is looking at the statues, frescoes and
mosaics of our great religious figures. Drinking is
already underway. The Sorcerers, no doubt bored by the
King's speech, are keen to get on with the business of
enjoying themselves. Normally in a crowded inn I'd use
my body weight to force my way through, but here I'm
rather more circumspect. It's absolutely forbidden for a
Sorcerer to blast anyone with a spell at the Assemblage
– it would lead to immediate expulsion – but I don't want
to offend anyone unnecessarily. Not yet anyway. I'll get
round to it soon enough.

I grab a beer and a small bottle of klee and head back
to the main hall, where I look around to see if there are
any faces I recognise. I'm due to meet Cicerius but I want
to get my bearings first and maybe see if I can learn
anything useful. The main room of the Royal Hall is
vast. Frescoes decorate the walls and ceilings, and a
huge and intricate mosaic depicting the triumphs of
Saint Quatinius covers the floor. In every corner there
are statues of past heroes of Turai. The stained-glass
windows are noted for their beauty and contain some
of the finest surviving work of Usax, Turai's greatest
artist. Fine though the stained glass is, it doesn't let in
a great amount of light, and torches are lit at regular
intervals along the walls.

The great room is full of Sorcerers of every description. Each is wearing his or her best cloak, which makes
for an impressive collection of rainbows. In the middle

of the floor a group of Turanians are holding court, welcoming old friends and allies. Old Hasius the Brilliant, Chief Investigating Sorcerer at the Abode of Justice, stands beside Harmon Half Elf and Melus the Fair. Next to them Gorsius Starfinder is guzzling wine and Tirini Snake Smiter – our most glamorous Sorcerer, and without a doubt the only one to wear a rainbow cloak made of transparent muslin – is showing off her smile to some younger admirers.

All Turai's most powerful Sorcerers, standing in a group like they haven't a care in the world. I immediately feel irritated. Close to them are some of our younger adepts: Lanius Suncatcher, the new Chief Sorcerer at Palace Security, along with Capali Comet Rider and Orius Fire Tamer. They irritate me as well. Lisutaris, Mistress of the Sky, doesn't seem to be here yet. Still wrapped around her water pipe, no doubt. As Turanian candidate for head of the Guild, the woman is going to be a disaster. There again, I can't see many of these people staying sober for the whole week.

Despite the gathering of so many magic workers under one roof, there's no real sorcery going on. Though Sorcerers are not as a rule modest, it would be regarded as bad taste to show off one's powers in such company. Here and there someone might use his illuminated staff to check under his seat for his tankard or place a large object discreetly inside a magic pocket, but there are no demonstrations of great power. Today is for meeting old friends, relaxing, and hearing news from round the world. Demonstrations of power can wait, and so can the election, which won't happen for a few days yet.

I'm still waiting for Astrath's report on the piece of

paper. He's decided to attend the Assemblage so I'm hoping to learn something from him later. I wonder if the message was genuine. I hope not. Covinius means trouble. Even for an Assassin he seems to be almost intangible. No one has ever seen him, and that bothers me. In what guise is he planning to appear? Though the Sorcerers are strict about who they admit to the Assemblage, an experienced Assassin like Covinius would have no trouble in assuming a convincing identity. The worrying thought strikes me that he might actually be a Sorcerer. I've never heard of a sorcerous Assassin, but there's always a first time. It's hard enough gaining any information about the Assassins Guild here in Turai. As for their equivalent in Simnia, who knows? The best I can hope for is that if Covinius does show, he'll kill someone else and leave Lisutaris alone. If that happens, some other Investigator can sort it out.

Cicerius appears at my side, resplendent in the green-edged toga which denotes his rank.

'Where is Lisutaris?' he enquires.

'Not here yet.'

'Not here yet?' The Deputy Consul is incredulous. 'How can she be late at a time like this?'

Cicerius can't quite understand that not everyone is desperate to do their duty for Turai all the time. He scans the room, tutting in frustration.

'Come with me,' he instructs. 'While we await the arrival of our candidate, I shall introduce you to your fellow Tribunes, and Tilupasis.'

He leads me across the floor of the main hall. I pass by many faces I recognise, people who were apprentices at the same time as me and are now powerful Sorcerers.

Cicerius ushers me into a small side room, one of the many which adjoin the hall. There we find Tilupasis, Visus and Sulinius. Cicerius introduces us formally.

Tilupasis is thirty-five, with nothing flashy in her appearance. She's wealthy, fashionable enough, but not much given to frivolity. A politician's wife and, since the death of her husband, something of a politician herself. I know our Senators take her seriously. She has the ear of the Consul, and friends at the Palace, and the ability to do people favours.

Visus and Sulinius are both around twenty, young men not yet begun on their careers. Sulinius is the son of Praetor Capatius, the richest man in Turai, and Visus is also of aristocratic parentage. They both look fresh-faced and handsome in their white togas, and eager to perform their tasks well. Becoming a Tribune of the People in order to attend the Sorcerers Assemblage is an unconventional start to a political career, but if they do well, Cicerius will look favourably on their subsequent careers.

Tilupasis informs the Deputy Consul that the Assemblage has begun satisfactorily. The Sorcerers are settling in well. More importantly, Tilupasis has already made a count of probable votes, and thinks Lisutaris is in with a chance.

'Sunstorm Ramius is the favourite to win, but there are a lot of Sorcerers here who haven't decided who to vote for. I'm certain we can get Lisutaris elected provided she herself puts up a good showing.'

Cicerius is pleased. He entreats his two young Tribunes to work hard for Turai. He tells me to let him know the moment I suspect any hint of treachery by any other delegation.

'Above all, be sure to act in a manner which brings only credit to Turai. It is vital that we show our visitors that Turanians are people of high moral standards. Do nothing which could be interpreted otherwise.'

Cicerius departs. Tilupasis turns to us.

'Disregard everything the Deputy Consul just said,' she tells us briskly. 'Turai needs to win this election and I'm here to make sure we do. If we can gather enough votes fairly, all well and good. If not, we'll buy them. I have an endless supply of gold, silver, wine, whores, pretty boys, dwa and thazis to keep the Sorcerers happy. Personal favours, political favours, anything. Whatever they need, we provide. Understand?'

The two young Tribunes gape. This is not what they were expecting. I'm unsurprised. It's exactly what I was expecting. You don't win a post like head of the Sorcerers Guild by fair play and good behaviour. Cicerius knows it, though he's not intending to dirty his hands with the details. That's Tilupasis's job, and from her introduction I'd say she was going to be good at it. She starts handing out detailed instructions to Visus and Sulinius as to which Sorcerers they are to approach.

I'm becoming increasingly uncomfortable. I never like being told what to do, and I fear I'm about to be ordered about in a manner quite unsuitable for a Private Investigator. My mood, already poor, worsens.

'Thraxas. I'm not depending on you to charm anyone, or manoeuvre for votes. We'll take care of that. I need you to look after Lisutaris and inform me immediately if you get wind of anything going on which may damage her chances.'

'Fine. I'll start in the Room of Saints. I could do with another beer.'

I'm hoping this might annoy her.

'A good choice,' says Tilupasis, unperturbed. 'Let me escort you there.'

She leads me out into the main hall. I'm wearing my best cloak but I'm still shabby beside her. Tilupasis is conservatively but fashionably dressed in a white robe with just enough jewellery to let people know she's got wealth on her side. The hall is now crowded and we pause to allow two blonde-haired female Sorcerers to pass.

'From the far north,' says Tilupasis. 'I already have their votes.'

'Did it cost much?'

'A little gold, a dragon-scale necklace or two. They were quite reasonable.'

Her eyes come to rest on one of the more exotic figures in the hall, a tall young woman in a cloak which is mainly gold, with the rainbow pattern visible only at the collar. The woman is dark-skinned and has hair so long as to make me suspect it's been sorcerously enhanced, stretching down almost to her knees. In amongst the dark mass of hair are several golden streaks and some beads which brilliantly reflect the torchlight. I've never seen so much hair on one person. It's an impressive sight. Beneath her rather spectacular golden cloak she's wearing a somewhat more functional tunic and leggings, marking her out as a visitor from outside the city. Very few Turanian women ever wear male attire, apart of course from Makri, and some of the lower-class workers at the markets.

'Princess Direeva?'

'Yes. One of the most powerful Sorcerers in the Wastelands.'

'Not an associate of Horm the Dead, I hope?'

Horm the Dead, a renegade half-Orc Sorcerer, almost destroyed Turai last year.

Tilupasis shakes her head.

'Her lands are far south of his. I don't think they're friends.'

Turanians tend to be suspicious of anyone who lives in the Wastelands, the long stretch of ungoverned territory that separates us from the Orcs in the east.

'Better to have her as a friend than an enemy, I suppose,' I mutter.

'More than that. Princess Direeva is of huge importance in this election. She carries a great many votes.'

'She does?'

'Of course. Her father's kingdom, the Southern Hills, is rich in sorcery. It has to be, being so close to the Orcs. Without magical protection they'd have been overrun long ago. There are ten Sorcerers here directly under her sway. But that's not all. The Wastelands are full of tiny regions that look to them for leadership. When you count up all the Sorcerers from these regions, it comes to something like thirty votes. That could be enough to sway the election. Right now I believe she favours Darius, the Abelasian, so winning over Princess Direeva is one of the most important tasks I have.'

The Princess stands rather aloof from the crowd. She's attended by two apprentices in blue cloaks but makes no attempt to mingle with the other Sorcerers. Tilupasis excuses herself, and heads over to begin her

offensive on Direeva. I'm surprised that the young
woman has thirty votes under her control. Already I'm
feeling slightly baffled by the complexity of the election.

I've spotted Sunstorm Ramius on the far side of the
room and I'm keen to get an impression of the Simnian.
He's a man of medium height and build, around fifty-
five but showing no effects of age. His beard is short and
well trimmed and he stands erect with something of the
manner of a soldier. Ramius won himself a fine reputation during the last Orc Wars and he looks like a man
who wouldn't flinch in the face of danger. Around him
are a large collection of friends and admirers, and from
the way they hang on to his words I can tell that he carries a lot of weight round here.

Charismatic and powerful, I reflect. Bad news for
Lisutaris. But good to know. Apart from my official business here, there's the ever-important matter of gambling on the result, and if I can't succeed in getting
Lisutaris elected I'm at least planning to back the
winner. Honest Mox has been taking bets on the outcome of this election for weeks now, but I've been holding off till I get a chance to study the form in person.
My first impression is that Sunstorm Ramius is probably worth his place as favourite.

I hang around on the fringes of the group who surround Ramius. They're talking of the election and I
listen keenly, because there are other candidates to con-
sider. Lisutaris, Rokim, Darius and Ramius may be the
early favourites, but that's not to say there won't be a
strong showing from anyone else. Surprise candidates
have been known to win the post before, creeping
through the pack when the Assemblage has been unable

to make up its mind. Or bribing their way to power, though the Sorcerers will never admit that this has happened.

I'm heading back to the bar for a fresh tankard of ale when a slight stir in the hall heralds the arrival of Lisutaris, Mistress of the Sky. She enters quite grandly, as befits her rank, with a young female apprentice beside her and Makri bringing up the rear. Lisutaris is extravagantly coiffured and wears her finest rainbow cloak over a white robe which trails elegantly behind her as she walks. She has silver Elvish bangles, a silver tiara, a necklace of three rows of emeralds and a pair of gold shoes that must have cost the equivalent of a shipload of grain.

Behind her Makri is wearing her full light body armour, something I've rarely seen. Usually when she gets into a fight in Twelve Seas there's no time to be donning armour. She brought it with her from the Orc lands and it's made of black leather partly covered with chainmail, which will turn most blades. Makri carries her helmet under her arm, and while she isn't wearing a blade – this is not allowed at the Assemblage – I've no doubt that Lisutaris will be holding one discreetly for her in a magic pocket. Anyone with an experienced eye can see that the wearer of such a suit is a person who knows how to fight; a worthwhile bodyguard. It makes for an impressive entrance. Lisutaris looks like a Sorcerer who means business.

I make my way over to greet them. Lisutaris is already surrounded by Sorcerers and, not for the first time, Makri also finds herself the object of some interest. Makri's reddish skin tone gives away her Orcish blood

– any Sorcerer would sense it anyway – and I can see that people are already wondering who this exotic creature is that walks behind Lisutaris wearing Orcish armour with the gait of a warrior.

'Nice entrance.'

'You think so?' says Makri. 'I was worried about the armour. But Lisutaris wanted her bodyguard to look businesslike.'

'Probably a wise move. Why are you late? The water pipe?'

'Only partly,' says Makri. 'Lisutaris was having her hair done by Copro.'

'I guess that explains it. How did you like our finest beautician?'

'He's okay,' says Makri, noncommittally. 'He offered to show me his new range of make-up from Samsarina. I told him I didn't need it.'

After her tough upbringing in the gladiator pits Makri still professes some contempt for the softness of our Turanian aristocracy, though in recent months she's moderated her hostility towards make-up, particularly in the field of colouring her nails.

'Does Lisutaris have your swords?'

Makri shakes her head.

'I've got them in my pocket. She lent me a magic purse.' She pats her hip. 'I've got two swords, three knives and an axe in here.'

A magic purse is a container of the magic space. You can put anything in there and it loses all mass and volume, which is very handy for carrying hidden weapons. It's a small manifestation of the magic space in which some of the sorcerous tests will later be carried out. Normally it's illegal to walk around Turai with a magic purse, but the Consul has suspended this law for the duration of the Assemblage.

Two young Sorcerers – Samsarinan, from their clothes – are attempting to edge their way past me to greet Lisutaris. Or possibly to introduce themselves to Makri. I leave them to it. Maybe if Makri gets involved with someone else she'll stop being miserable about the Elf.

I'm picking up a beer when a heavy hand pounds me on the back.

'Thraxas? Is that you?'

I turn round to find a large Sorcerer with a red face and a bushy grey beard smiling at me. I don't recognise him.

'It's me. Irith.'

'Irith Victorious?'

'The same! You've put on weight!'

'So have you.'

I slap him on the back enthusiastically. I haven't seen Irith Victorious for more than twenty years. When I was a mercenary down in Juval, Irith was a hired Sorcerer in the same army. It was the first time I met Gurd, the war was messy and confused and just about the only good things were the klee, provisions and occasional good times supplied by Irith Victorious. He was a slim youth in those days, but from the size of his waistline I'd say he'd carried on with the good times.

'What are you doing now?'

'I made good. King's Chief Sorcerer in Juval. You wouldn't have thought that was going to happen when the Abelasians were chasing us through the jungle! What are you doing here?'

Irith knows I never made it as a Sorcerer. When he learns I'm working for the Deputy Consul he roars with laughter. I find myself roaring with laughter too. I always liked Irith.

'There's six Sorcerers from Juval here and we're looking for a good time. Come and meet them!'

I go to meet them. They turn out to be six of the largest, most jovial Sorcerers ever made, each with a loud voice, a large belly and a mission in life to get as much ale inside him as possible, all the while shouting in a loud voice for more beer, more stories about the old days and more serving girls to sit on his knee.

'The election?' yells one of them, who's drinking a huge flagon of ale while another hovers at his side. 'Who cares? Hey, can anyone else do this?'

He mutters a word and the floating tankard rises and starts emptying beer into his mouth. I'm extremely impressed. It's one of the finest spells I've ever seen. His companions bellow with laughter and start trying to emulate the feat. Soon beer is flowing in all directions. Waitresses are scurrying this way and that with fresh supplies and Irith Victorious is claiming in the loudest of voices that he doesn't care what anyone says, he was the real champion at the last Juvalian Sorcerers' drinking contest and anyone who says otherwise is an Orc-lover.

'The Juvalian drinking contest is as nothing compared to the feats of Thraxas of Turai!' I bawl, and start on a fresh tankard.

'Turai?' screams Juval. 'No one can drink in this city. Too cold! I've been as cold as a frozen pixie since I got here. Southern heat, that's what makes a drinker!'

'Southern heat? I've seen a two-fingered troll drink

more than a Juvalian Sorcerer. Haven't you finished that tankard yet?'

I call for more beer.

'And charge it to Cicerius!'

We toast the Deputy Consul, and then the Deputy Consul in Juval, or some such official. I don't quite catch the title.

'Anyone betting on the election?' I enquire, some time later.

Irith is a gambler but he's not as enthusiastic about betting on the contest as I thought he might be. He knows – as does any Sorcerer who's interested – there's a woman working in the kitchens as a cook whose actual purpose is to act as a runner, taking bets to a bookmaker, but he doesn't fancy the odds.

'Sunstorm Ramius is the strong favourite and they're only offering two to one on. Hardly seems worth it. I can never get excited about an odds-on bet.'

I nod. Risking a stake of twenty gurans to win only ten isn't that attractive a prospect to a fun-loving Sorcerer like Irith. Myself, I might go for it at the chariot races if I was certain I was backing the winner. Here at the Assemblage, I'm not so sure. Having seen Tilupasis swinging into action, it doesn't seem impossible that Lisutaris might win. I heard Tilupasis telling young Visus in strong terms that she didn't care how old the Chief Sorcerer from Misan was, it was his duty to show her round the city and make sure she was having a good time. As the elderly Sorcerer departed on Visus's arm she looked pretty happy, so that's probably a few more votes for Turai. Furthermore, I'm on Lisutaris's side and I have a lot of confidence in my abilities.

'Number one chariot,' I tell Irith.

'What at?'

'Investigating. Drinking. Fighting. Getting votes. Lots of things. Sharp as an Elf's ear. Where's the beer?'

Providing Lisutaris, Mistress of the Sky, can avoid appearing in public looking like she's just unwillingly detached herself from her water pipe and is having trouble putting one foot in front of the other, I reckon she's in with a chance. Most people like her, she's maintained her good reputation and she can muster a lot of charm when she has to. A few beers later it's as clear as day that I should be placing a hefty bet on the Mistress of the Sky, so I head for the kitchens to do just that, picking up a plate of venison and a huge peach pie on the way back. I get back to drinking with the Juvalians, and entertain one and all with a fine story of my exploits in the war between Juval, Abelasi and Pargada, twenty-four years ago.

'It was the first time I met Gurd, and we gave the Pargadans hell, I can tell you.'

Some hours later a tired-looking attendant suggests to us that as the Royal Hall has now completely emptied of Sorcerers, it may be time for us to go home. I clamber to my feet, bid farewell to Irith and his companions, step lightly over the one or two Juvalian Sorcerers now lying prostrate on the floor, and stumble out the building. I'd say the Assemblage has gone well so far. Far more enjoyable than I anticipated. I wonder what happened to Lisutaris and Makri. I shrug. Powerful Sorcerer and ferocious warrior. They can look after themselves.

At the door I run into Tilupasis. She looks as fresh and elegant as she did at the start of the day.

'Get many votes?' I ask.

'I believe so. And you?'

'I may have secured the support of the Juvalians.'

'You mean you out-drank them?'

'I did. It was a close-run thing, but I was drinking for Turai.'

Tilupasis laughs, quite elegantly.

'Good.'

'Good?'

I was hoping she'd be annoyed. It still bothers me that I'm obliged to be here working for the government.

'I have Visus and Sulinius to charm those who need to be charmed. But for those who need to be drunk into submission, I have you. I told Cicerius you would be a good man to have on our side.'

Tilupasis departs. Going to snuggle up with the Consul maybe. I have a peculiar feeling I've been outsmarted somehow. To hell with them.

Outside, the only landus I can find doesn't want to take me south of the river. I'm obliged to raise my fist and inform the driver that his landus is going south, with or without him. We set off through the snow. The streets are quiet. I'm cold. It wasn't such a bad day.

Astrath Triple Moon sends me a message apologising for his non-appearance at the Assemblage, claiming illness. The message ends with the brief sentence, *Paper came from Hanama.*

I mull this over with my morning beer. Astrath has good powers of sorcerous investigation and his results can generally be trusted. My hunch was correct. It was Hanama who warned Lisutaris about Covinius. This means I'll have to talk to her. Talking to Assassins is never something I enjoy doing.

I finish my beer, warm up my cloak and set off through the snow for the Assemblage. Once there I nose around for a while, check that Makri is looking after Lisutaris's back, then get round to drinking with Irith and his companions. In the rooms and corridors of the Royal Hall, the electioneering is gathering pace. So far I've had little involvement in the machinations of Tilupasis, although she does ask me to escort young Sulinius to a secluded location behind the hall.

'He's carrying a lot of gold and I don't want him to get robbed.'

The gold buys the votes of four Sorcerers from Carsan. Tilupasis is well satisfied.

'Let the Simnians try to match that.'

'Are they busy with bribery as well?'

'Of course. So are the Abelasians. But they lack the advantage of being at home. I have access to the King's vaults. We can out-spend them.'

The only other task I'm given is to call in at a local Civil Guard station to bail out two Samsarinans who found themselves in some trouble after an argument at the card table in a tavern. Tilupasis refunds their losses, promises to show them a more hospitable venue for gambling the next night and charms them sufficiently to make some inroads on the Samsarinan delegation. Samsarina have their own candidate, Rokim the Bright, but Tilupasis hopes to persuade them to switch their eighteen votes to Lisutaris if things seem hopeless for their candidate.

'Eighteen second-choice votes,' she says. 'At present they're attached to the Simnian, but I'm hoping we can sway them.'

Tilupasis is proving to be a highly efficient organiser and has boundless energy. Her main worry is Princess Direeva. In a tight contest the thirty Sorcerers under her influence are looking more important than ever, but they're intending to vote for Darius Cloud Walker, the Abelasian. Direeva has known him for a long time, and trusts him.

'I can't seem to get to Direeva. Her representative rebuffed a very generous offer. She doesn't appear to want for anything. She wasn't interested in gold and she didn't seem to take to either Visus or Sulinius.'

At least Lisutaris is holding up, just about. Accompanied by Makri, she greets her fellow Sorcerers, quite charmingly from what I can tell, disappearing only occasionally to indulge her need for thazis. So far she has not disgraced Turai by falling over in public. I've informed Tilupasis and Cicerius about the possible involvement of a Simnian Assassin. Cicerius is sceptical.

'Palace Security would have notified me if Covinius had entered Turai,' says the Deputy Consul. 'I can't believe that Lisutaris is in danger of being assassinated. The Sorcerers' election is keenly contested but there has never been an assassination. Who is meant to have hired him?'

'I don't know yet. I'll check it out as soon as I can.'

Tilupasis promises to discreetly inform the other Turanian Sorcerers of the warning so they can watch out for Lisutaris, just in case the threat turns out to be real. Which, along with Makri, gives her quite a lot of protection. I've sent a message to Hanama requesting a meeting, but have had no reply as yet.

I excuse myself from Tilupasis as it seems like a long time since I had a beer. Close to the Room of Saints, I bump into Makri.

'Any trouble?'

Makri shakes her head.

'No trouble.'

At this moment Princess Direeva appears at our side. Ignoring me, she introduces herself to Makri.

'I am Princess Direeva,' she says. 'And you are?'

'Makri.'

The Princess nods.

'I thought so. Champion gladiator of all the Orc lands, I believe?'

Princess Direeva is apparently impressed.

'I understand you were undefeated for five years?'

'Six,' says Makri.

'Really? And you once fought a dragon in the arena?'

'I did.'

Direeva seems intrigued. Her extraordinary hair sways gently as she talks, making the gold streaks and glittering beads sparkle in the light. There may be a touch of Orcish blood about the Princess herself. Though only Human Sorcerers can stand for the post of Guild leader, there are various Sorcerers in attendance with Elvish blood in their veins, so I suppose a little Orc isn't such a surprise. The Sorcerers are not so formal as many of the city's Guilds. Makri would be bounced right out of a meeting of the goldsmiths, but goldsmiths are always very concerned about etiquette.

I've heard Makri bragging about her accomplishments in the arena enough times already, and Princess Direeva shows no interest in talking to me, so I slip off. In the Room of Saints Tilupasis is encouraging some Pargadans to drink more wine. She asks me what Princess Direeva wanted with Makri.

'A friendly chat.'

'Really?'

Tilupasis's eyes light up.

'Excellent. We may have found something the Princess is interested in.'

I spend the rest of the day drinking with Irith Victorious. He asks me how I'm coping with my official duties.

'It's all right. Better than rowing a slave galley. It wasn't like I had anything else planned for the winter.'

One of Irith's companions teaches me an improved

warming spell for my cloak. So now I'm warm and I
have plenty of free beer. I'm starting to enjoy this
assignment.

The light fades early and I arrive home in darkness.
I take care climbing the stairs to my office. I may be full
of beer but Thraxas, number one chariot among Turai's
Investigators, has never been known to fall off his own
staircase. I'm nearly as happy as a drunken mercenary.
These Sorcerers from Juval know how to enjoy themselves. Maybe I should move down there. Be better than
this lousy city.

'Better than this lousy city!' I yell into the darkness.
There's no one around and I take the opportunity to
bellow the last verse of an old army drinking song before
entering my office in a cheerful manner and finding
Makri, Lisutaris and Princess Direeva all unconscious
on the floor. Darius Cloud Walker is lying dead beside
them with a knife in his back. I blink. It isn't a sight I
was expecting.

The sheer awfulness of the situation almost paraly-
ses me. The room stinks of dwa and thazis. I'm full of
beer. I can't cope with a dead Sorcerer. I'm still trying
to take it in when there's a knock on the door and a
voice I recognise shouts my name.

'Thraxas. We want to talk to you.'

It's Karlox, an enforcer for the Brotherhood. I mutter
a foul curse at Makri for landing me in this situation.
From the look of her face I'd say she's been indulging in
more dwa than she can handle. If the overdose doesn't
kill her I swear I'll do it myself.

My first thought is to kill Karlox, get on a horse, ride
out of town and keep going. The situation is so grim as

to defy description. When Cicerius hired me to help Lisutaris he wasn't expecting me to lure her rivals to my office and have them murdered, which is what this is going to look like. I'm heading for the scaffold in the exotic company of Makri, Lisutaris and Princess Direeva, and that's going to make a fine story for the *Renowned and Truthful Chronicle*.

'Open up, Thraxas,' shouts Karlox. 'I know you're in there.'

Karlox may be dumb as an Orc but he's a loyal member of the Brotherhood, not the sort of man to give in easily. I've a shrewd idea he's here investigating the recent death of their dwa dealer, and that's a big enough problem in itself. Makri killed him and at this moment she's unconscious at my feet and there's an important Sorcerer dead on the floor. It would be easy to panic.

I'm not a man to panic. I remain silent and quickly weigh up the situation. I doubt that Karlox is here alone. He knows he couldn't get the better of me without help. If he's here with a gang, he'll be able to break down the door, minor locking spell or not. The one thing I can't afford to happen is for any witnesses to see Darius lying alongside Makri. Particularly as it's Makri's knife that's sticking in his back.

If I move the body I'll be in endless difficulties later. If I don't move it I'll be in endless difficulties right now. Karlox beats on the door and I can hear him giving orders to start breaking it down. I hoist the unfortunate Darius over my shoulder and stagger to the inner door. Darius doesn't weigh that much. The shock of these events has sobered me up just enough not to fall and break my neck as I make my way down the stairs and through to the back of the tavern. To my surprise, Gurd and Tanrose are still about, making preparations for tomorrow's food.

'What—?'

'Can't stop. Go upstairs and look after Makri till I get back. The Brotherhood are about to break the door down.'

Gurd picks up his axe and they depart swiftly. I carry on through to the yard. Ideally I'd like to dump the body as far away as possible, but I can't risk being seen from the front of the tavern so I can think of nothing better to do than heave the body over the wall into the next yard. It's a high wall and I'm panting with the exertion. The snow billows around me, muffling any sound.

I pray that no one has seen my actions. Not that it will matter in a day or two, when the Sorcerers' companions start working their spells, looking for Darius. I've just committed a serious crime and I've no idea how I'm going to escape the consequences. Without pausing to catch my breath I hurry back upstairs to find Gurd and Tanrose confronting Karlox and six companions. They've forced the door, breaking the lock.

Gurd is outraged at the damage to his property, but the Brotherhood men are more interested in the sight of Makri, Lisutaris and Princess Direeva lying on the floor. My room is still thick with thazis smoke and reeks of burnt dwa.

'Been having a party?' rasps Karlox.

I unsheathe my sword and stand beside Gurd. With his axe in his hand the old Barbarian is still a formidable sight.

'Time to leave,' I say.

'Where did you get the dwa?' says Karlox, which is quite a shrewd question for such a stupid guy.

I'm not planning on giving him an answer, though it's a question I'll certainly be putting to Makri. I tell Karlox brusquely that he's got about ten seconds to leave my office or suffer the consequences. He eyes my blade, and Gurd's axe.

'Why so upset, fat man? We're just asking a few polite questions about the death of one of our men. You got something to hide? Or are you just wanting some time alone with the doped girls?'

His men guffaw.

'You've given me plenty to report,' says Karlox. With that he turns and strides out of the room, followed by his men. I immediately shut the door and place my locking spell on it, for all the good that will do.

'What's going on?' asks Gurd, but I'm already bending down over Makri. I'm mad as hell at the woman but I don't want her to expire from dwa. She's completely inexperienced in its use. Or I thought she was.

Lesada leaves, from the Elvish Isles, serve me mainly as hangover cures but I've seen an Elvish healer use them to bring a person out of a dwa trance. I crush a couple in some water and pour some down Makri's throat. She coughs, sits up and looks around her curiously.

'What's happening?' she says.

'A good question.'

She looks round the room. I ask her if she notices anything missing.

'Like what?'

'Like a Sorcerer maybe?'

'Right. Darius. Where is he?'

'He's lying in a snowdrift in the next yard. Did you kill him?'

Makri looks puzzled.

'Of course not. Why would I?'

'Who knows? But when I got here Darius was dead on the floor and your knife was still sticking in his back. The Brotherhood arrived and I had to hide the body. If we don't move fast we're all heading for a swift execution. So help me wake up these two and tell me what's been going on.'

Gurd and Tanrose want to stay and help but I banish them from the room. The less they're involved the better. I set about trying to revive Princess Direeva, while Makri gets to work on Lisutaris.

'What were you thinking of, taking dwa? You know what happened to Minarixa.'

Makri shrugs.

'I was depressed.'

I don't have time to be outraged. Makri tells me that after the Assemblage ended Lisutaris said she didn't want to go back to Thamlin. 'She said she'd show Princess Direeva the bad part of town. Direeva seemed keen to accompany us.'

'Why did you bring Darius?'

'He just sort of tagged along. I think he liked Direeva.'

Lisutaris and Direeva come slowly back to consciousness, aided by Lesada leaves and deat, a foul herbal drink traditionally taken to sober up. They're both confused and don't yet realise the urgency of the situation.

'I need to sleep,' says Lisutaris.

'You need to sleep? You'll be going for a very long

sleep if we don't do something about this. As soon as Darius is missed, his Sorcerer buddies will start scanning the city for him. They'll locate his body soon enough. And when they do they'll start looking back in time to find out what happened. That might take days or weeks but they'll succeed in the end. Thanks to you invading my office I'm now involved in this disaster, and if we ever get out of it, next time you want to take dwa and hang around with dead guys, stay well away from me.'

'Yes, fine, it's an aggravating situation,' says Lisutaris, coldly. 'But you ranting isn't going to help. What are we going to do?'

'Firstly you could tell me who killed Darius Cloud Walker.'

Everyone looks blank. All three claim that he was still alive last time they could remember.

'So someone just waited till you'd conveniently all drugged yourselves into a stupor then snuck into my office and used Makri's knife to kill him? The Civil Guards are going to love that story.'

'Did you examine the body?' asks Lisutaris.

'Of course not. The Brotherhood were breaking the door down.'

We fall silent. The tale of a mysterious stranger isn't impressing anyone here. It's not going to impress the Sorcerers Guild or the Turanian authorities.

'Why did you leave the Assemblage without telling me?'

'You were having such a good time with the Juvalian Sorcerers, that's why,' says Makri.

'Indeed,' says Princess Direeva. 'Such a good time

that I do not see how you can criticise others for their pleasures.'

'My pleasures didn't involve a dead Sorcerer who was second favourite for head of the Guild. Congratulations, Lisutaris, you just lost a rival. Which makes you a pretty good suspect. Anyway, we've sat here talking long enough, it's time to do something.'

'Why must you do anything?' enquires Direeva. As she sits on the couch her hair trails on the floor. It must be inconvenient on occasion.

'To save my own skin.'

I'm mostly concerned about Makri but I'm not about to say that. And lingering at the back of my mind in an annoying manner is the thought that if I'm to help Lisutaris win the election, which I was hired to do, I can't let her be involved in any of this. Keeping her out of it is not going to be easy, but I never give up on a client.

'Lisutaris, can you put some sort of sorcerous shield over the night's events? Cover everything so it can't be looked at?'

The Mistress of the Sky considers this. I know she's aching for some thazis. If she lights another stick I'll be tempted to slug her.

'Probably, for a while. I've hidden events before. But if the whole Sorcerers Guild starts looking I'm not going to be able to shut them out for long. Even on his own, Old Hasius the Brilliant would get through eventually.'

'I too have hidden events,' says Princess Direeva. 'I will add my powers to yours.'

'That will buy us some time. Meanwhile I'll try and find out who killed Darius. That doesn't get us off the hook, seeing as we're concealing a crime, but it will help. If I can find proof against the killer we might be able to divert attention from any of you being involved.'

'How do you know we weren't?' asks Direeva.

The young Princess doesn't seem to be treating this as seriously as she should. Possibly she feels that if she finds herself in trouble she can always claim diplomatic immunity and ride back to the Wastelands. Maybe she's right, but that's not going to help anyone else.

'I don't. You're all suspects. I'm just hoping I can find a better one.'

I rise to my feet.

'Get busy on the spell. I'm going to move the body further away. Even without sorcerous help the Civil Guard aren't fools. If they find Darius lying dead right next to the Avenging Axe they'll know for sure I had something to do with it and that will lead back to you. And whatever you do, don't get stoned again, it will lead to disaster.'

I pause at the door and turn to Makri.

'Where did you get the dwa?'

'I stole it from the dealer.'

'Very moral behaviour. At least he was selling it at a fair price.'

Outside it's bitterly cold. I haven't had time to re-charge my warm cloak. Snow is falling in thick sheets and there's not a soul in sight. It takes me a while to get a horse saddled up and fitted on to a wagon, and longer to retrieve the now frozen body of Darius. I sling it in the cart, cover it with a blanket and set off. My mood is grim. It wasn't helped by the difficulty I had removing Makri's knife from the corpse.

The Sorcerers Guild is not going to give up easily on this one. It might take them one day or three months but I have no doubt that some time in the future they will be staring at a picture of me riding in a cart with Darius's body. That's going to be hard to explain and it's not going to do much for Lisutaris's chances in the election.

Almost worse is the realisation that I'm going to have to report all this to Cicerius. He's my client. I've withheld information from Cicerius before but there is no way I can keep this from him. For all I know the death of the Abelasian Sorcerer might lead Turai into war. I can't let that happen without warning the Deputy Consul. I dread to think what the man is going to say, and try as I might, I can't think of a means of explaining the situation that doesn't put me in a bad light. Thinking it over while I'm looking for a suitable snowdrift in which to dump Darius, I don't come up with anything I like.

CHAPTER
EIGHT

I'm used to being abused by officials. Often on a case I end up being told by a Prefect or Captain of the Guard how much better Turai would be without me. I've been lectured by the best of them, but nothing compares to the lecture Cicerius gives me when I wake him up at three in the morning to inform him that Lisutaris, Mistress of the Sky, has just got herself mixed up with the mysterious death of Darius Cloud Walker.

This man is noted for the power of his rhetoric. In the courts he regularly tears his opponents to shreds. Some of his speeches have become so famous that copies of them are used in schools to teach students how to construct an argument. Cicerius's argument on this occasion demonstrates mainly that as a protector of Turanian interests I am as much use as a one-legged gladiator, if that.

'I hired you to help Turai, not plunge us into war with the Abelasian confederacy! Never in my most fevered imaginings could I have dreamed of the chaos that would result from involving you in this affair!'

'Steady on, Cicerius,' I protest. 'I'm not to blame. It wasn't me that got stoned in Twelve Seas with Darius. It was Lisutaris.'

'You were meant to be looking after her. And what

were you doing? Drinking beer and trading jokes with these degenerate Sorcerers from Juval! Did I not specifically warn you not to do that?'

'Very probably. I wasn't expecting things to go wrong so quickly.'

Even as I speak I know this sounds feeble.

'You yourself warned of some involvement by an Assassin. Did you expect him to wait until you were ready?'

Once again I am subjected to Cicerius's invective. I have to raise my voice to stop him.

'Okay, it's bad. I thought that having Makri as a bodyguard would keep Lisutaris out of trouble, and that turned out to be a mistake.'

At the mention of Makri's name Cicerius fulminates some more about the foolishness of placing trust in a woman with Orcish blood. I find myself defending her, which I don't feel much like doing.

'Makri's had a few distractions. But if an attempt is made on Lisutaris's life, you'll still be pleased she's got Makri to protect her. And it's all very well coming down on me like a bad spell for messing things up, but if it wasn't for me we'd be in a lot worse position. If I hadn't got rid of the body the Brotherhood would have found Darius lying there with Lisutaris and Direeva, and what would have happened then? At the very least you'd be paying blackmail money to the Brotherhood till the King's vaults were empty. And there were seven Brotherhood men, they wouldn't have all kept quiet about it. The news would be all over the city by now. At least I've bought us some time.'

Cicerius is aware that the respite is temporary. He

knows as well as I do that when the Sorcerers start looking they'll eventually find out the truth.

'You have bought us time? For what?'

'For me to find the killer.'

'And if that turns out to be Lisutaris? Or your companion?'

'It won't.'

'How can you be sure?'

'I'm not sure. But I've talked to them both and my intuition tells me they're innocent. As for Princess Direeva, I'm not so certain.'

'If an unknown assailant did enter your office and kill Darius, have you not made everything worse by moving the body and hiding the crime?'

'There was no time to work things out when the Brotherhood were beating on the door. As far as I knew, either Direeva or Lisutaris had stabbed Darius, and I couldn't let that be discovered. Anyway, no matter who did kill him, would you really have wanted that scene to be made public? It would have ended Lisutaris's chances of election.'

Cicerius shakes his head.

'Had she been taking dwa?'

'I don't think so. Direeva had.'

'This curse is going to destroy us.'

Cicerius's son was involved in a dwa scandal last year, and when we were on Avula, the Deputy Consul was badly shaken to discover that the drug had now taken root on the Elvish Isles.

'If things carry on like this the Orcs will sweep us away. What do you propose doing to rescue Turai from this calamity?'

'Lisutaris and Direeva are making a hiding spell.'

'Can we trust Direeva?'

'I don't know. Ask Tilupasis, she's been working on her. We have to take the risk, it'll cover our tracks for a while. The spell would be a lot stronger if they got some help from Old Hasius.'

'You mean involve the Chief Sorcerer at the Abode of Justice in covering up a murder?'

Cicerius is a stickler for the law. He's been known to go against his own party to uphold the constitution. And yet such is the seriousness of the matter for Turai that he doesn't immediately dismiss my suggestion.

'To save the city I might even be prepared to sanction such an illegal action. But I doubt if it could be kept secret. Hasius's apprentice is a supporter of Senator Lodius. If Lodius learns of this we're finished.'

Senator Lodius leads the opposition party, the Populares. They're fierce opponents of Cicerius and would leap at the opportunity to catch him out in such an illicit plan.

'All right, Hasius is out. And Gorsius is too unreliable. But Melus the Fair is a friend of Lisutaris. She might be able to help, and you could trust her. She wouldn't sell out Lisutaris because they're companions in the Association of Gentlewomen.'

'Kindly do not bring that organisation into the picture,' says Cicerius acidly. 'They are nothing but trouble.'

'As you wish. But I think Lisutaris could do with her help. Anyway, with the hiding spell working I've got some time to investigate.'

'How long?'

'I don't know. It depends on the alignments of the moons at the time of the murder. If they're unfavourable it might take the Sorcerers Guild a week or so to break through. Lisutaris is going back to her villa to check her books. Which is where I'm heading right now. She is going to try and look at the events herself before she starts hiding them. If she can get a good picture of the murder we'll be a step ahead of everyone else and I might be able to clear things up before everything goes to hell.'

Cicerius is far from soothed. With the situation being as it is in Turai, it's hard to know who he can trust. He'd like to get the Civil Guard to discreetly investigate but many of the guards are in the pay of either the Brotherhood or their rivals the Society of Friends, and those that aren't might well be supporters of the Populares.

'I'd say it's safest to tell no one.'

'And trust you to fix everything?'

'No. Trust me to find out the truth, then get Tilupasis to fix everything. She's an efficient woman. You think I could have some more wine before I set off? It's cold out there.'

'Get drunk on your own time,' says Cicerius, with feeling.

I set off, leaving a highly agitated Deputy Consul behind me. I'm none too calm myself. Cicerius might have been right about calling the guards straight away. But my intuition told me to move the body and I've lived on my intuition for a long time now. I ride towards Truth is Beauty Lane, home of the Sorcerers. The wind pierces my cloak like a series of sharp knives. I can't ever remember being so cold. I'd never have taken the damned case if I'd known it was going to involve so much outdoor activity.

Lights are burning in Lisutaris's villa, and despite the lateness of the hour a servant takes my horse for stabling while another leads me inside. The house reeks of thazis. I'm starting to object to the aroma. I find the Mistress of the Sky sitting at her water pipe in the company of Makri and Princess Direeva. The walls are hung with Elvish tapestries of green and gold, and numerous well-tended plants surround the large windows that look out over the gardens. It's a beautiful room, decorated by one of the fashionable designers now found necessary by Turai's upper classes. Warm too, though there is no fire. Such is the ingenuity of Turai's architects that large villas now have systems for leading hot air through pipes under the floors to warm the houses. Unlike the frozen masses in Twelve Seas, the wealthy of Turai never have to shiver.

No torches burn on the walls. The bright illumination in the room is provided entirely by Lisutaris's illuminated staff, which rests in a corner, bathing the room in light.

Makri has removed her armour to display the man's tunic she generally wears. Princess Direeva's tunic and leggings are somewhat similar and it makes for an odd contrast with Lisutaris's flowing robes.

'How was the Deputy Consul?' asks the Sorcerer.

'He regrets nominating you for the post. And Makri, I wouldn't count on his help for getting into the university.'

Makri's face falls. She has a serious ambition to enter

the Imperial University, and without some unusually powerful assistance that will never happen. Seeing her disappointed face, I'm oddly pleased. Revenge for all the trouble she's been causing me recently.

Lisutaris motions towards the water pipe.

'Do you never do anything else?' I say, angrily.

'As you wish,' says Lisutaris.

'I wasn't refusing. I just wondered if you never did anything else.'

I take a long pull at the pipe. The thazis is so strong that I'm obliged to sit down. I do feel calmer.

'You are just in time,' announces the Sorcerer. 'We have the hiding spell ready. Before using it I shall look for the killer.'

Beside her is a golden saucer full of kuriya. In this dark liquid, an experienced practitioner can sometimes read the secrets of the past. It's a difficult art. I've occasionally gleaned secrets from the kuriya but my success rate is low. However, my powers are as nothing compared to Lisutaris's, and I'm optimistic that we may well learn the truth.

Before using kuriya I'd have to spend a long time getting myself in to the correct state of mind. Lisutaris is far beyond this. With no preparation, not even a deep breath, she waves her hand over the saucer. The room immediately goes cooler and the black liquid starts to glow. We crane our necks to see the picture that begins to form.

It's a picture of my office. Very clear. You can see yesterday's dirty plates lying on the table. As the picture spreads to fill the saucer I observe Makri and Direeva lying unconscious on the floor. Darius Cloud Walker is nearby, also comatose. Lisutaris doesn't seem to be around. The door opens and she enters. She treads softly through the room and bends down over Makri. She reaches down and comes up with a knife. And then she pounces on Darius and sticks the knife in his back. Next, she disappears from the room, leaving the Sorcerer bleeding to death.

The picture fades. I look around at my companions. All three of them are struck dumb. Lisutaris looks like she's just encountered the darkest demon of hell.

'Well, that seems fairly unequivocal,' I say. 'No room for argument there. So what are we going to do now? And why the hell did you have to stab him with Makri's knife? If you hated the man that much, couldn't you just have blasted him with a spell?'

The Mistress of the Sky is still unable to speak. She stares at the now dark liquid, unblinking, horrified.

'Snap out of it,' I tell her. 'And get busy with the hiding spell. You better make it good, because if anyone ever needed a hiding spell, it's you.'

CHAPTER
NINE

I awake feeling unusually comfortable, and very warm.
I realise I'm not at home. I'm in a guest room at
Lisutaris's villa. Lisutaris the killer. I'd never have picked
her for a murderer. There's a bronze statue by the
window. My clothes are draped over it. I get out of bed
and get dressed. Outside the room a servant asks me if
I'd like breakfast.

'I'll take a beer and whatever you got on a plate. Is
Lisutaris up yet?'

She isn't. Downstairs I pick up my beer, and some
roasted fowl from a selection of silver platters in the
dining room, and finish them off quickly. I'm not planning on hanging around. Unfortunately, before I can
make my exit Lisutaris appears, a small stick of thazis
in her hand. She doesn't look like she's slept well.

'I didn't kill him,' she says.

She said that last night as well.

I don't reply.

'Don't you believe me?'

'No.'

'Someone faked that magical picture.'

I continue not to believe her. It looked pretty damn
convincing to me and it would stand up in court.

'I'm telling you, someone faked it.'

'No one could fake that.'

'I thought you always supported your clients.'

'I do. That's why I haven't turned you over to the Guard.'

'But you don't believe I'm innocent?'

'No.'

Makri enters the breakfast chamber.

'What's going on?'

'Thraxas believes I killed Darius Cloud Walker. He's unhappy to be stuck with a murderer for a client.'

'Lisutaris isn't a murderer,' says Makri. 'You have to help.'

'I don't have to do anything.'

We stare at each other in silence. The Mistress of the Sky inhales from her thazis stick.

'Those pictures were good,' she says. 'Even with all my power I couldn't prove they were faked. They'll fool other Sorcerers.'

'There's no reason to think they were faked,' I point out, harshly. 'And even if they were, what happened to the real past? A Sorcerer can hide the past but no one can erase it. You looked in the kuriya ten times or more and you couldn't find the real events. Or what you say are the real events. So we're talking two major discrepancies here, neither of which can be done by sorcery. One, erasing reality, and two, faking a new reality. Temporarily hiding the past is one thing, but erasing and faking can't be done. You know that better than me. Why don't you tell me what really happened?'

'You've known me for a long time,' says Lisutaris. 'We were standing on the same piece of city wall when it collapsed under dragon attack.'

'Kemlath Orc Slayer was standing there as well,' I point out. 'And last year I got him exiled from the city.'

'But he was guilty!' explodes Makri. 'Lisutaris didn't kill Darius. Why would she? You have to help. No one else knows how to investigate things like you.'

I take another beer. I really don't like this.

'How good is the hiding spell?' I ask, after a while.

'Good,' answers Lisutaris. 'Better with Direeva's power added to my own.'

'You don't sound certain that will last.'

Lisutaris isn't certain. Princess Direeva departed the villa last night after seeing the pictures of Lisutaris knifing Darius. Darius represents the nation of Abelesi, and they're friends of Direeva's.

'If Direeva thinks you killed him she's not going to keep helping.'

I can see Tilupasis will be hard pressed to get Direeva's votes for Turai, but that might be the least of our problems now. I ask Lisutaris about the alignment of the moons, important in sorcerous enquiries concerning the past.

'Not so good. The Sorcerers will have the alignments in their favour in two or three days.'

Lisutaris sits down heavily as if crushed by the weight of her troubles. I finish my beer. Somewhere south of here, Darius Cloud Walker is lying in a snowdrift. He deserved better.

'I suggest you recruit Melus to boost the hiding spell. Say nothing to anyone. And pack a bag.'

'Why?'

'Because the most likely outcome is that we're all fleeing the city, one step ahead of the Civil Guard.'

I grab another beer and walk out of the villa. I know I'm making a mistake. There's no way this one is turning out well. Last night there was another heavy fall of snow. The land around the city will be impassable in this weather. Unless you're a Sorcerer, of course. I'll probably end up climbing the scaffold myself while Lisutaris makes her escape. I just can't see any good outcome. It's going to need something superhuman to prevent it. I'm a forty-three-year-old Investigator, badly overweight, and I drink too much. No one would accuse me of being superhuman.

Back at the Avenging Axe, Gurd looks at me questioningly.

'Who did it?' he asks.

'Lisutaris, looks like.'

'What are you going to do?'

'Get her off the hook.'

Gurd raises his eyebrows. He knows that protecting a murderer is not a job I'd volunteer for.

'Can you do it?'

'I'm number one chariot in this business.'

'But can you do it?'

I shake my head.

'No one could do it.'

Upstairs in my office I sit and stare out at the snow. After a while I get out my klee and sip the fierce spirit till I feel better. I set up my niarit board and play through a game or two. The room feels cold so I stoke up the fire. It doesn't make me warm so I lie on the couch and drag a blanket over me. I really should be doing something. I drink some more klee and fall asleep.

I'm woken by Makri. She says she's come to apologise.

'What for?'

'For taking dwa and getting unconscious when I should have been watching Lisutaris. I'm sorry.'

I haul myself upright.

'Sorry? No need to apologise to me. You can do what you like.'

'Okay, I said I was sorry.'

'Stop apologising. I don't care what you do.'

'Stop giving me a hard time,' protests Makri.

'I'm not giving you a hard time.'

'Yes you are. You're deliberately making me feel bad by saying I don't need to apologise.'

'You don't.'

'Stop doing that,' says Makri, and looks cross.

'Makri, you can fill yourself full of as much dwa as you like. I don't care.'

'Well, that's fine. I don't care if you care or not.'

'I don't.'

'You shouldn't.'

'I won't.'

'Then we're fine,' says Makri.

'Completely fine.'

Makri storms out of the room. I pick up my klee and wonder what I'm meant to do at the Assemblage today. Look for clues? Protect Lisutaris? Kill her other main rivals?

Makri storms back into the room.

'What's the idea of going on and on about me taking dwa when you drink so much?' she demands.

'I wasn't going on and on.'

'You're being intolerable. I'm going to tell Tanrose.'

'You're what?'

'I'm going to tell Tanrose.'

'You? The number one gladiator and genius philosophy student? You're going to run away and tell tales?'

'Okay!' screams Makri. 'I was feeling bad about Seeath! I just wanted to not feel bad for a little while! Stop tormenting me!'

Makri grabs the bottle of klee and takes a slug. I pick up my cloak. There's no time to charge it up, which means I'm in for a cold journey to the Royal Hall.

'You want me to put some stuff in this magic pocket?' asks Makri.

'What?'

'Lisutaris let me keep it for the week. I've got two swords, three knives and my axe in here. You have to be prepared when you're a bodyguard.'

'And you're a great bodyguard.'

'Stop insulting me,' says Makri. 'I said I was sorry.'

We have to trudge for a long way through the frozen streets before we find a landus to take us up town. It takes us ages to travel up Moon and Stars Boulevard. There is little traffic on the streets but the road is partially blocked near the harbour by a collapsed aqueduct and the landus has to pick its way carefully through a mess of fallen masonry and huge blocks of ice. Workmen, moving slowly in the freezing cold, are trying to clear the way.

'Samanatius teaches here,' says Makri, and looks concerned.

I have no mental energy to waste on Samanatius.

'Are you sure you can't remember anything else about last night?'

Makri shrugs. She's wearing the floppy green hat she brought back from Avula. It's ridiculous.

'I told you everything. Lisutaris wanted to show Princess Direeva some interesting bits of the city. So we came to Twelve Seas. Darius was with us. He was friends with Direeva so he tagged along. I took them to the Avenging Axe. We went in your office because my room is small and cold, and after a while we got to drinking klee—'

'You were drinking klee? Whose klee?'

'Yours, of course. I figured you wouldn't mind; after all, you're meant to be helping Lisutaris.'

'And you all passed out and next thing you know Darius is dead?'

'That's right.'

'And you didn't see anyone else the whole time? Didn't sense anyone following you in Twelve Seas?'

'No.'

Snow falls from the bleak sky. Without the warming spell my cloak is useless. I shiver.

'What about Direeva? How was she with Darius?'

'Friendly.'

'You think she might have resented his attentions?'

'Maybe. But not enough to kill him. He wasn't trying to force himself on her.'

'You fell asleep before Direeva. You don't know what happened after that.'

Makri admits this is true but she doesn't believe that anything bad enough could have occurred to make Direeva kill the Sorcerer. I doubt this myself, though I'm still suspicious of the Princess.

'I notice Direeva seemed to take to you.'

Makri looks embarrassed. She doesn't reply, and changes the subject.

'You know those pictures of Lisutaris killing Darius were faked.'

'I don't know that at all. Faking a scene like that and sending it into the past would be a fantastically difficult thing to do. It's the sort of thing you read in stories about Sorcerers, but I'm not certain there's any Sorcerer in the world who could really do it. So where does that leave us? The same pictures will appear when anyone else looks. If it really didn't happen, the Sorcerer who forged it has strength I've never encountered before, or access to some spells no one else knows.'

Makri understands how bad this all is. When the Sorcerers Guild clear away the hiding spell, Lisutaris will be handed over to the authorities and sent for trial. Despite the evidence Makri is still convinced that Lisutaris didn't kill Darius.

'Why?'

'Intuition.'

I don't dismiss Makri's intuition but I trust my own better. And it's not sending me anything very positive right now. Maybe it's the cold.

'What a mess,' I mutter.

All the while I'm wondering about Covinius, the Assassin. Could he have anything to do with this? I need to talk to Hanama, and quickly. We arrive at the Royal Hall. Lisutaris hasn't yet turned up.

'She'll be having her hair done by Copro,' Makri tells me. 'She's hired him for every morning of the Assemblage. Wants to make a good impression.'

'She's going to make a hell of an impression soon.'

All around the Sorcerers are arriving, greeting each other. Many of them are notably less ebullient than yesterday. The mood will pick up when their hangovers fade. I look around for Irith Victorious. I'm planning on discreetly pumping him for information on Darius Cloud Walker. Juval borders Abelasi and the Sorcerers should know each other well. Maybe someone else wanted Darius out of the way.

Before I leave Makri I bring up the subject of the Turanian Assassins Guild. In particular, Hanama, number three in the hierarchy.

'You're friendly with Hanama.'

'No I'm not.'

'Well, you're as friendly as a person can be with an Assassin. I need to talk to her but she's not answering my messages. Before I'm reduced to storming their headquarters, how about you have a word with her?'

'I'm not friendly with her,' protests Makri.

'You meet at gatherings of the Association of Gentlewomen.'

'She doesn't go to meetings,' says Makri.

She's lying. I guess it's meant to be a secret.

Tilupasis takes the bad news much better than Cicerius. For her it's just another problem to be solved, like buying votes.

'You must keep it quiet and find out the truth,' she instructs, like it's the easiest thing in the world. 'Once you find out the truth, Kalius and Praetor Samilius will be able to arrest the murderer without involving Lisutaris. It need not spoil her chances of winning.'

'It will spoil them plenty if she really did it.'

'Nothing will spoil Lisutaris's chances of election

while I'm running her campaign,' says Tilupasis firmly. 'If she's guilty of murder then you will have to find some way of disguising the fact.'

'And how am I meant to do that?'

'You're a sorcerous Investigator. It's what you do.'

'What I do is catch petty thugs, slug them and send them to jail. Large-scale conspiracy isn't my forte. And if the Sorcerers Guild catches me trying to hoodwink them they'll be down on me like a bad spell.'

'I have great confidence in you,' says Tilupasis. 'Keep me informed of all developments and let me know if you need money. I'll instruct my operatives to learn what they can to assist you. Now, how is your companion Makri getting along with Princess Direeva? I'm very optimistic about this.'

'I doubt that Makri will enjoy being used as bait for Direeva's votes.'

What Makri might enjoy doesn't concern Tilupasis. She departs to carry on the campaign and I depart for a beer.

Irith Victorious is sitting at a table, looking a little the worse for wear.

'How are you today, Irith?'

'Not quite as happy as an Elf in a tree,' he replies. 'Won't feel myself till I get a few drinks in. Care to join me?'

'Of course.'

Today there are some organised events at the Assemblage. Classes for learning new spells, swapping lore from around the west, that sort of thing. Irith tells me he isn't quite up to learning anything new right now, though he's in the market for a magic pocket which can store beer without it going stale.

I'm looking for information on Darius. As a means of raising the subject I tell Irith I placed a bet on Lisutaris.

'Rash behaviour, Thraxas. Sunstorm Ramius is the man, I'm sure. Though I'd rather see Darius or Lisutaris in the post. Even Rokim, though I'm not keen on Samsarinans as a rule. Ramius is too much of an old soldier for me, he'll have the Guild declaring war on the Orcs at the first excuse. Me, I like my life more peaceful. You think Lisutaris is keen on going to war?'

'Only if the thazis plants are threatened.'

'I might vote for her. I admire a woman with a respectable hobby.'

Other Juvalian sorcerers drift in, each in a similar state to Irith. I pick up some useful information. Mainly of the negative sort, however. Darius has no obvious enemies. Gets on with most people, apart from apprentices. As Sorcerers are always firing their apprentices, that's not much to go on, but I file it away to check out later. I nose around for more but as it's not yet known that Darius Cloud Walker is now firmly rooted to the ground, I can't press too much for fear of giving myself away.

Sunstorm Ramius strides through the room, greeting us as he passes.

'Just off to teach some Samsarinans how to purify poisoned water with a simple spell,' he informs us. 'Care to come along?'

The Juvalians decline. They're not quite in the mood for instruction today. Ramius smiles indulgently. I get the impression he doesn't entirely approve of the manners of the Juvalians, but as a man who's looking for votes he can't go around being rude to the electorate.

'What sort of candidate is he?' says Irith. 'Didn't even offer to buy us a drink. Anyone seen Darius? He ought to be good for a beer or two. Hey, Thraxas, is Lisutaris handing out any free thazis?'

I grin at the large Sorcerer.

'I take it you're not planning on much studying at the Assemblage?'

His companions guffaw at the notion.

'I haven't learned a new spell in fifteen years,' replies Irith. 'I've got plenty already. Who needs more? Are you going to talk all morning or are you going to finish that beer?'

A few hours later, slightly the worse for wear, I wander off in search of Lisutaris, finding her in a corner of the main hall, sitting beside Makri. Makri is again wearing her full armour but the effect is spoiled by her floppy green hat, which is the sort of thing sported only by small Elvish children.

Makri tells me she bought a new stud for her nose.

'It's magic. Look, if you touch it it goes gold. Touch it again it goes silver. Then it goes gold . . .'

'. . . and then it goes silver. That's great. Any information?'

I'm looking at Lisutaris. She's looking at the ceiling. Or possibly the sky. I frown.

'I take it your recent troubles haven't led you to lay off the thazis?'

Lisutaris slumps forward on to the table.

'She's under a lot of stress,' says Makri.

I glance around. Approaching fast is a delegation of Sorcerers from Mattesh.

'For God's sake, Makri, can't you keep her under

control? If these Sorcerers see her like this they're never going to vote for her. Get her out of here.'

Makri stands up. She sways, clutches at her head, and sits down again.

'Sorry,' she says.

I glare at her.

'As a bodyguard you're about as much use as a eunuch in a brothel.'

'I've been under a lot of stress.'

The Sorcerers draw near. I hoist Lisutaris to her feet and start walking her rapidly in the other direction.

'Tell me about your new spell for protecting a whole city!' I boom, trying to give a good impression while I drag the number one Turanian Sorcerer to the safety of a side room. Makri struggles along behind us. I dump the Mistress of the Sky on a couch. Makri slumps beside her. I take out my flask of klee and pour a healthy dose down my throat.

'Have you been encouraging Lisutaris to drink?' comes an angry voice behind me.

It's Cicerius. He saw us heading this way and followed us in.

I protest my innocence. Cicerius looks at us like we've just crawled out from under a rock. He demands to know why I've been spending the day drinking when I should be trying to get Lisutaris out of the mess she's in. I feel confused, angry, full of beer and bereft of a good reply. I slump down beside Makri.

'I've got a new nose stud,' says Makri. 'You touch it it goes gold. Then it goes silver.'

'A fine trio you make,' rages the Deputy Consul. 'None of you can even stand. God knows what I was thinking when I entrusted the welfare of our great city into your hands.'

Cicerius's assistant Hansius rushes through the door.

'Deputy Consul!' he gasps. 'Word from Twelve Seas. The Civil Guards have just found the body of Darius Cloud Walker! He's been murdered!'

Outside, the Assemblage is already in uproar as the news spreads.

'Need more thazis,' mumbles Lisutaris, then closes her eyes. I notice that her hair is particularly finely arranged. And her make-up is just perfect. The early morning beauty sessions are really paying off.

CHAPTER TEN

I pour some kuriya into a saucer. No one speaks. Makri looks uncomfortable. Cicerius is agitated. Tilupasis remains calm. We're gathered in Cicerius's private room at the Royal Hall and I'm preparing to show them what happened at the Avenging Axe.

'What you are about to see is hidden from all other eyes by the spell cast by Lisutaris, Mistress of the Sky, and Princess Direeva. I've only got access because Lisutaris has given me a key.'

I take out a scrap of parchment and intone a brief incantation, Lisutaris's key. Cicerius and Tilupasis draw closer to the saucer. The air cools. A picture starts to form. My untidy office. I really should clean it up some time. Makri, Direeva and Darius are unconscious on the floor. Lisutaris enters, stabs Darius, then departs. The picture fades. Seeing it again, I don't like it any better.

Cicerius controls his agitation. Though sometimes excitable, he's not a man to panic in a crisis any more than me.

'How many people have seen that?'

'Just us. And it's well hidden from everyone else. The Sorcerers will get through eventually but it will take a while.'

'It looked very real to me,' continues Cicerius. 'Are

you convinced by Lisutaris's protestations of innocence?'

I shrug.

'I've taken her on as a client.'

'You do not sound convinced.'

Makri breaks into the conversation.

'She's innocent! I was there, I know she didn't stab
Darius.'

'You were unconscious.'

'I was the last to fall asleep. Lisutaris didn't do it.'

Tilupasis wonders about the magic required to falsify
the past.

'My knowledge of sorcery is limited. Is it possible that
the pictures are, as Lisutaris claims, fakes?'

'Maybe.'

'Please be more specific,' says Cicerius.

'Well, there are three different things involved here.
Hiding, erasing, and making. Hiding means concealing
the past. Plenty of Sorcerers can do that, at least for a
while. The other two are not so easy. Lisutaris and
Direeva searched for the real events before they made
their hiding spell, but they couldn't find them. They
couldn't find anything else apart from the pictures of
Lisutaris killing Darius. So if there were other real
events, someone has erased them. But that's impossible.
No one has ever perfected such an erasement spell. I
guarantee you could ask every Sorcerer at the
Assemblage and they'd tell you the same. The obvious
conclusion is that there was no erasement, which would
mean the events as depicted are true, Lisutaris is the
killer.

'The same goes for a making spell, something to

create the illusion of events happening, a good enough illusion to fool a Sorcerer when he checks back in time. Again, no such spell has ever been perfected. It's a difficult thing even to imagine, painting a convincing picture of real events and placing it in the past. What we saw there was my office, complete with junk. Could someone fake that in every detail? I doubt it. Again, the obvious conclusion is that we're looking at the real events.'

'Whether Lisutaris murdered Darius or not, we can't let it be known,' says Tilupasis.

I point out that not everyone feels so comfortable with covering up a murder. Tilupasis gives the slightest of shrugs. She's quite comfortable with it. We look towards Cicerius.

'If the Sorcerers Guild will eventually discover the truth, it might be better for Turai to come straight out and admit that this has happened,' he says. 'Lisutaris would hang, or be sent into exile, Turai would lose influence, but at least we would not be found guilty of complicity in the murder of the Chief Sorcerer of another country. If we try and cover this up and it goes wrong, the Abelasian confederacy and the other states in the south will turn against Turai. We already have numerous enemies.'

We fall silent while Cicerius weighs up his options. The Deputy Consul is in charge here. It's his decision, and for once I don't feel like barging in with my own opinions.

'If Lisutaris is innocent, as she claims, what chance do you have of uncovering the real murderer?'

'A reasonable chance. Maybe less. I've no leads and

I'll be up against sorcery no one has encountered before. Which is not to say I won't find anything. Criminals generally leave some traces behind, even sorcerous criminals. The problem is time. We don't know how long it will take for the Guild to break through the hiding spell.'

Cicerius drums his fingers lightly on the table. Finally he makes a decision.

'Carry on with your investigation. We shall continue with our efforts to have Lisutaris elected as head of the Guild.'

Hansius appears at the door, Cicerius is needed for a conference with Lasat, Axe of Gold. He departs swiftly.

'I must return to my work,' says Tilupasis. 'Now that Darius is no longer in the running, I should be able to win over some of these southern votes. Keep watching Lisutaris. And Makri, be nice to Princess Direeva. This is now more important than ever. With Darius out of the running we have an excellent chance of winning her over.'

'Not if she decides to believe that Lisutaris killed Darius.'

'You must persuade her otherwise,' instructs Tilupasis.

She hurries off.

'What exactly do I have to do to get Princess Direeva's votes?' asks Makri.

'I don't know. I was never any good at politics.'

I stare at the now blank pool of kuriya. After the spell the temperature in the room has again risen. The authorities have made it warm for the Sorcerers. Anything to keep them happy.

'It's unfortunate the body was discovered so quickly.'

'You should've dumped it in a deeper snowdrift,' says Makri. 'Do you have any suspects?'

'Lisutaris. Maybe Sunstorm Ramius. He had something to gain from Darius's death. Got rid of a rival.'

I'm not fooling myself. Darius wasn't really a rival to Ramius. There was no sign of him picking up enough support to overhaul the Simnian. Nonetheless, I find myself suspicious of Ramius. He's arrogant, powerful and successful, and that's three things I dislike in a Sorcerer.

'It's time to go to work. Have you shaken off the thazis?'

'Yes.'

'Does the Imperial Library have much about sorcery?'

'The largest collection in the west,' says Makri. 'How can you possibly not know that?'

'I've been cultivating ignorance for a long time. Take Lisutaris home then meet me there as soon as you can. I need to do some research into spell-casting and I'm terrible at using a catalogue.'

There is great agitation in the main hall as the Sorcerers congregate to discuss the murder. They come pouring from all corners of the building, workshops abandoned. Even the Juvalians emerge from the Room of Saints, drinks in hand. Illuminated staffs are fired up all over the hall, as if to cast light on the affair. Sunstorm Ramius is already deep in discussion with other important Sorcerers. It won't be long before they start looking for the killer. Again I get the urge to ride out of town. When they conjure up a picture of me dumping that body, the whole Guild will be down on me like a bad spell. If the Sorcerers don't just blast me on the spot, the Civil Guards will prosecute. Either way, my prospects are poor.

Astrath Triple Moon is standing alone on the fringes of the crowd.

'Any news on the knife?'

The Sorcerer is very worried.

'No. It's been wiped. Is it the knife which . . .'

His voice tails off. I tell him I'd rather not give him any more details. Astrath accepts this. He'd rather not know. He promises to keep on working but he's deeply troubled to find himself involved in such an affair.

'I owe you a lot, Thraxas, but if the Guild really gets on my back it's going to be difficult to lie to them.'

I take the opportunity to ask Astrath if he knows of any spell, or any Sorcerer, who could create a sequence of fake events lasting almost a full minute, and send it back into the past. He doesn't.

'I don't think it could be done. Not by us, or the Elves, or the Orcs. Every detail of a long scene? There would just be too many things to control. And what about the real events? It's one thing to hide them for a while, but unless you completely erased them somehow they'd keep bursting through any illusion.'

The news spreads that Darius was found in a snow-drift, stabbed to death. Those Sorcerers who are familiar with Turai explain to those who are not that Twelve Seas is the bad part of the city near the harbour, where crime is rampant. There's a lot of nodding of heads. The immediate impression is that the Abelasian must have gone there seeking either dwa or a prostitute, neither of which would be particularly strange for a Sorcerer on holiday.

Princess Direeva and her apprentice remain aloof from the masses. There's no telling how the Princess will react if she finds herself being questioned by the Guards. Will she maintain silence, to help Makri and Lisutaris? Or tell what she knows, claim diplomatic immunity and depart swiftly? Already with Direeva and Astrath it seems like there are too many people who might be indiscreet. Even if Lisutaris's spell miraculously hides the events of the murder for weeks, I can't see the Civil Guard being baffled for long. They know how to follow a trail. Nor can I see the addled Mistress of the Sky standing up to questioning. I curse the day I ever became involved with the woman. It would have been better all round if the dragons she brought down had fallen on top of her.

It's time to visit Hanama. There's a Messengers Guild post in the entrance hall, placed there for the convenience of the Sorcerers. The young messenger who takes my scroll looks surprised when he sees that it's addressed to the headquarters of the Assassins Guild, but he hurries off, keen as always to do his duty. These young messengers are always keen. I've no idea why.

I hurry from the Assemblage and pick up a landus outside. Shortly afterwards I'm sitting in a tavern on the outskirts of the notorious Kushni quarter. Kushni is a hive of drinking dens, gambling dens, dwa houses, whorehouses and anything else disreputable you might wish for. In the summer it's a seething, sweltering mass of decadent humanity. Even in the depths of winter, trade goes on at an unhealthy pace. The Assassins have their headquarters nearby. I've informed Hanama that if she ignores this message I'm going to march in and call for her in a loud voice. I figure that ought to bring her out. No Assassin likes hearing their name shouted out loud, they're a private sort of people.

A young whore with red ribbons in her hair sidles up to the table. I ignore her. Her young male companion then approaches. He's also got red ribbons in his hair. I don't think the Whores Guild admits men. I could be wrong. I ignore him as well. A dwa dealer offers me some Choirs of Angels, cheap. I tell him to get lost. The dealer's friend gets insistent. I take a dagger from my pocket and lay it on the table. They sneer at me and mouth a few insults but they leave me alone. There are plenty of willing customers to cater for. No need to argue with a big angry man with a knife.

Hanama arrives in the dark garb of a common market worker. Each time I've encountered her I've been surprised by how young she looks. From her many reported exploits she can't be much under thirty, but she's a small, slender woman, dark-haired but very pale-skinned. With the aid of a little disguise she could pass as a child. The thought of Hanama dressing up as a child before disposing of another victim makes me shudder. I loathe the Assassins. Hanama is as cold as an Orc's heart. The fact that I fought beside her last year doesn't make me like her any better.

Hanama refuses my offer of beer.

'Staying sober? Got an assassination coming up?'

Not the best introduction perhaps, but it's hard to find the right tone when you're talking to a woman who has famously killed all sorts of important people. It's said she once killed an Elf Lord, an Orc Lord and a Senator all in one day. Hanama stares at me, pale and expressionless. She's not pleased at my method of bringing her to a meeting. I wonder whether I could knock her out with a sleep spell before she got her knife in my throat. I'm not carrying any spells. I'd better not offend her too much.

'Why did you insist on seeing me?'

'I'm looking for some information about Covinius.'

'An Assassin from Simnia, as is public knowledge, I believe.'

'But public knowledge doesn't go any further. Like whether it's a man or a woman. Or what Covinius looks like. Or whether he actually comes from Simnia.'

'I know no more about him.'

'What brings him to Turai?'

'I did not know that he was in Turai.'

'Then why did you send a message to Lisutaris warning her?'

This has to take Hanama by surprise but you couldn't tell from her expression. She denies it coolly. I tell her to stop wasting time.

'I know you sent the message. You might be number one chariot at murder but when it comes to covering your tracks you're a washout. I worked out it was you in a couple of minutes, and I've got sorcerous proof to back me up.'

The tiniest hint of colour touches Hanama's cheeks for a second or two. I think I might actually have embarrassed her.

'Don't feel bad. Investigating's my business. No one else knows you've been sending messages.'

If Hanama's Guild knew she had she'd be in trouble. The Assassins generally strive to avoid becoming embroiled in the world of politics. Neither would Hanama's companions be pleased to know of her involvement in the Association of Gentlewomen.

'I'm presuming you warned Lisutaris because of that Association?'

Hanama remains silent. I point out that as I'm responsible for Lisutaris's well-being, along with Makri, it would make a lot more sense to tell me what she knows. Hanama considers it while I calculate the chances of leaving the tavern alive if I'm forced to black-mail her.

'You know your buddy Lisutaris is quite likely to end up dead at the hands of Covinius?'

This seems to sway her.

'An informant who works for my organisation was fatally wounded last week. Before dying he informed us that Covinius the Simnian was heading to Turai. He had encountered him in the course of his work. The nature of this informant's mission is secret, and unconnected with either Lisutaris or the Sorcerers Assemblage, so I am unable to tell you any more. But it did occur to me that if Simnia were bringing an Assassin with them, Lisutaris would be the likely target. She is Ramius's main rival.'

I'm dissatisfied with this. Other than confirming that Covinius is in town, Hanama hasn't really told me any-thing.

'There is nothing more to tell. I do not discuss our private affairs with anyone. Sending the message was the most I could do.'

Hanama stands up and leaves swiftly. I toss some money on the table for my beer, and depart, angry.

Talking to Assassins always bothers me.

It's not far to the Imperial Library. This is a magnificent piece of architecture but it's a place I rarely visit. All those scrolls make me feel inadequate. And I don't like the way the assistants walk around so quietly in their togas. They make a man feel like he doesn't belong.

There's a whole room devoted to sorcerous learning but that's as far as I get. When I start trying to work out the catalogue I develop a serious mental block and am obliged to wait till Makri shows up, which takes a while. When she finally waltzes in I'm annoyed to see the staff greet her in a friendly manner. She grew up in an Orcish slave pit. I'm a native-born citizen of Turai. They ought to show me more respect.

'What do you expect?' whispers Makri. 'You once spilled beer over a manuscript.'

'Not much beer. You think they'd have forgotten by now. How's Lisutaris?'

'Glued to the water pipe. She's taking it all badly. You know, I'm starting to think she might not be such a great candidate for head of the Sorcerers Guild. I like her a lot but I can't see her spending much time looking after Guild affairs.'

'You just realised that?'

'Well, you're the one who betted on her,' Makri points out.

'That was before I realised that helping her election would mean covering up a murder. I'm going to have to work hard to pick up my winnings.'

'Is that why you took her as a client?'

'It tipped the balance. Did you leave her safe?'

Makri thinks so. Lisutaris's house is full of servants

and attendants and Makri left instructions that they
should be wary of strangers.

'Not that that's going to help much if the great
Assassin Covinius decides to pay a visit. I've seen
Hanama. She didn't tell me much. But Covinius is def-
initely in town.'

'Did he kill Darius Cloud Walker?'

'Who knows? I'll have to try and find out more, which
isn't going to be easy.'

A passing library assistant frowns at me. I lower my
voice. 'I need to find out what kind of spell could possibly make it appear as if Lisutaris killed Darius. I've been
racking my brains and I looked all through my own
grimoire, but I can't think of anything. Neither can
Astrath.'

Makri seems distracted. I study my companion suspiciously.

'Did you take a turn on the water pipe?'

'Of course not. Stop treating me like I'm Turai's
biggest drug abuser. There were special circumstances.
I was depressed. Did you know that Jir-ar-Eth the Avulan
Sorcerer is here?'

'What about it?'

'You told me no one could travel from the Elvish Isles
to Turai in winter.'

'Jir-ar-Eth set off early, shortly after we left.'

'Then why didn't See-ath send me a message with
him?'

'Possibly Lord Kalith's Chief Sorcerer felt he had more
important things to do than carry love letters. Do you
have to go on about See-ath all the time?'

'It's important,' says Makri.

I shake my head helplessly.

'Try and concentrate, we've got work to do.'

I describe to Makri what I'm after and we get busy at the catalogue, looking for a spell. Two spells probably, one to hide the real events and one to create the false ones. It's sounding more and more unlikely. The pictures of Lisutaris killing Darius were very clear. Just because I can't think of a motive doesn't mean it didn't happen. I've come across stranger things. Perhaps the thazis is driving her mad. At such extreme levels, who knows what it might do?

'Did Lisutaris share your dwa?'

'Stop going on about dwa,' hisses Makri. 'I said I was sorry.'

We struggle through tome after tome, scroll after scroll. Faced with this task I quickly tire. I hate this catalogue. I'd rather be on a stake-out in a freezing alleyway.

'Can't they organise it in a way a man can understand?'

'It's perfectly logical.'

'What do these numbers mean? I can't make any sense of it.'

'It's the classification system,' explains Makri. 'It tells you where to find things.'

'Why isn't it clearer?'

'It's very clear. You just don't understand it.'

I struggle on, working my way through books listing spells for every conceivable occasion. If I wanted to learn how to attack a Troll, I'd be fine. If I needed to know how to tell what the weather is like two hundred miles away, I could locate the right incantation. I even come across a spell for testing the strength of beer, and that's something I'd be interested in. But for what I'm looking for, there's nothing.

'This is hopeless. I've said all along it couldn't be done. Okay, I might be about the worst magic user in Turai. I can't do much more than heat up a cloak or send an opponent to sleep. But I understand the principles of sorcery, and its limitations. I think we're going to have to face it. Lisutaris is guilty.'

'You don't really believe that,' protests Makri. 'You just can't stand being in the library any longer. You can't send a woman to the gallows just because you don't understand the classification system.'

'Don't bet on it. Anyway, I can't concentrate any more. If I don't eat soon I'm going to expire. I suggest we go to the hostelry across the road, and try again later.'

Makri isn't hungry.

'And I don't like giving up on research. I want to go all through the catalogue.'

I'm forced to admire her persistence, but I can't carry on myself.

'Meet me in the tavern when you've run out of energy. Maybe once my belly's full I'll come up with an idea.'

The Imperial Library stands in a magnificent square, flanked by an enormous church and the Honourable Merchants Association's building. All these workers need refreshment and there are several small taverns tucked away round the corner. I choose The Scholar, which, despite its name, seems a welcoming enough establishment. The short walk from the library to the tavern is an ordeal. The wind slices through me and snow whips into my face. By the time I arrive my cloak is encrusted with tiny particles of ice and I hang it close to the fire to dry. At this time in the afternoon the tavern is empty, save for two young men, probably students, who sit at a table with two small jars of ale, studying a scroll. I order the special haunch of salted beef, then take my beer and sit in a prime spot in front of the fire to thaw out.

Another few winters like this will finish me off. Fleeing south towards the sun might not be such a bad idea. I'm in a tough spot. Already the most powerful Sorcerers will be turning their attention to the matter of Darius. They'll find their way blocked by Lisutaris's spell, but for how long? What if Lisutaris was too addled by thazis to cast it properly? The Civil Guard might be looking for me at this very moment. For the first time in my career I start to think I may be in over my head. I can't fight the Sorcerers Guild. I was foolish to try. I pick at my salt beef without much enthusiasm, finishing it only with the aid of an extra portion of sauce and another beer.

The door slams, an icy gust rushes into the tavern and Makri staggers in.

'Move over from that fire, Thraxas, I'm as cold as the ice queen's grave.'

Before she has time to even sit down, the landlord appears and brusquely informs her that women are not permitted in this establishment. Makri gapes.

'Are you serious?'

He's completely serious. It's their regular policy. In truth, it's not that unusual in some of the more respectable sections of the city.

Makri has not been herself recently, With the emotional upset over See-ath and the overindulgence in substances – for which I blame Lisutaris – she's not really been exhibiting the hard edge I've come to expect. In some ways that's not such a bad thing. Makri continually getting into fights can be wearing on a man. On the other hand, Makri being emotional is pretty wearing as well. As the landlord asks her to leave she snaps right back into character and places her face as close to his as she can get, which is close enough, though he's a large man and quite a lot taller than her.

'I just struggled through the snow to get here. I'm not planning on leaving right now.'

The landlord makes the unforgivable mistake of laying his hand on her shoulder to lead her out. Makri immediately lands him such a fearsome kick in the groin that the students at the far end of the tavern shrink back in terror. The landlord collapses to the floor. Makri grabs a table and hurls it on top of him. She glares down at his prostrate body.

'I will be taking this matter up with the Association of Gentlewomen,' she says.

Outside the snow is falling faster and heavier.

'Can you believe that?' yells Makri, over the howling wind.

We struggle down the street till we reach another tavern, The Diligent Apprentice. Makri marches in. I follow with my hand on the hilt of my sword, ready for trouble. A friendly-looking landlady greets us as we enter. Makri seems almost disappointed.

'Are you going to complain about me hitting the land-lord?' she demands, as we sit down with two beers and two glasses of klee.

'No. I didn't like the tavern much anyway.'

A year ago I'd have objected plenty. Now, I'm more sympathetic. Or maybe I'm just used to it.

'Did they really not serve women? Or just women with Orcish blood?'

'I don't know. Probably both. It wasn't much of a place. Their haunch of beef was adequate at best. I think I'll pick up another meal while I'm here.'

Makri grins.

'I always get depressed when life is too peaceful. All those years being a gladiator, I suppose. I need to fight every now and then, and it's been a long time since I was in a fight.'

I point out to her that only a few days ago she killed a dwa dealer.

'Right. I forgot about that. Well, it wasn't really what you'd call a fight.'

'And soon after that you got in a brawl with those three dock workers.'

'What are you doing, keeping records?'

'How are you ever going to manage if you get to the Imperial University? They frown on violence.'

'I can probably wean myself off it.'

Makri drinks heartily of her ale.

'Don't get too cheerful, Makri, we're still in a hell of a situation. The Sorcerers Guild could be looking at pictures of our involvement in a murder right now.'

Makri slaps the table.

'I almost forgot. I found a spell!'

'You did?'

Makri brings out a sheet of paper and reads from it.

'"A spell for wiping out events in the past. With this incantation an experienced practitioner can erase all traces of events, so that they can never be seen, even by sorcerous enquiry."'

Makri looks up from her notes.

'You wouldn't believe the obscure place I found this in. I swear no one else could have located it. It wasn't in the main sorcery collection, it was hidden away in—'

'Yes, Makri, I already know you're number one chariot in the library. Let me see the spell.'

I study Makri's copy. It's very interesting, a spell the like of which I've never encountered. It claims that if worked properly it can erase almost a full hour.

'I'm certain no one in Turai has ever worked this. Where did it originate?'

'Developed in the Wastelands, according to the catalogue. The Southern Hills.'

I raise my eyebrows. Princess Direeva lives in the Southern Hills.

'We might be on to something. But this doesn't account for everything. It might work for erasing events but it's not a spell for creating new ones.'

'I'm sure it's relevant,' says Makri. 'You know how when things happen during an investigation and it seems like a coincidence, you generally get suspicious? Well, take a look at the ingredients for the spell.'

She hands over another sheet of paper. The spell requires a healthy dose of dragon scales.

'And only recently you were hunting for a dragon-scale thief.'

It is a coincidence. And Makri's correct. In my line of work, coincidences always make me suspicious.

CHAPTER ELEVEN

The landus driver doesn't want to take us to Twelve Seas. These uptown drivers hate to go south of the river.

'I'm a Tribune of the People.'

'Never heard of you.'

It takes a lot of argument to persuade him. I'm deep in thought as we travel down Moon and Stars Boulevard. I want to follow up the dragon scales, which means I have to talk to Rezox. As I just put him in prison he isn't going to be keen to talk to me. Not in a friendly manner anyhow. Some abuse, possibly. I tell the landus to stop, and then hurry into a small way-station which acts as a forwarding post for the Messengers Guild where I quickly scribble a message to the Deputy Consul.

We travel on our way. The driver complains about the cold. Makri complains about the cold. She ought to put on a little weight.

'If you weren't so scrawny you wouldn't feel it so much.'

'Princess Direeva said I had a perfect figure.'

'I bet she did. Keep working your charms, you'll get her votes.'

'I don't want to charm anyone into voting for Lisutaris,' says Makri. 'The whole thing is corrupt and I don't approve.' She shivers. 'Are you claiming you don't feel the cold?'

I scoff at the suggestion

'You call this cold? It doesn't compare to the conditions I experienced up in Nioj. I've camped out for a month in weather worse than this.'

'You're a liar,' says Makri, still quite cheerful after her fight.

There is great confusion at the corner of Quintessence Street where the aqueduct has collapsed. Workmen are still struggling to clear the area but there seems to be some other sort of activity going on. A gaggle of citizens are arguing furiously and Civil Guards are arriving on the scene. I urge the driver to edge his way past but Makri calls for him to halt.

'What's happening here? These men are standing in front of Samanatius's academy.'

Samanatius's so-called academy is a miserable hall surrounded by equally miserable slums. Makri insists that she's going to take a look.

'Fine, you can walk the rest of the way.'

Makri departs and the landus driver manoeuvres his way into Quintessence Street and along to the Avenging Axe. Inside the tavern I fill up with food and beer and enquire of Gurd if anyone has been here asking questions. No one has, which means that Lisutaris's hiding spell is working for now. I'd like to spend a few hours in front of the fire but I can't stay for long, though I refuse to leave the tavern till I've recharged my magic warm cloak. I can't stand more outdoor work without some protection, no matter how much I brag to Makri about the weather not affecting me.

In my office I find Casax waiting, along with Orius Fire Tamer. Casax is head of the local chapter of the Brotherhood. A very important man in Twelve Seas. All crime is controlled by the Brotherhood. Since Casax took over, crime has been doing very well. Orius Fire Tamer is a young and recently qualified Sorcerer who seems to have hooked up with the Brotherhood.

'Don't you know how to knock and wait politely?' I demand.

'Never learned that,' answers Casax.

He's wrapped in an enormous fur. He doesn't look cold. I notice he's grown his hair a little longer, and tied it at the back. Casax has a fair complexion, but he's weatherbeaten, a man who started out at the docks a long time ago and worked his way up. A calm, strong, intelligent man, and very dangerous.

'Having a good time at the Assemblage?'

'The time of my life.'

'Orius tells me you've been enjoying yourself,' says Casax.

I'm uncomfortable. A Brotherhood boss doesn't pay social visits for no reason.

'You've been enjoying yourself a lot recently. Rolling around with Lisutaris and Princess Direeva, from what I hear.'

'You've been hearing things that are none of your business.'

Casax raises his eyebrows a fraction. Last year I found myself more or less on the same side as Casax in a case involving the chariot races. A fortunate occurrence, and since then the Brotherhood have left me alone. It doesn't mean much. The Brotherhood are never well disposed towards Investigators.

He leans forward.

'You know anything about the death of a dwa dealer?'

'Which one? They die a lot.'

'Orius here thought he might be able to pick up a little Orcish aura round the death scene.'

I glance at the Sorcerer, then back to Casax.

'So?'

'Your young companion is part Orc. And handy with a sword.'

'Plenty of people are handy with a sword in Twelve Seas. And she's not the only girl in town with Orc blood.'

Casax glances round the room.

'Is this it?'

'What do you mean?'

'I mean is this all you have? Tiny rooms full of junk? Furniture fit for a slum?'

'It suits me fine.'

'You don't have something salted away? Gold in the bank?'

I look at him blankly.

'Why do you do it?' he asks.

'Do what?'

'Investigate.'

'I got thrown out of my last job for being a useless drunk.'

'You could still do better for yourself. Rezox would have paid you to let him go. So would plenty of others. You could live a lot better.'

The Brotherhood boss rises to his feet.

'If you came here to give your pet Sorcerer a chance to see what he could learn, you're going to be disappointed,' I tell him.

Orius Fire Tamer sneers at me.

'You think you have any power to affect me?'

'I think I could toss a knife in your throat before you got a spell ready, kid.'

Casax almost grins.

'He might, Orius. He's a tough guy, Thraxas. Not so tough that he'd bother me, but tough enough. When he's sober.'

He turns to me.

'If your Orc friend killed my dealer I'll be down on her like a bad spell. Not that I miss the dealer. But I've got a position to maintain. You understand.'

They depart. I open my klee. The bottle is almost finished. I make a mental note to buy more. Makri appears.

'Was it about the dealer?'

'So they said. But I think Casax was more interested in what Lisutaris and Direeva were doing here. He won't learn anything from Orius. That runt isn't going to get through a hiding spell cast by Lisutaris. What's the kid think he's doing, linking up with the Brotherhood? When I was his age—'

'Thraxas,' says Makri, loudly. 'Be quiet. I have something important to tell you.'

'If this is about See-ath, I don't—'

'It's not about See-ath. It's about Samanatius. They're trying to evict him.'

'What?'

'The landlord wants to demolish the block. He's using

the collapse of the aqueduct as an excuse. He's been trying to get rid of Samanatius and the other tenants for months now, he wants to make money on the land.'

I'm staring at Makri in bewilderment. I can't think why she's telling me this. It almost sounds like she expects me to do something about it.

'You have to do something about it.'

I finish off my klee.

'Me? What? Why?'

'The owner got the go-ahead from Prefect Drinius, but it's illegal to demolish the block without permission from the Consul's office.'

I shrug.

'Happens all the time. If the local Prefect says its okay, the owner's not going to wait for the Consul to screw things up. Just mean another bribe to pay.'

'They can't evict Samanatius! He's a great man.'

I don't care one way or the other about Samanatius.

'You have to stop it.'

'Makri, what gives you this bizarre idea that I could do anything? I'm an Investigator, not a planning inspector.'

'You're a Tribune of the People. You can halt any building work by referring it to the Senate for adjudication.'

My head swims.

'What?'

'It's part of the power invested in the Tribunes. They could do lots of things to protect the poor. Stopping landlords from demolishing buildings was one of them.'

'You're crazy.'

'I'm not. I looked it up in the library.'

'That was a hundred and fifty years ago.'

'Their powers were never rescinded.'

'But I'm not a real Tribune. It's only a device to get me into the Assemblage.'

'It doesn't matter,' declares Makri firmly. 'Cicerius made you a Tribune and it's legal. You now have the full power of the Tribunate behind you and you have to do something.'

I grab for the klee. It's empty. There must be a beer round here somewhere.

'Makri, this is insane. I'm sorry your buddy's getting evicted but I can't stop it. What the hell is Cicerius going to say if I suddenly start using my supposed power to order the local Prefect around? The Senate would go crazy. So would the Palace, probably. I'd have the whole government on my back. Who is the landlord anyway?'

'Praetor Capatius.'

'Capatius? The richest man in Turai? Controls about forty seats in the Senate? Sure, Makri, I'll take him on any time. Easy as bribing a Senator. I'll just tell him to please stop behaving badly. Be reasonable.'

'You can do it,' insists Makri. 'It's part of your power.'

'I don't have any power,' I roar, frustrated by her insistence. 'And have you forgotten what else is going on right now? I'm in the middle of a case that's quite probably going to end up with me rowing a slave galley and Lisutaris dangling on a rope. I've got Sorcerers, the Deputy Consul, and an election to worry about, not to mention Covinius, deadly Assassin, in case you've forgotten. And you expect me to march up to Prefect Drinius and say, "Excuse me, you have to stop this eviction because I'm a Tribune of the People"?'

'Yes.'

'Forget it.'

'Samanatius will not be evicted.'

'I can't prevent it.'

'I'll kill anyone who tries,' threatens Makri.

'Good luck. Now excuse me, I've got an investigation to be getting on with.'

I grab my warm cloak and depart swiftly. Stop the eviction indeed. Use my powers as Tribune of the People. That would certainly give the local population something to laugh about. They'd still be laughing when Praetor Capatius hired twenty armed men to chase me out of Twelve Seas.

It takes a long time to find a landus. I'm cold. I wish I had more beer inside me. I wish I wasn't always having to visit the Deputy Consul. For a man who paid out good money only a few days ago to hire me, he shows a great lack of enthusiasm to see me when I finally roll up at his house.

'What do you want?'

'Beer. But it's usually in short supply round here, so I'll take whatever you've got.'

'Have you disturbed me merely to request alcohol? I have an important appointment with Tilupasis.'

'She's an efficient woman, Tilupasis. Sharp as an Elf's ear. You ought to make her a Senator. I need to talk to Rezox. I threw him in the slammer a week or so back and I need some quick access. It's to help Lisutaris.'

For all that he's a crusty specimen and was a poor soldier, Cicerius can move quickly when he needs to. He's known for his quick wits in the Senate. As soon as I hold up the possibility of helping Lisutaris, he moves into action, dashing off an official letter and granting permission for me to visit Rezox in prison. And when I mention that Rezox may not be forthcoming with the important information, he replies brusquely that he can deal with that if necessary.

'His crime was to steal dragon scales from a warehouse? Tell me on the way why this is important. If he seems disinclined to co-operate, I can offer him his freedom.'

I wasn't planning on taking Cicerius along with me but he insists. Inside he's no calmer than me. We're just waiting for the scandal to blow up in our faces. The Deputy Consul lives in fear of anything damaging the interests of his beloved Turai. Furthermore, the repercussions of Lisutaris's arrest would hand a huge slice of harmful ammunition to Senator Lodius, head of the Populares. The opposition party will use Lisutaris's downfall to smear Cicerius, and by association Kalius, the Consul, and even the King.

We hurry to the prison in Cicerius's official carriage.

'Powdered dragon scales form part of a rare spell for erasing the past.'

Cicerius still maintains that things would never have gone so badly wrong if I had looked after Lisutaris properly.

'It could be worse. Certain members of the population of Twelve Seas are suggesting I use my Tribune's powers to stop Praetor Capatius carrying out an eviction.'

Cicerius is incredulous.

'What? You will do no such thing.'

'Don't worry, I wasn't planning to. Although they

have a point. It's hardly fair of the Praetor to use the cover of a fierce winter to evict the poor. You'd think the man had enough money already without tearing down his slums.'

I know this will annoy Cicerius. Capatius is a strong supporter of the Traditionals and a huge contributor to their funds.

'Presumably Capatius is set on improving the people's housing conditions.'

I laugh, which annoys him.

'Capatius is set on improving his bank balance. Which is odd really, seeing as he owns his own bank. Doesn't it bother the Traditionals that some of your supporters spend their whole life bleeding the poor?'

'I do not intend to discuss Turanian politics with an Investigator,' says Cicerius.

He doesn't mind discussing politics when it suits him. We've arrived at the prison. We hurry inside. A Captain of the Guards salutes the Deputy Consul and leads us to Rezox. Cicerius's assistant Hansius, arriving before us, has arranged for the interview in a private room. He's an efficient young man, Hansius. He'll go far.

In detention, Rezox looks about as miserable as a Niojan whore, and the sight of me coming for a visit doesn't cheer him up any. Cicerius begins to speak. Not having time for long speeches, I interrupt.

'Rezox. I need to know who you were passing the dragon scales on to. Spill it and Cicerius will get you out of jail.'

'Is that true?'

'Sure it's true. Cicerius has the green-edged toga. He can authorise it. So long as you tell me now.'

Rezox weighs things up. If he's worried about the morality of selling out his partner, it doesn't delay him for more than five seconds.

'Coralex,' he replies. 'Up at the top of Pashish.'

'Coralex?' says Cicerius. 'I know of him. He's a respectable importer of wine.'

Coralex is the biggest disposer of stolen property in Turai. I thought everyone knew that.

'Cicerius, you're much too trusting. Okay, I'm off to see Coralex.'

Before departing, I inform Cicerius that the threat from Covinius is now very real.

'I don't know if he had anything to do with Darius's murder but I know he's in Turai. There's a strong chance his target is Lisutaris.'

'Why do you say that?'

'He's a Simnian Assassin, isn't he? Sunstorm Ramius might be favourite to win the election but that doesn't mean the Simnians won't try to get rid of the opposition.'

'I regard that as highly unlikely,' replies Cicerius. 'Simnia has never attempted assassination in the Sorcerers' contest.'

'There's a first time for everything.'

'Might his purpose in Turai be unconnected with the Assemblage?'

'It might but we ought to assume the worst. Can you provide any more of a bodyguard for Lisutaris?'

The Deputy Consul nods.

'Is Coralex really a disposer of stolen goods?' he asks.

'One of the biggest.'

Cicerius shakes his head sadly.

'My household has purchased wine from his warehouse. Some citizens have lost all sense of morality.'

I depart swiftly on the trail of the dragon scales. My sense of morality went into decline a long time ago. It kept getting in the way of my work.

CHAPTER

TWELVE

Honest Mox's bookmaking establishment is closed for the first time in living memory. The gambling fraternity of Twelve Seas are stunned. I'm standing outside in the snow with about twenty others, looking forlornly at the locked front door

'What happened?'

'His son just died. From dwa.'

The frustrated gamblers shake their heads. It's almost too bad to contemplate. We never thought we'd see the day when Mox had to close. There's a general feeling that if we can make our way here through the bad weather, Mox ought to at least be able to keep his shop open.

People start drifting away, heading north towards the next bookmaker. It's a frustrating occurrence. I was planning to lay off a little money on Ramius. As Lisutaris is likely to be slung out of the competition I really wanted to cover my losses with another bet. I've no time to visit another bookmaker. I need to see Coralex in a hurry. I curse. This job just gets worse and worse.

The wind howls down from the north. By the time I reach Coralex's house in Golden Crescent, home of the richest merchants, I'm about as angry as a Troll with a toothache. The servant who answers the door tries to keep me out and I just walk over him. They don't build many domestic servants that can stand up to me. Another functionary attempts to hold me back and I bat him out of the way. Coralex appears at the top of the stairs. I've encountered him before in the course of my work, though I've never invaded his home before. I march up the stairs and grab him by the throat.

'Coralex. I'm in a hurry. You got some dragon scales recently from a crooked merchant named Rezox. I want to know who you sold them to.'

'Throw this man out of the house,' yells Coralex.

An employee hurries into view, a more formidable specimen than the domestic servants. He's tall and he carries a sword. I slam Coralex into him then grab him by the scruff of the neck and tumble him downstairs.

I turn back to Coralex.

'As I was saying. What happened to the dragon scales? Stop stammering, I don't have time. I'm here with the backing of Deputy Consul Cicerius, and if I have to toss you downstairs, the Deputy will move Heaven, Earth and the three moons to see I don't get prosecuted. He's already very upset by what he just learned about you.'

The merchant hesitates. I touch my dagger.

'Spill it.'

Coralex spills it. At his age, he isn't going to get off lightly from a trip down the stairs. A man of his wealth naturally has a very long staircase.

I leave the house with a lot of information, and curses raining down on me from Coralex, his wife, and a very pretty daughter who probably doesn't know that her father deals in stolen goods. Outside the snow catches me in the face. I shake it off. Now that I've really offended someone, I feel like I'm working well. I have a list of the people who've recently bought dragon scales, and as these are not easy to come by there's a good chance that the mysterious spell-worker will be among them.

Back in Twelve Seas I buy a bundle of logs from a street vendor, stoke up the fire, open a beer and prepare to study the list. I'm interrupted by a knock at the door. I wrench it open and am surprised to find Senator Lodius, leader of the opposition party in Turai and sworn enemy of Cicerius. I've never spoken to Lodius. He did once violently denounce me to the Senate after I'd run into some trouble while working for Cicerius. The *Chronicle* ran a full report, listing many of my previous misdemeanours.

'Are you busy?' he enquires, politely.

The Senator is a man of medium height, about fifty or so but well preserved. He has something of an aristocratic air, though he styles himself leader of the democratic Populares party. He's not particularly imposing in appearance but he's handsome enough for a political leader, with blue eyes, short grey hair neatly styled and a well-cut toga just visible under a thick woollen cloak. He's a powerful speaker when he has to be and he has a lot of support in this city.

'I'm busy. But come in anyway.'

I don't know why he's here. Lodius is far too important to be visiting me. I've never liked the man – he always gives me the impression of a politician who'd hitch his wagon to any cause which might bring him to power – but if he's here to offer me some lucrative work I might be prepared to change my opinion.

The Senator is accompanied by two assistants, or

bodyguards more likely, as Turanian politics is inclined to be violent. I kick some junk under the table, draw out a chair and motion the Senator to take a seat. Surprisingly, he accepts my offer of beer. He takes the bottle, doesn't mind that I don't have any goblets to hand, and gets right down to business.

'I understand you are busy, at the Sorcerers Assemblage?'

At the mention of the Assemblage I'm immediately on my guard.

'I wish you success,' he says. 'It will be a fine thing for the city if our candidate is elected.'

I'm expecting Lodius to start in with some criticism of Cicerius and the Traditionals, but that doesn't seem to be what he's here for.

'I am hoping, however, that you will have time to perform another function. Have you heard of the impending demolition of the buildings around the collapsed aqueduct?'

'Yes.'

'Are you aware that the proposal to clear the area will make four hundred Turanians homeless?'

I wasn't, though the way landlords crowd people into the slums, it's not really a surprise.

'Praetor Capatius wishes to develop the land for profit,' continues Lodius. 'As the richest man in the city and a strong supporter of the Traditionals, the Praetor has of course no regard for the rights of the ordinary citizen.'

By this time I'm eyeing the Senator warily. I don't like where this is going.

'Are you aware of your powers as Tribune of the People?'

'I've a rough idea.'

The Senator nods. Then he asks me what I'm planning to do.

'I wasn't planning to do anything.'

'Surely you do not wish to see these people made homeless, particularly in the middle of such a fierce winter?'

'I'd sooner they were warm and cosy. But I'm not really a Tribune. I was only given the post so I could get into the Assemblage.'

'Nonetheless, you have the power. Are you afraid that Cicerius would disapprove of you acting against his friend Capatius?'

'Not particularly. I just don't see myself as a politician. And I'm busy.'

'Too busy to help your fellow citizens?'

If there's one thing you can be sure of it's that Lodius doesn't care about his fellow citizens either, but I don't seem to have the opportunity to point this out. He's backing me into an awkward corner.

'Yes. I'm too busy. I'm already helping Turai by assisting Lisutaris. I can't be rescuing the whole city. You're head of a political party, why don't you stop the evictions?'

'I don't have the power. By some quirk of history, only the Tribunes can do that. A Tribune can insist that every legal step is followed to the letter in the matter of city development. Naturally, that was not what Cicerius had in mind when he nominated you, but the fact remains that you can prevent the eviction by referring the matter to the Senate. Once that has been done, I will take over.'

'Would this have anything to do with you needing four hundred votes in a vital ward that has an election next year?'

'I am concerned only with the plight of the poor.'

We stare at each other for a while. I'm wondering what pressure Lodius can bring to bear. While I don't relish having him as a political enemy, Cicerius and the Traditionals still have more power. The Consul, Turai's highest official, is always a Traditional, and they're the party of the King. The last thing I want to do is end up an enemy of the King. The whole thing is extremely aggravating for a man who tries to stay out of politics. I inform the Senator that, sad as I am to see hardship among my fellow citizens, I'm not about to enter the political arena by vetoing Praetor Capatius. Senator Lodius sips his beer, and turns to speak to one of his assistants.

'Ivitius. Tell me again what you saw when you were visiting your cousin in Quintessence Street.'

'Thraxas the Investigator dumping a body over a wall,' says Ivitius.

'And what night was that?'

'The same night Darius Cloud Walker was killed.'

Lodius turns back to me.

'A very troubling affair, as you know. I understand that the Sorcerers Guild is currently extending its full powers in an effort to find out what happened to Darius Cloud Walker. But from what I hear, someone has cast a mystical shield over the events of the night in question. The Sorcerers are baffled, at least for the moment. Of course, they are lacking specific information. All they know is that the body was found in a snowdrift in Twelve

Seas. If they had more facts – for instance, the exact location of the killing, and the identity of those around the victim at the time – I have no doubt that they could quickly learn the truth concerning his death.'

I can't think of anything to say. I'm all out of words.

'My carriage is outside,' says the Senator. 'I will take you to the site of the eviction. Nothing formal in the way of documentation is required. It is merely necessary for you to speak to the person in charge, one Vadinex, an employee of Capatius's. Tell him that you are referring the matter to the Senate. Work will then cease, pending investigation.'

I still can't think of anything to say. I get my cloak. We ride in silence along Quintessence Street. The snow and ice are thick on the ground, but Lodius has a sturdy carriage pulled by two equally sturdy horses and we reach the site of the eviction a lot quicker than I'd like to. The snow is falling on a dismal scene of workmen, city officials, lawyers, civil guards and poor tenants, all arguing bitterly. Despite the cold, violence is in the air as the Civil Guards hold back the crowd. Some of the slum dwellers scream from upstairs windows, aiming their anger at Vadinex, the man in charge.

I knew Vadinex in my army days. He stands about six and a half feet tall and he's built like a bull. Once at a siege he won a commendation for being the first man over the wall. Praetor Capatius uses him for difficult assignments, and evicting a few poor tenants is all in a day's work for him.

I really don't want to be doing this. I notice Captain Rallee among the guards, and make my way towards him. Before I get there, a figure bursts through the crowd brandishing an axe. It's Makri, clad in a thick cloak and her floppy hat, and bristling with weapons.

'You're not going to evict Samanatius,' she yells.

An elderly figure in a plain cloak, presumably the philosopher himself, steps forward through the blizzard to lay his hand on her shoulder, indicating I think that he doesn't wish to see violence done. Vadinex confronts her, flanked by his helpers. Makri raises her axe. I step forward.

'Stop!' I yell.

I have a loud voice when necessary, and a lot of bulk. It's hard to miss me, even in a snowstorm.

'I'm halting this work. As Tribune of the People, I am referring the matter to the Senate.'

There is general astonishment. Captain Rallee actually laughs. Vadinex doesn't seem so amused.

'What the hell are you talking about, Thraxas? Get out of my way.'

Various others now step forward in support of my statement. Several cold-looking lawyers, accompanied by armed men, courtesy of Lodius, announce that the eviction cannot now go ahead.

'The Tribune has spoken.'

Everyone looks at me. I feel foolish. Senator Lodius has now stepped into the fray. As people recognise him they realise that this is not a joke. Captain Rallee addresses Vadinex.

'It's legal,' he says. 'The matter has to go to the Senate. You can't carry out the eviction.'

Vadinex starts to protest but Captain Rallee cuts him short.

'I said it's legal. And if you keep me standing here in

this snowstorm any longer, I'm liable to throw you in prison for assaulting a Civil Guard. Eviction over. Everybody go home.'

Vadinex eyes me with loathing.

'The Praetor will be down on you like a bad spell for this,' he growls.

Makri hurries over.

'Stay away or I'll kill you,' she spits at him.

Vadinex always had a short temper. Were the area not so thick with Civil Guards, he'd quite likely attack her. I'd like to see Makri killing Vadinex. The way the huge man looks at her before he departs, she may yet get the chance. He moves off, taking his companions with him.

'Thraxas, you were great!' enthuses Makri. 'I knew you'd come through in the end. Come and meet Samanatius!'

I shake the elderly philosopher's hand. He thanks me warmly, but when he looks into my eyes I know he knows I'm not here of my own free will. All around, tenants of the slums are congratulating me for rescuing them from Vadinex.

'Good work,' booms Senator Lodius, and gets round to letting everyone know that he is the man responsible for their salvation. The congratulations fail to give me a warm glow. Makri might be as happy as an Elf in a tree that Samanatius has a reprieve, but I've got other things to worry about.

'Where's Lisutaris? You're meant to be protecting her.'

Makri tells me she's asleep in her room at the Avenging Axe. Direeva is with her.

I frown.

'I'm starting to get suspicious of Direeva. I don't like the way she keeps sticking to Lisutaris.'

'Tilupasis likes it. Tilupasis seems to have a lot of influence, even with the Consul.'

'She ought to. They're having an affair. Well, according to scurrilous rumour anyway, and I generally trust that. Do a good job for Tilupasis and she might help with the university.'

'I already thought of that.'

I ask Makri if Tilupasis is a supporter of the Association of Gentlewomen, but Makri doesn't think she is, which strikes her as odd.

'Maybe she thinks she's doing fine already,' I suggest.

Makri isn't enjoying her employment as bodyguard.

'I expected I might have to kill the occasional attacker and maybe fight off a few Assassins. I never thought it would involve being nursemaid to a woman who can't stand upright after lunchtime. What were you thinking of, nominating her for head of the Sorcerers Guild?'

'I didn't nominate her. Cicerius did. Is she still going at the water pipe?'

'Like a hungry dragon chewing on a carcass. How does she ever remember any spells? I mean, you can't remember them even when you're sober.'

'She studied more than me.'

'It was hell at the Assemblage. I had to keep dragging her away from visiting Sorcerers so they wouldn't see how doped she was. Isn't she meant to be impressing people?'

Despite her recent lapses, Makri does have something

of a puritanical streak, which now appears to be resurfacing. She thinks that people should get on with their work, and Lisutaris is certainly failing to do this. I agree that Lisutaris can't be impressing the Sorcerers with her performance.

'The delegation from Turai are doing their best. The other two Tribunes have been spreading hospitality around to the extent that some of our guests are now so sated with sex, alcohol and dwa that they'd vote for anyone they were told to. It's not going to be enough to defeat Ramius in the vote, but remember, our candidate only has to make it into the top two.'

'But those two go into some sort of final contest,' Makri points out. 'How is Lisutaris going to manage that?'

'Who knows? It wouldn't surprise me if Tilupasis is working on some way of cheating right now.'

At the Avenging Axe, Makri goes to check on Lisutaris. I've barely time to load up with stew, venison and yams before I'm back at work, studying the list of recipients of dragon scales. It's an interesting collection, containing the names of quite a few aristocratic Turanians. These rich ladies like to make their hair sparkle with dragon scales, but it seems as if they prefer to buy them at a discount, even if it's illegal. Coralex and Rezox were doing a good trade. Clients include Praetor Capatius, Prefect Galwinius, several other Senators and various high-up city officials. Rich merchants too, including, I note, Rixad. I'm not surprised. He was keen to keep his wife happy, and nothing says I love you better than a sprinkling of well-cut dragon scales.

Unfortunately, few people on the list have any knowledge of sorcery. I can't see Capatius or Galwinius huddled over a cauldron, cooking up a magical brew. The name of Tirini Snake Smiter catches my eye. She might be buying dragon scales for making spells. She is a Sorcerer. But she's also a woman who loves to display herself to her best advantage, and I'm inclined to believe she wanted to make her hair sparkle rather than work some malevolent spell. Tirini would be an unlikely murderer. She never dabbles in politics, or crime, to my knowledge, being more concerned with party-going, temporary romances and generally enjoying herself. She has a lot of power, but the most notable thing she's done with it recently is light up the trees in her garden in a fantastic display for a reception she held. The *Renowned and Truthful Chronicle* was impressed. They liked the fireworks too. I don't see her as a murderer.

The only other name of note is Princess Direeva. Direeva has recently bought dragon scales from Coralex. I muse on this. In my eyes Direeva is already a suspect for the murder of Darius. No known motive but plenty of opportunity. And now it turns out that she's been clandestinely buying the main ingredient for a hitherto unknown spell of erasement.

Unfortunately Direeva also wears beads made from dragon scales in her hair. If I confront her she'll simply say she needed some new jewellery. She does have a lot of hair to decorate.

I need a drink. After a lifetime as a private citizen, suddenly being obliged to act in an official capacity has unnerved me. I'm grateful it's midwinter. People have enough problems worrying about staying alive without paying too much attention to the startling sight of Thraxas suddenly appearing as a minor politician. With any luck it will soon be forgotten about. It had better be, I'm not planning on defending anyone else's rights.

Next morning at Lisutaris's villa I find Makri sitting
in front of a well-laden breakfast table.

'Lisutaris still unconscious?'

'No, wide awake.'

I'm surprised.

'What happened? The water pipe break from over-
use?'

'Lisutaris never starts on the water pipe till Copro's
been to do her hair. She needs to be fully alert for the
morning beauty treatments. Copro wouldn't like it if she
wasn't paying attention. He's quite temperamental.'

Discussing Copro, I feel quite temperamental myself.

'I need to see her.'

'You can't see her yet. Copro doesn't like to be interrupted when he's working.'

'Goddammit, are you serious? I'm trying to get her off
a murder rap and she's too busy getting her hair done?'

'You can't expect an important Sorcerer to turn up
at the Assemblage with her hair in poor condition,' says
Makri. 'It's hardly going to impress people.'

'They're voting for top Sorcerer, not fashion woman
of the year.'

'No one's going to vote for her if they think she's not
making an effort,' asserts Makri.

'So how come you're a fan of Copro all of a sudden? I thought you didn't like him.'

I stare at Makri suspiciously.

'There's something different about you.'

'No there isn't.'

'Yes there is. Your hair is different.'

'Just a little rearrangement,' says Makri, defensively. 'Copro said it would show off my cheekbones better—'

'Your cheekbones? What's got into you? When you arrived in Turai you couldn't stop talking about how stupid the rich women were.'

'I'm just fitting in,' says Makri, calmly. 'As Lisutaris's bodyguard I can't be arguing with her hairdresser. It would create all sorts of difficulties.'

She studies her fingernails.

'Do you think I should get my nails done as well? I'm not really happy with this colour.'

'What's wrong with it?'

'It clashes with the chainmail.'

Makri holds her fingers over a piece of chainmail, and peers in the mirror.

'Thraxas, you remember how I said I'd like to be blonde after we saw all those blonde Elvish women? What do you think?'

'Will you stop talking like this? Yesterday you were going to chop up Vadinex with your axe, and today you're twittering on about your hair.'

'I do not see the two things as mutually exclusive,' protests Makri.

'Life was easier when you were an ignorant Barbarian.'

'I was never an ignorant Barbarian.'

'Well, you didn't used to ramble on about hair and make-up. When you arrived in this city all you wanted to do was attend the university.'

'I still do. I may wear a little eyeliner when I get there.'

'What happened to Makri the demented swordswoman?'

'Make your mind up, Thraxas. Only last week you were lecturing me about killing the dwa dealer. You want me to kill someone? Fine. Just point me in the right direction.'

'I don't want you to kill anyone.'

'Don't worry about me,' says Makri, warming to the topic. 'I'll kill anyone that needs killing. Orcs, Humans, Elves, Trolls, dragons, snakes, mythical beasts—'

'Will you shut up about killing things?'

'What, so now I'm not meant to talk about killing people *or* make-up? Is there any subject you'd be happy with?'

'Solving a murder would be a good choice. How long is Lisutaris going to be?'

'I think she's scheduled for a manicure as well. Copro brought his best assistant, and a nail specialist.'

Quite a long time apparently. Makri is showing little interest in the food in front of her, so I pile up a plate for a good second breakfast, meanwhile silently cursing Copro and his ilk. When I was young the city wasn't full of beauticians. Old Consul Juvenius would have thrown Copro off the walls, and a good thing too.

'So what do you think?' says Makri.

'About what?'

'Dying my hair blonde.'

'I think you'll look like a cheap whore. Stop asking me about it.'

'Do you have to be so unpleasant? Looking after Lisutaris is stressful. I need some relaxation.'

Unable to take any more of this, I carry my plate over to the window and stare out at the ice-covered garden. If Makri asks me one more time about her hair I'm going to turn her in as an accessory to murder. There's some commotion in the long hallway and a messenger rushes in calling for Makri. He hands her a slip of paper. Makri breaks the seal and looks concerned.

'Bad news at the Assemblage.'

'The Sorcerers have got through—?'

'No. Sunstorm Ramius has dispatched Troverus to take Princess Direeva to dinner. Tilupasis is very concerned.'

Makri rises to her feet.

'I have to intercept them.'

'Who is Troverus?' I ask, feeling confused.

'Handsomest young man in Simnia, according to all reports. Tilupasis has been worried about him all along. That Ramius, he's cunning.'

Makri starts making ready to leave. She has a determined look in her eyes.

'I won't have it. No "handsomest young man in Simnia" is going to charm Direeva into voting for Sunstorm Ramius.'

Makri hurries to don her armour, and throws her weapons into the small purse which contains the magic pocket. All the while she's muttering about the perfidy of the Simnians.

'It's underhand tactics. I'll show them.'

'I thought you weren't keen on this vote-winning business. You said it was corrupt.'

'It is. But I refuse to be defeated,' states Makri. 'Look after Lisutaris till she gets to the Assemblage. And whatever you do, don't insult Copro. He's extremely temperamental.'

Makri takes a final, dissatisfied look at her nails, then hurries out. I sit down to finish off the food on the table, and ring for beer. The young servant who arrives has a noticeable rural accent. No doubt a sturdy and sensible woman from the outlying farmlands.

'What do you think of Copro?' I ask.

'He's a great man, and a boon to the city,' she replies. 'They should make him a Senator.'

I study her face.

'Was there much beauty treatment back on the farm?'

She shakes her head.

'That's why I moved to the city.'

The city is doomed.

Lisutaris's apprentice emerges from her private chambers. I learn that the Sorcerer will be ready in a little while.

'How long is a little while?'

'No more than an hour.'

Eventually Lisutaris emerges, accompanied by Copro and his two helpers.

'Thraxas.' Lisutaris greets me graciously. She is wide awake, the first time I've seen her like this since the Assemblage began. Copro is still fussing round her with a comb. He's thin, dark, a little younger than I imagined. And not quite as lisping, though I wouldn't want him on my side in a sword fight. I doubt he'd handle a blade as well as his comb. I note with displeasure that beneath his long hair, jewelled earrings glisten on his earlobes. A number of guilds in Turai use plain gold earrings as a mark of rank, but few men would wear jewels in their ears, apart from the foppish sons of wealthy Senators.

Copro motions extravagantly towards Lisutaris.

'Do you like it?'

'It's wonderful. Lisutaris, we have to get to the Assemblage. Cicerius is starting to complain about your nonappearance. And Tilupasis is giving me a hard time.'

Lisutaris tells me she'll be ready in an instant, and departs upstairs.

'I love your friend Makri,' says Copro. 'Such a savage beauty.'

I grunt, and sit down.

'She really should let me do more with her hair.'

Makri has a vast unruly mane, remarkable in its own way. I can't see her taking to any of the controlled styles favoured by Turai's aristocrats. To my disappointment, Copro agrees with me.

'Of course, such a woman as Makri would not suit such a stylised coiffure. Her magnificent features would only be diminished. But a little styling to bring out her radiance, her force of character. A style the Abelasians call Summer Lightning. It would be breathtaking. I already did much the same for Princess Direeva.'

'You attend Direeva?'

'Princess Direeva insists on the best. I have often been called to the Southern Hills to assist.'

Not really wanting to engage in conversation with Copro, I busy myself with my beer, but Copro apparently finds me more interesting than I find him, because he sits down facing me at the table.

'You have such a fascinating job. Is it dangerous, tracking down all those criminals?'

'Yes.'

'Is it exciting?'

'No. But I need the money.'

Copro studies me. I'm just waiting for him to make some crack about my appearance. I've got long hair tied back in a ponytail, and if he suggests styling it I'm going to sling him out the front door. He asks me some more questions about my work and I grunt some replies. All the time I'm wishing that I wasn't here in Lisutaris's villa, and remembering that when I did live in the better part of town, I never felt all that comfortable about it. Finally Copro gives up on me and converses with Lisutaris's apprentice about new styles just in from Samsarina. Summer fashions, apparently, although I can't see why they want to talk about summer fashions when we're still in the middle of winter.

Copro arrived in Turai with nothing, and now he's rich. For all the hand-waving and vacuous conversation, I'd be willing to bet he's a shrewd enough operator underneath, and smart enough never to be singed by a dragon.

Tiring of the conversation, I go in search of the Sorcerer. Servants look on with disapproval as I approach her private chambers, but I ignore them and find her in her room, sucking on her water pipe.

'Time to go,' I say, and drag her to her feet.

She looks at me with surprise.

'I can't believe you just laid your hand on me.'

'It was either that or kill the beautician.'

'The last time anyone laid a hand on me I punished them with a heart attack spell.'

'I'd be surprised if you could remember a spell for a runny nose. Don't you ever get sick of thazis dreams? Get your warm cloak on and call the carriage. We're due at the Assemblage. You've got an election to win. Cicerius is paying me to make it happen. So let's go.'

Lisutaris looks with longing at the water pipe.

'Touch that pipe again and I'm going to slug you.'

'I'd kill you if you did.'

'And then who'd get you off the murder rap? Face it, Lisutaris, you need me. So let's go.'

Lisutaris looks at me with dislike.

'I didn't realise how unpleasant you were.'

'Then you're the only person in Turai who didn't. I'm famous for being unpleasant. Now get ready before I pick you up and throw you in the carriage.'

Lisutaris bundles about a hundred sticks of thazis into a magic pocket and starts smoking them on the way to the Assemblage. We're hardly out of Truth is Beauty Lane when her head starts lolling about. I grab the thazis from her hand and toss it out the carriage window.

'What the hell's the matter with you? You used to be a good Sorcerer and now you're about as much use as a eunuch in a brothel.'

She shakes her head slowly

'I'm worried I might have killed Darius.'

'You seemed sure you didn't.'

'I'm not so sure now,' she says, and takes another thazis stick from her magic pocket. Lisutaris, Mistress of the Sky, is starting to fall apart. By the time we get to the Assemblage she's unsteady on her feet. Tilupasis intercepts her at the door and leads her off to some private room before the other Sorcerers can see the state she's in. Makri and Princess Direeva are looking on.

'She wasn't like this ten years ago,' says Direeva. Her hair sways gently. The dragon scales, finely cut by a jeweller, sparkle brilliantly in the torchlight.

'Just our bad luck that Sunstorm Ramius is a clean-living sort of Sorcerer.'

Direeva enquires if I've made any progress on the case. I'm noncommittal.

'I'll get there in the end. Depends how much time I have. How is the hiding spell?'

'Strong enough,' replies the Princess.

Last night Melus the Fair visited Lisutaris's villa to add her power to the incantation, strengthening the spell. I hope we can trust Melus. She's sharp as an Elf's ear and has close ties to Lisutaris, but it's one more person who might give us away. The weight of events is getting to me. Makri wonders what would happen if Lisutaris managed to win the election and was then found to be implicated in the murder.

'Hard to say. As far as I understand the Sorcerers' rules, the head of the Guild can't be expelled. Lasat, Axe of Gold, is the temporary leader, but once he confirms the new Sorcerer in their post they can't be removed. And given that important upper-class citizens in Turai are usually allowed the opportunity to slip off into exile before being convicted of a serious crime, Lisutaris might still end up as head of the Guild, exiled in another city.'

'Could she ever return to Turai?'

'Maybe, when the heat died down. I think Cicerius is hoping for something like that, if I can't clear her name. Won't help you or me, though.'

I'm firmly of the Turanian lower classes. Even my name marks me out as such. If I'm implicated in a murder, no one will look the other way while I flee the city.

Makri has intercepted Princess Direeva before her appointment with Troverus. She's doing her best to keep her entertained with tales of her exploits in the gladiatorial arena. Direeva seems interested.

'I too have often had to fight. When my grandfather died my uncle attempted to seize the kingdom from my father. It took two years of continual warfare till he was in control. My uncle hired an army of Orcish mercenaries, and it was only with help from the Abelasians that we overcame them. Darius Cloud Walker was our ally. We will miss him.'

A cunning look comes into Makri's eyes.

'Yes, it's a terrible loss. But now you have thirty votes to spare, I expect you'll be transferring them to Lisutaris.'

'Is that why you have been hospitable?' says Direeva, slightly stiffly.

'Of course not,' replies Makri, a little flustered. 'I'm naturally hospitable to any woman who can lead an army. But now your friend has been brutally murdered, you have to vote for someone. I mean, it's a shame your old ally ended up in a snowdrift with my knife in his back, but you can't dwell on the past. Voting for Lisutaris seems like the natural thing to do . . . given that Darius was unfortunately killed in Thraxas's office . . . just the other night . . . with my knife . . .'

Makri's voice tails off. She holds up her hand.

'Do you like this nail varnish? I'm not sure about it.'

Direeva laughs, quite heartily for a Princess.

'If you get exiled from Turai you can stay with me in the Southern Hills,' she says. 'I may vote for Lisutaris. Having seen Turai, I'd say it's vital to you that Lisutaris becomes head of the Guild. I did not know that your strength was so diminished. You're extremely vulnerable to attack from the Orcs.'

'They haven't recovered from the beating we gave them last time,' I say.

Princess Direeva isn't so sure.

'It's difficult to predict when a new leader may arise to unite the Orcish nations and lead them against the west.'

I've been through one major Orc war and I don't expect to live out my days without seeing another, so I'm interested in Direeva's opinions.

'You weren't expecting it last time,' she continues. 'King Bhergaz of Aztol was of no special importance till the neighbouring country asked him to intervene in their succession dispute. He put his own cousin in charge, got control of the eastern trade route, started dealing in gold and slaves and became rich. Next thing anybody knew he was calling himself Bhergaz the Fierce and raising an army to conquer the region. Once he got Rezaz the Butcher on his side he became effective leader of the Orc lands only six years after ascending to the throne of Aztol. And you remember what happened after that.'

I certainly do. Without the timely intervention of the Elvish armies, Turai would now be a province of Aztol.

'The Kingdom of Aztol hasn't recovered from defeat,' continues the Princess. 'But Gzak is growing stronger.

It's a rich land and a lot of Orcs still look up to Gzak for its victories last century.'

'So you think Gzak will invade?' asks Makri. She doesn't sound too distressed by the prospect. Here in Turai she can never find enough Orcs to kill.

'It's possible. But hard to predict. It takes something special to unite the Orcs. Last century Ormizoan the Great started his career as leader of a small band of rebels. The same magnetism that made his followers stand by him in difficult times eventually made him war leader of the entire east. The Orc lands are rarely peaceful. Who knows if one of the current warring rebel Princes might be destined for greatness? Have you heard of the young Prince Amrag of Kose who just overthrew the King? He was abandoned as a bastard child, so the story goes, but his brilliant guerrilla warfare proved too much for the army to contend with. He has a reputation as a very charismatic Orc.'

I nod. I've heard of Prince Amrag. Charismatic, savage and successful, so they say.

'Isn't there some weird story that he's not entirely Orc?'

'What do you mean, not entirely Orc?' asks Makri.

'Mixed blood,' answers Direeva. 'A little Human perhaps. Some of the wilder stories even say he has Elvish blood, though I find that impossible to believe. But even the fact that such stories gather around Amrag shows he's an Orc to sct their imaginations rolling.'

I get a brief vision of the horrors of the last war. I banish it with an effort. There's no time to dwell on that, or on what may be to come.

'I have to do something about the current crisis. I'm

no closer to finding the murderer. And now we know Covinius is here, Lisutaris is in terrible danger.'

'I'll see if Hanama can learn any more,' says Makri, unexpectedly.

'What changed your mind?'

'You helped Samanatius.'

Poor Makri. If she wasn't so naive she'd know I'd never have gone near the eviction without being blackmailed into it.

Makri turns back to Direeva but the Princess has now switched her attention to a young man wearing a well-cut rainbow cloak whose bright golden hair tumbles over his shoulders in a raffish manner. Troverus, we presume.

'Where'd he come from?' demands Makri, not pleased at being outflanked by the young Simnian Sorcerer. 'You think he's handsome?'

I shrug.

'I don't think he's that handsome,' says Makri. 'Look at all that girly blond hair.'

'You like girly blond hair.'

'Yes, it's really nice, now you mention it,' says Makri. 'Excuse me, I have to get between them.'

With the determined look of a woman who is not about to be easily defeated, Makri plants herself firmly between Direeva and Troverus and eyes the Simnian like a hostile attacking force.

'I understand that venereal disease is rampant in Simnia,' she says. 'How do you cope with that?'

I leave her to the struggle. Things may be bad but at least Tilupasis doesn't have me trying to charm anyone. The Assemblage continues to be the one bright spot in a frozen city. If the murder of Darius has cast a shadow over proceedings, you wouldn't guess it from the behaviour of Irith Victorious and his jolly Juvalian companions. Behind the scenes the senior Sorcerers may be working assiduously, but in the main hall, behaviour has become riotous. Cicerius is shaken.

'I was not quite prepared for this,' he admits. Nearby, some dark-skinned southern Sorcerers are engaged in a contest to see who can levitate the largest barrel of beer.

'At least we have their vote,' says Cicerius, moving swiftly to avoid a floating river of ale. 'We sent a wagonload of beer to their lodgings.'

With Darius out of the way, it seems certain that Ramius will win the vote. Lisutaris is still favourite to gain second place, ahead of Rokim, but there's been an unexpectedly good showing by a Sorcerer named Almalas.

'A Niojan, of all things,' says Cicerius, animatedly.

Nioj, our large northern neighbour, is one of the biggest threats to Turai's security. If they gain control of the Sorcerers Guild we might as well surrender to King Lamachus.

'How can a Niojan be making gains?' I ask. 'No one likes Niojans. They're religious fundamentalists. Their church isn't even that keen on sorcery. They don't drink, don't have fun, don't do anything except pray.'

'Sober habits are not universally despised,' retorts Cicerius.

'We're talking Sorcerers here. Whoever heard of a Sorcerer voting for a man who doesn't drink?'

Cicerius admits it's strange.

'Has he been spreading his Niojan gold around?'

'Quite probably. But remember, many northern states look to Nioj for protection from the Orcs. Almalas's sober habits may not be so unwelcome to those who worry about imminent attack. Also, he is a war hero, at least as much as Lisutaris or Ramius, possibly more so. Tales of him leading troops into battle have been widely circulated.'

'I remember Almalas. I guess he was a good enough commander. His sorcery wasn't on a par with Lisutaris's, though.'

'He is at least able to walk around, which helps,' says Cicerius, in a withering tone. 'What about the hiding spell?'

'Still in place. It's been boosted by Direeva and Melus the Fair.'

'Have you eliminated Princess Direeva from suspicion?'

'No. I haven't eliminated her from anything. I still don't like the way she's sticking close to Lisutaris. I have some other leads, though. There's an apprentice used to work for Darius who got the boot after being accused of embezzling funds and left threatening to kill Darius. The apprentice was last heard of in Mattesh, still practising sorcery and threatening revenge. And I've got a lead on the erasure spell.'

The air starts turning orange and gold as the southern Sorcerers begin to show off their illuminated staffs. Three days into the convention, inhibitions are fading and there's more magic in evidence. The Royal Hall is not a place to visit if you don't like surprises.

'I can hardly bear to go into the main room,' confesses

Cicerius. 'Every time I do I seem to get covered in beer or wine.'

'At least they're celebrating. Better than them all trying to solve the murder.'

Cicerius's assistant Hansius approaches briskly. He leans over to whisper in the Deputy Consul's ear, though as the nearby Sorcerers have now started up a raucous drinking song, it's difficult to hear anything. Cicerius listens briefly before dismissing Hansius.

'Bad news. Sunstorm Ramius and Old Hasius the Brilliant have let it be known they are close to uncovering the hidden events. Ramius of course is keen to do this. It will enhance his reputation.'

'Couldn't you do something to get Old Hasius off the case? He's sharp as an Elf's ear when it comes to looking back in time. Isn't there some matter at the Abode of Justice which requires his urgent attention?'

'Unfortunately not,' replies Cicerius. 'The King has granted permission for Hasius to remain here and help. He naturally wishes to give all possible aid to the Sorcerers Assemblage.'

'I take it the King doesn't actually know that our own candidate is prime suspect?'

Cicerius shakes his head, and looks grim.

'You must at least hold them off till after the election,' he tells me. 'We depend on it. Now, about this matter of Praetor Capatius and the eviction.'

I'm expecting Cicerius to chew me out over this one, but the Deputy Consul for once seems to perceive that I was in an impossible position.

'It was clever of Senator Lodius to spot that you could aid him in this matter. It did not occur to me when I nominated you as Tribune of the People that this might happen. I regret that it has granted the Populares party a small victory. However, in the scheme of things it does not matter too much. But whatever happens, do not be drawn into further such actions.'

'I'll try my best.'

Tilupasis joins us, neatly sidestepping a levitated goblet. In the midst of the uproar she remains unruffled. She gives a brief report to the Deputy Consul. Two days away from the vote, things are looking reasonably good, but she's worried about the growing support for Almalas.

'Sareepa Lightning-Strikes-the-Mountain seems quite taken with him. God knows why.'

Cicerius is perturbed. Sareepa Lightning-Strikes-the-Mountain is head of the Sorcerers Guild in Mattesh, our southern neighbour.

'They have a lot of influence in the League of City States. Sareepa probably controls twelve votes. We can't let them go to Nioj.'

'Didn't we already pay Sareepa?'

'She gave the gold back,' explains Tilupasis. 'After listening to Almalas talking about a Sorcerer's duty to God and state, she says she regrets even considering taking an immoral bribe.'

Tilupasis spreads her arms in despair.

'What am I meant to do with a senior Sorcerer who suddenly gets religion?'

'Increase the bribe?'

'It won't work.'

'Send a young Tribune to her private chambers.'

'I already tried. She sent him away. And she

instructed her delegation that thazis and dwa would no longer be tolerated. The woman's gone mad with moral behaviour. Damn that priest Sorcerer.'

Tilupasis lays her hand on my shoulder.

'Thraxas, didn't you know Sareepa Lightning-Strikes-the-Mountain when you were an apprentice?'

'Sure. She used to distil klee in a cauldron and invite young mercenaries to sample it, as I recall. The woman was never more than one step away from being slung out of the apprentices' college. Weird that she should suddenly become respectable.'

'You have to change her back.'

'Pardon?'

'Get her drinking again. Once she's got some klee inside her she'll forget this Niojan ethical nonsense and take the bribe.'

I point out that I'm already busy doing various other vital tasks, and besides, I'm not what you'd call a skilful diplomat.

'No one's going to vote for Turai on my recommendation.'

'How important are Sareepa's votes?' Cicerius asks Tilupasis.

'Absolutely vital.'

Cicerius draws himself up to his full height, adjusts his toga, and turns to me.

'I'm ordering you to get her drunk,' he says. 'Don't argue. You're the man for the job.'

CHAPTER FOURTEEN

I rith Victorious is lying belly-up on the floor of the drinking area. His companions are laid out beside him on a bed of tangled rainbow cloaks. Tilupasis ordered the closure of a busy local tavern in order to divert its entire supply of ale to the Juvalian Sorcerers. When that proved insufficient she ordered the next tavern to close, bringing in its beer and klee as reinforcements. Finally overwhelmed by the flood of free alcohol, the Juvalians are now rarely conscious and spend their days in a stupor, awakening only to drink. They've promised to cast their votes for Lisutaris.

Not far away, the five members of the Misan delegation lie dwa'd out of their heads, courtesy of Tilupasis. She had the drug brought in from the confiscated supplies stored at the Abode of Justice. Officially these mounds of dwa should have been destroyed, but Tilupasis seems to have the authority to do just about anything.

Four Sorcerers from the far western state of Kamara who once strode confidently into the Royal Hall are now unfit to leave their private quarters after a forty-eight-hour orgy of unprecedented degeneracy. Some of the Kamaran tastes were, strictly speaking, illegal in Turai, but not beyond the organisational powers of Tilupasis and the city's efficient brothel keepers. The Kamarans have promised that when they recover, they'll be sure to vote for Lisutaris.

What Sunstorm Ramius makes of all this I don't know. I'm certain his Simnian delegation has also been indulging in bribery but I can't imagine it's on anything like the vast scale of corruption wrought by Tilupasis on behalf of our city. Thanks to us, the Sorcerers Assemblage has descended into an unparalleled orgy of illicit gold, extravagant drunkenness, wanton sex and extreme drug abuse. It makes a man proud to be Turanian.

'You Turanians are a filthy, degenerate nation,' says Sareepa Lightning-Strikes-the-Mountain.

I've sought her out to say a friendly hello. So far it's not going well.

'I cannot believe the way the Sorcerers are behaving. I blame Turai, the entire city is corrupt.'

'It's really not so bad . . .'

'It is vile,' insists Sareepa. 'Thank God for Almalas. He is a beacon of light in this foul den of corruption.'

Is this really the same Sareepa Lightning-Strikes-the-Mountain I used to know? When we were fifteen she'd already worked her way through the male population of the district and was looking to neighbouring towns for new lovers.

'Why are prayer calls ignored at this Assemblage?' she demands.

'A little laxity is common at such events.'

'A little laxity? Not for the Niojans. They pray six times a day. Would that others would follow their example. Thraxas, you must escape from this iniquity. I will introduce you to Almalas.'

'Could we perhaps discuss this over a bottle of wine?' I venture, remembering my mission.

Sareepa looks as if she's about to explode.

'Wine? Do you realise—'

At this moment some Sorcerers stumble between us in drunken pursuit of a levitated beer barrel.

'A flagon of klee to the man who brings it down,' shouts one of their number, and starts firing bolts of light from his staff.

Sareepa is rendered temporarily speechless. Realising that alcohol is not the best subject to be discussing, I turn the conversation to Darius's apprentice.

'Left Abelesi with a powerful hatred for Darius. Settled in Mattesh, I believe?'

Sareepa knows the apprentice in question.

'Quite a powerful Sorcerer these days. He's here with us.'

'With you? How?'

It turns out that said apprentice finished his studies, took up Matteshan citizenship, and is now a fully fledged Sorcerer in attendance with the rest of the delegation.

'He still hated Darius,' agrees Sareepa. 'But don't go suspecting him of murder. My delegation is firmly under my control.'

I ask for an introduction anyway, which Sareepa agrees to make, providing I'm sober. The woman really hates alcohol. It's a sad state of affairs.

'Have you ever come across a spell for making a new version of reality and sending it back in time?' I ask.

'There's no such spell,' replies Sareepa. 'No one could do that.'

Moments later I'm apprehended by a furious Makri.

'You know what happened? I was just telling Direeva how I once killed three Trolls with my bare hands in the arena, and that creepy Troverus smiled in this really annoying manner and said he'd come to the Assemblage to forget about unpleasant things like fighting and then whisked Direeva off for dinner!'

'Couldn't you have stopped them?'

'I was too taken aback by anyone wanting to forget about fighting,' complains Makri. 'By the time I recovered, they were gone. Damn that Troverus. I don't trust him at all. Right this moment he's charming Direeva over a bottle of wine, and who knows what'll happen after that? And he's not that handsome anyway. See-ath was a lot better-looking and he never said he was bored with my fighting stories. I hate these smooth-talking Simnians. What am I meant to do now?'

'I've no idea. Ask Tilupasis, she's the expert.'

'Come and help. You could detain Troverus with some tedious war story while I charm Direeva.'

'Can't do it. I need to go out and investigate.'

As I leave the hall I pass a tall man with a long beard who's wearing the most sober rainbow cloak ever woven. It's hard to imagine a rainbow cloak could be so dull. He's talking in a deep voice to a large crowd of younger Sorcerers who appear to be hanging on his every word, which is some achievement, with the uproar on all sides. Almalas, I presume. Niojan Sorcerers never take on fancy names. I listen to him for a while, but as he seems to be talking about honour, duty and such like, I quickly lose interest.

The rest of the afternoon is spent travelling round the frozen city, checking out people who bought dragon scales from Coralex. It gets me nowhere. I'm not even sure what I'm looking for. Someone who's been buying scales but doesn't look like they'd wear them in their hair. Someone who looks like they could work an erasure spell never before used in Turai. No one I visit fits the bill. Just a lot of aristocratic women with plenty of jewellery. Or merchants' wives on the way up, also with plenty of jewellery. Even a Captain of the Guards, who's buying jewels for a girl he'll never be rich enough to marry.

The last name on my list is Rixad, the merchant whose wife I was recently tailing. He isn't pleased to see me. People who once hired me often aren't, even when I've done a good job for them. The results are the same as everywhere else. Rixad bought the scales for his wife. His wife likes plenty of decoration. Rixad makes it clear he's not keen for me to hang around. Now he trusts his wife again he doesn't want her finding out he was checking up on her.

He'll always be checking up on her. He should have married someone less demanding. She should have carried on as an actress till someone better came along.

Outside the snow is still falling. As I walk through the northern outskirts of Pashish I notice two legs protruding stiffly from a snowdrift. A beggar, frozen to death. And it's not even a bad part of town. Thinking of the wealth that's pouring into the Assemblage, I get annoyed. A little of that money could have housed a beggar for the winter instead of disappearing down the throat of some corpulent freeloader. Like Irith. Like me. I stop feeling annoyed and start feeling depressed. I want to go home but I have to call back to the Assemblage to check up on Lisutaris and report to Cicerius. I shiver.

I've learned two new spells for warming my cloak but it never seems to keep out the cold.

I make my report to Cicerius, including my failure with Sareepa Lightning-Strikes-the-Mountain.

'You must try again.'

'Okay, I'll try again. Where's Lisutaris?'

'Unconscious. Sulinius and Visus took her to my private room.'

'Is she losing votes, being so stoned?'

Cicerius no longer knows. With half the Assemblage now permanently under the influence of dwa or thazis, it might even be in her favour.

'And we've spread plenty of gold around.'

The Deputy Consul nods. He doesn't look that happy about it.

'You wish you had a nice clean candidate like Almalas?'

'Yes. But I don't.'

'Don't worry, Cicerius. If Lisutaris is elected, you'll get plenty of credit.'

Cicerius nods. He'll enjoy getting the credit. He's not enjoying the process.

At this moment Makri and Lisutaris wander past. Makri has discarded her body armour and is wearing only her chainmail bikini. It's the smallest bikini ever seen in the west. It's not even on properly. Lisutaris is fully dressed but completely drenched, possibly from an unsuccessful experiment with beer levitation. Both have huge thazis sticks hanging from their lips, creating a mushroom-shaped cloud of smoke above their heads.

Cicerius looks at them with horror.

'Were Visus and Sulinius not—'

'I broke out,' says Lisutaris, her speech slurred. 'Had to console Makri.'

'Failed with Direeva,' says Makri. 'Sorry about that. Simnian outmanoeuvred me. Tell Tilupasis she should have him killed.'

'Thraxas has to charm Sareepa,' says Lisutaris.

'Tough assignment,' says Makri. She laughs. Her thazis stick falls from her lips and is extinguished by the beer that drips from Lisutaris's cloak. Lisutaris mutters a word and the thazis flies from the floor into Makri's hand, and relights itself. At least the Mistress of the Sky hasn't completely forgotten how to work magic.

It's fortunate that entry into the Assemblage is so closely regulated. Were the ordinary citizens of Turai to see their leaders freely distributing illegal substances, there would be consternation. Or jealousy, maybe.

'You're looking as miserable as a Niojan whore,' says Lisutaris. 'Have some thazis.'

'Please take them home,' says Cicerius, sounding as close to desperate as I've ever heard him.

They want to go to Twelve Seas rather than Thamlin. I don't argue. It's as well for me to be close to Lisutaris. Makri isn't in a state to do much in the way of guarding her. I sneak them out a side door and into an official carriage. On the journey back to Twelve Seas, Makri wakes up.

'Did you bring my armour?'

'Yes.'

'Keep it safe,' says Makri, and goes back to sleep. She's clutching her armour. I've wrapped my cloak around her to stop her freezing. The carriage takes a long, long time to make the journey. The streets are next to impassable and the driver has to coax the horses through the falling snow. I'm cold as the ice queen's grave. I've been cold for weeks. I'm sick of it.

Getting my companions up the stairs to my office is difficult. Before we're more than halfway up, a large band of men emerge from the snowstorm.

'Thraxas!' they call.

I take out my sword. I don't recognise them. Not the standard Brotherhood thugs of Twelve Seas. There must be thirty of them, all armed.

'What?'

'We're here on business.'

'Whose business?'

'Praetor Capatius's business.'

Their leader steps forward

'The Praetor outranks you, Tribune. It wasn't very bright to go against him.'

'It wasn't very bright of the Praetor to send you after me. I'm working for the Deputy Consul and he outranks the Praetor.'

'Really?' says the leader. 'How about that?'

Thirty armed men advance towards me. Hearing the voices, Makri once more wakens. She sees the situation and quickly pulls a sword out of her magic pocket. As she raises it, it slips from her hand and clatters down the stairs.

Makri has never dropped her sword before.

'Damn,' she says, and pulls out another blade. She loses her footing on the icy stairs and tumbles down in a heap. The men laugh at the sight. Makri attempts to rise, but can't make it to her feet. Capatius's men advance.

'Don't you believe in the legal process?' I say, mean-while descending the stairs to stand over Makri's prone figure. Were I on my own I'd already be inside the tavern with a locking spell on the door, but I can't leave my companions out here. Even without the threat of Capatius's men, they'd freeze to death soon enough.

The situation is hopeless. Faced with overwhelming odds, I've generally managed to overcome my opponents with a simple sleep spell. Due to the freezing weather, I'm not carrying any spells. Just a sword. Good as I am with a sword, I'm not going to be able to beat thirty men. Only Turai's richest aristocrat would hire thirty men. It's far too many, by any standards. I'm going to die as a result of my unwilling opposition to the eviction. I knew I should have stayed out of politics.

The first man is no more than three feet away when a voice comes from behind me.

'I'm cold.'

It's Lisutaris, Mistress of the Sky. She's cold.

'What's happening?'

'We're being attacked.'

I raise my sword to parry the first blow. Suddenly the thirty men are tossed backwards like feathers in a storm. Seconds after preparing to meet my death I'm looking at a bundle of unconscious thugs. I glance round. Lisutaris, still unable to make it on to her feet, has raised herself to her knees with the aid of the railings.

'Good spell,' I call.

'You're welcome,' replies Lisutaris. 'I can't get up. Help me inside.'

I toss Makri over my shoulder and march upstairs.

'At least you can still do sorcery,' I say as I take Lisutaris inside.

'Of course I can still do sorcery. I'm number one

chariot. Put some logs on the fire. It's freezing in here.'
I throw some logs on the fire. Lisutaris waves her hand
and they burst into a roaring blaze. I wish I could do
that. I should have studied more.

CHAPTER
FIFTEEN

Next morning I'm sitting over a beer and a plate of stew at the bar with Gurd and Tanrose. Tanrose makes excellent stew, flavouring it with herbs she grows in the back yard. Gurd and I have cooked a lot of stew on our campaigns round the world but we never had any particular talent for it. For all that I detest Twelve Seas, it's a comfort to be able to eat good meals made by Tanrose.

The Avenging Axe is not yet open and would be quiet were it not for the furious sounds of combat emanating from the back yard.

'Makri is madder than a mad dragon,' says Gurd.

Fortunately Makri is not angry with me. Not even with the filthy city of Turai. She's angry with herself. She is appalled to have fallen over in front of an opponent. Early in the morning Tanrose was surprised to discover a bleary-eyed but fully armed Makri preparing to do battle with the wooden targets in the yard. Since then she's been practising her weaponry, oblivious to the biting cold.

The noise of battle halts as Makri rushes in to pick up one of the long knives she keeps secreted behind the bar.

'You haven't eaten,' says Tanrose. 'Have some stew.'

'No time,' says Makri. 'I fell over. I'm a disgrace.'

Makri hurries out, clutching her knife. I carry on with my stew, and take another ale.

'She pushes herself too hard,' says Gurd. 'Even the best warrior can't fight all the time. Look at Thraxas. He was a fine companion in war and he spent half his time too drunk to walk.'

There's some truth in this. But I was a better horseman in those days.

'Makri is getting stranger,' I muse.

'Stranger?'

'In the past week she's been miserable about See-ath the Avulan Elf. Then she was the determined bodyguard. Right after that she was getting stoned with Lisutaris and right after that she was back to being organised, rescuing Samanatius. Then she was being intellectual at the library and right afterwards getting stoned again. Now she's back to being mad axewoman. I don't understand it. She should just pick a personality and stick with it. It's not normal, changing all the time.'

'Perhaps it's the mixed blood,' suggests Gurd.

I'm inclined to agree.

'I expect it will drive her mad in the end.'

'Pointed ears.'

'Always leads to trouble.'

'Nonsense,' scoffs Tanrose. 'She's just young and enthusiastic.'

'Enthusiastic? About everything?'

'Of course. Makri is full of passion. Don't you remember what that was like?'

'No, I don't remember. Another beer if you please, Gurd.'

I wonder if I was ever passionate about my wife. My

memory seems hazy on the subject. Lisutaris appears in the bar. She spent the night on Makri's floor and her fine robe is crumpled. Her make-up is smeared and her hair is badly in need of attention.

'I'd better get back to Thamlin and clean up before the Assemblage. Big banquet today. And then the vote.'

She shows no enthusiasm for the banquet or the election.

Lisutaris sits with us at the bar. She refuses the breakfast offered by Tanrose. Though Tanrose is becoming used to the odd collection of characters who pass through the Avenging Axe these days, she's still surprised by the sight of Turai's leading Sorcerer, as purebred an aristocrat as Turai can offer, slumped unhappily at the bar, looking like a tavern dancer after a rough night.

'How is the Assemblage?' asks Tanrose, politely.

'Awful,' replies Lisutaris. 'They're trying to kill me.'

I'm perturbed. The Mistress of the Sky's nerves don't seem to be what they once were. An excess of thazis can lead to feelings of persecution, I believe.

'We're not certain anyone is trying to kill you,' I say, in an attempt to be reassuring.

'We are. Yesterday a Simnian Sorcerer whispered something in my ear. I did her a favour a long time ago and she came to repay it. She told me that Sunstorm Ramius definitely did hire an Assassin before he left Simnia.'

'Can you trust that information?'

'Yes.'

So now we have it confirmed. Ramius has engaged the services of Covinius to kill Lisutaris.

'We'll protect you,' I say. 'No client of mine is falling to an Assassin.'

Lisutaris turns her head to stare at me.

'Any idea what Covinius looks like yet?'

'No.'

She shakes her head sadly. Lisutaris is suffering. She was okay in battle but the thought of an Assassin on her tail and the pressure of the Sorcerers Guild trying to break the hiding spell is really getting to her. It's getting to me too.

I call Makri in from the back yard. She's caked with sweat and the falling snow has dampened her hair so the points of her ears show through.

'Time to be a bodyguard. Ramius did hire an Assassin.'

'Good,' says Makri. 'I'll kill him.'

She's back in fighting mode. I hope it lasts.

All over Turai there's great interest in the outcome of today's election, though few people in the city are aware of what has really gone on at the Assemblage. Even the *Renowned and Truthful Chronicle*, normally privy to most of the city's dirty secrets, has remained strangely silent about the scandalous happenings, which is odd. The *Chronicle* loves scandal, and they're sharp as an Elf's ear at dredging it up. Even the Royal family has trouble keeping its affairs out of the news-sheet. Possibly Tilupasis is responsible. She's well informed and not overburdened with scruples. It wouldn't surprise me if she's blackmailing the editor.

I'm fretting about my appearance at the Royal Hall. For one thing I'm not going to be admitted to the feast, which is galling for a man who likes his food. For another there's the ever-present risk that Old Hasius and his friends are suddenly going to pierce the hiding spell. I haven't made any progress on finding the real murderer of Darius, unless the real murderer is Lisutaris, in which case I don't want to make any progress.

And then there's the matter of Sareepa Lightning-Strikes-the-Mountain. I'm meant to be winning her over. A hopeless endeavour. That woman is never going to vote for Lisutaris. Not after yesterday's display of inebriation. Damn Sareepa. If there's one thing I can't stand it's a person who gives up drinking. It shows a great weakness of character.

Makri's having problems of her own in the vote-winning department. As she leaves with Lisutaris she's muttering that a certain blond-haired Simnian Sorcerer is going to find himself on the wrong end of a sharp sword if he keeps on being charming to Princess Direeva.

'How about if I just kill him? We could pretend he was the Assassin. Could you fake some evidence?'

They depart to visit Copro, who's going to have his work cut out getting Lisutaris into shape for today's appearance. I don't like the beautician any better than I did before. He should go back where he came from, wherever that is. He might be number one chariot at styling hair, but what sort of achievement is that for a man? The amusing thought strikes me that if Copro were not the useless specimen of humanity he is, his work would make him an excellent Assassin. Gets into all the best houses, and no one would ever suspect.

Only Sorcerers are allowed at the banquet, no exceptions allowed, so for a large part of the day I'm exiled to the Room of Saints. My two fellow Tribunes are with me, along with those other people granted access to the Royal Hall who aren't Sorcerers – personal staff, a few government representatives and such like. Hansius and Tilupasis drift around, carrying on with the hospitality to anyone that needs it.

Sulinius and Visus look tired. When Cicerius handed them over to Tilupasis they were expecting to be involved in some light diplomacy: showing our visitors round the city, making introductions, that sort of thing. They were surprised to find themselves plunged into an endless round of bribery and corruption. The young aristocrats have adapted well. It'll be good preparation for life at the Palace and their careers in the Senate. Both are worrying about the upcoming election.

'Tilupasis still isn't certain Lisutaris is going to make it. Rokim the Bright is still in the picture and Almalas has been taking votes from everyone.'

'Your companion Makri seems to be losing ground with Direeva.'

There's a certain tone in Sulinius's voice as he mentions Makri's name. When he becomes a Senator and gets his own villa, he's never going to let a woman with Orcish blood through the front door.

Visus asks me about Sareepa and I admit that I've made no progress.

'It's difficult. Sareepa's gone religious thanks to Almalas. Tilupasis should've given me more notice.'

'I managed to convert the Pagadan delegation in a single hour,' says Sulinius, grandly.

'That's because the Pargadans are notorious dwa addicts and you brought them a wagonload. Anyone could have done that.'

'Perhaps if you did not concern yourself with meddling in city politics . . .'

Sulinius is aware of my interfering with the Praetor's business. Not having any intention of apologising or explaining myself, I tell him sharply that if his father insists on throwing poor people out into the snow, he has to expect some opposition.

'And tell him if he tries sending any more men after me, then Lisutaris, Mistress of the Sky, will smite him with a plague spell.'

'Lisutaris would not come to your aid.'

'Oh no? I was fighting beside Lisutaris before you were born. She already blasted your father's thugs once. She'll help me again.'

I wonder if she really would. Having the Mistress of the Sky as head of the Sorcerers Guild would be no bad thing if she felt obligated to me for a few favours. Good reason to clear her name. Maybe I shouldn't have been rude to her. At least I wasn't violent.

The great door opens and a flood of Sorcerers, led by Irith Victorious, announce the end of the formal banquet. I hear him muttering a complaint about them only serving wine with the meal as he hastens towards the bar, showing surprising speed for a man of his size.

'Beer, and make it quick,' he yells at a waitress.

There are only a few hours left till the election. I take the opportunity to talk with the Matteshan Sorcerer who once served as apprentice to Darius.

'I didn't kill him, if that's what this is about,' he states flatly. 'I was with the other Matteshan Sorcerers all evening when he was killed.'

That's not such a great alibi. They'd lie for him if necessary.

'Darius got through a lot of apprentices, though. And none of them liked him much better than I did. I'm not the only Sorcerer who started off in Abelasi then went elsewhere after being sacked by Cloud Walker. My predecessor, Rosin-kar, swore he'd kill him one day. And the one before him left in disgrace. I think he's with the Pargadans now.'

Tilupasis approaches me as I head back for the Room of Saints.

'How are things progressing with Sareepa?'

'Badly.'

'You must try again.'

'I'm busy looking for ex-apprentices of Darius. They seem to have spread round the world.'

'Work on Sareepa.'

'Doesn't anyone want me to solve this murder?'

'Of course,' says Tilupasis. 'But the hiding spell will work for a little longer. It is more important that Lisutaris performs well in the election.'

I get the impression that if Lisutaris loses the election Tilupasis isn't going to care whether she's convicted of murder or not.

Makri rushes up and confronts Tilupasis.

'Can't you do something about this Troverus? He's sticking about as close as a poultice to Direeva. I can't get near the woman.'

'Keep trying,' instructs Tilupasis.

'Is that the best advice you have? It's not working. When you told me to charm Princess Direeva – and don't think I didn't notice there was something dubious in that whole concept – you didn't say I'd have a rival who wins prizes for being handsome.'

Faced with defeat, Makri clenches her fists in frustration.

'You can't trust a man as good-looking as that. He probably likes boys, right? Send him some boys to distract him.'

'He doesn't like boys. I made enquiries.'

'He doesn't? Well, send him some gold.'

Tilupasis shakes her head.

'Troverus is already wealthy. He doesn't want money.'

Makri explodes with anger.

'So how come I'm the only one that's up against someone incorruptible? It's hardly fair. What am I meant to do?'

'You could sleep with him,' I suggest.

'I don't want to sleep with him. He's creepy. Tilupasis, Thraxas is telling me to whore myself around the Assemblage just to get you votes. Well, forget it, I'm not doing it. I'm here as a bodyguard, not a comfort woman.'

'I really must go,' says Tilupasis. 'The Pargadans need more dwa. I trust the two of you to work things out.'

'Is that what Tilupasis wants me to do?' says Makri. 'She can forget it. I'm not going to sleep with just any Sorcerer that fancies a good time.'

'God help anyone who thinks he'd have a good time with you.'

'I didn't notice See-ath complaining,' retorts Makri. 'Anyway, your idea is stupid. Direeva isn't going to thank me for stealing her suitor, is she?'

A tall man in a toga greets Makri politely as he passes.

'Who's that?'

'A mathematician from Simnia. He's here with the delegation. He's the only civilised person I've met in this place. Yesterday he was telling me about his work on prime number theory. Do you know—'

'Fascinating, Makri. Nothing interests me more than mathematics. I have work to do. Sareepa has twelve votes.'

'Direeva has thirty,' counters Makri, and we go our separate ways.

The election is drawing near. Time for one last attempt on Sareepa. She's sitting at one of the top tables in the main hall, placed there by Tilupasis to flatter her. Sareepa herself appears calm, but her fellow Matteshan Sorcerers are unhappy. No doubt they've been forbidden by Sareepa to overindulge. I've never seen a group of Sorcerers more in need of a drink. Most of the people in the hall are carrying on with their previous intemperate behaviour. Goblets, tankards and bottles glint in the light of the flaming torches on the walls, and it's obvious the Matteshans are aching to join in the fun. Tough break, arriving at the biggest binge in the Sorcerers' calendar only to find that your leader has developed a puritanical streak.

I'm about to make one last desperate effort to end Sareepa's sober behaviour. Not just for the good of Turai. Sareepa Lightning-Strikes-the-Mountain has fallen under the thrall of Nioj. The woman needs help.

I'm carrying a bottle of the finest klee Turai can offer. Distilled in the mountains, this liquid could burn a dragon's throat. They don't make liquor like this in Mattesh. Before Sareepa realises what's happening, I'm standing beside her at the table, pouring it into the empty glasses of her delegation.

'What do you think you are doing?' demands Sareepa Lightning-Strikes-the-Mountain.

'Part of my Tribunate duties. A toast to the King of Mattesh.'

At these words Sareepa's companions' eyes light up. No Matteshan can refuse a toast to the King. It would be disloyal. They raise their glasses and look towards their leader expectantly. Very reluctantly, Sareepa raises her goblet, all the while staring at me in a manner which would cause grave concern were I not wearing such a fine spell protection necklace.

We drink. There is a moment's stunned silence as the fiery liquid hits their throats. Sareepa coughs violently. I fill up her goblet again in a manoeuvre so swift that only an expert at the bottle like myself could pull it off.

'A toast to the Queen!'

'The Queen!' yell the delegation, filling up their own glasses.

'A toast? To who?' enquires Sulinius, appearing at that moment, as I have asked him to.

'The Queen.'

Sulinius grabs a goblet.

'The Queen!!'

He drinks. Everybody drinks. You can't not drink when a foreigner is toasting your Queen.

'And the King!' says Sulinius, and drinks again.

I'm already filling glasses.

'To Mattesh!' I cry.

No Matteshan can refuse a toast to their country. It would be disloyal.

We drink. I break open another bottle.

'Let me see that,' says Sareepa.

I hand it over.

'Interesting . . . from the mountains?'

'Yes. Finest quality.'

The Sorcerers wait expectantly.

'A toast to the King,' says Sareepa, and starts pouring herself another large one.

An hour or so later, Sareepa Lightning-Strikes-the-Mountain is challenging the Simnians at the next table to a drinking contest.

'You Simnian dogs couldn't drink if you fell in a barrel of ale!' she roars.

Before leaving the Matteshan Sorcerers I ask them if any of them have heard of a spell for making a new version of reality and sending it back into the past. None of them have.

'There's no such spell.'

I'm getting sick of hearing that.

Tilupasis and Cicerius are waiting for me in the Room of Saints.

'What happened with Sareepa?'

'I got her drunk. Better have the apothecary standing by. Klee laced with dwa has been known to cause fatalities.'

'And her votes?'

'Heading for Turai. By the third bottle she was cursing all Niojans.'

Tilupasis roundly congratulates me.

'It was a fine plan.'

'Sharp as an Elf's ear,' I mumble, and look round for a chair. Even by my standards, I've drunk a lot of klee.

Makri is sitting at a table nearby, with Direeva and Troverus. Makri looks aggressive, Troverus looks unruffled and Direeva looks interested.

'I can out-drink any Simnian Sorcerer,' declares Makri, and downs the goblet of klee in front of her. Troverus does the same. Makri refills the goblets. They drink again, and then again.

'No one likes a Simnian,' says Makri. 'Direeva is never going to be impressed with a weakling like you.'

A few goblets later, Makri's face goes a horrible shade of green and she is obliged to hurry from the room. I find her in the corridor, throwing up into a pot plant.

'Goddammit,' she gasps, still retching.

'You were never going to win a klee-drinking contest,' I say, and hunt around in my bag for a Lesada leaf to make Makri feel better. Makri takes the leaf and washes it down with my beer.

'I couldn't think of anything else. Everything I do, Troverus does better. He knows more about art and culture than me, and he's been everywhere and done everything, and everything he says is witty. Princess Direeva is eating out of his hand. She's bound to vote for Ramius.'

As the leaf takes effect her colour returns to normal. I advise her to give up.

'Give up?'

'Why not? You don't really care who Direeva votes for.'

'It's not in my nature to give up,' says Makri, then vomits noisily into the pot plant again.

'I didn't become champion gladiator by giving up.'

She's sick once more. I wince. It's a painful sight.

'Give me another leaf.'

Makri hauls herself to her feet.

'I have an excellent idea,' she says, and stumbles off in the direction of the Room of Saints. I follow on, interested to see what Makri's new strategy might be. Possibly some learned disquisition of political theory, learned from Samanatius?

Makri weaves her way across to Direeva, knocking over several Sorcerers on the way. At the table she stands in front of Troverus, lays her hand on his rainbow cloak and yanks him to his feet.

'I'm getting really sick of you,' she says, and then punches him in the face hard enough for him to tumble unconscious to the floor. Princess Direeva looks startled.

'Don't vote for the Simnians,' says Makri to Direeva. 'I hate them. Turai is a disgusting city but Lisutaris is a good woman and she's given you a lot of thazis.'

'And if I need military help?' says Direeva.

'Call on me,' says Makri, and slumps down beside her. 'I'll sort them out. Number one chariot at fighting.'

Irith Victorious is occupying a large couch in the corner. I take him a beer and join him in a final drinking session before his fellow Juvalians drag him off to vote. The Room of Saints empties of Sorcerers. Makri appears at my side. She's unsteady on her feet and her speech is slurred.

'That seemed to go well,' she tells me.

In the distance, Troverus's companions are carrying him off to vote.

'You want this couch?' says Makri.

'You can have it.'

'I don't really need it. I've been practising with weapons. Stayed sober all day, more or less.'

Makri plummets to the floor. I help her on to the couch then sink into a nearby chair. Electioneering. It's tough.

I awaken to the sensational news that Sunstorm Ramius has won the vote, with Lisutaris in second place. Both of them will now go forward to the final test. Turai has accomplished the first part of its mission. Cicerius makes a gracious speech to everyone in the Room of Saints, thanking them for their support, and indicating that though most of the credit belongs to him, others were involved in an important capacity.

Some time later Tilupasis arrives at our side.

'Congratulations to you both,' she says.

Makri wakes and vomits over the edge of the couch. She's not the drinker I am. Tilupasis is unperturbed, and motions to an assistant to bring a cleaner.

'I'll call a landus to take you home. As long as we can keep Lisutaris's name clear for another day, we're in with a chance of having a Turanian head of the Sorcerers Guild. Is the hiding spell holding up?'

'Yes.'

'How long will it last?'

'I don't know.'

'Why not?'

'I'm too drunk to think.'

Tilupasis smiles. She smiles a lot. I doubt she ever means it but it seems to hide her insincerity, for some reason.

I help Makri to her feet and we head for the door. The Sorcerers will now carry on with their celebrations but I need a rest. As we pass through the main hall, Hansius hurries up to us.

'Trouble,' he says, and motions for us to follow. He leads us to a room at the far end of the hall I've not been in before, a room reserved for the senior Sorcerers. Inside the room, Old Hasius the Brilliant, Sunstorm Ramius, Lasat, Axe of Gold, and Charius the Wise are deep in conference with Cicerius. They're talking in low voices but I catch enough to know that we're in trouble.

'Lisutaris, Mistress of the Sky, killed Darius Cloud Walker.'

Cicerius protests.

'This is impossible.'

'We have seen clear pictures,' insists Ramius. 'She must be apprehended immediately.'

Ramius becomes aware of our presence, and looks round. He ignores me, but when he sees Makri he recognises her immediately.

'She was in the room with Darius when he died. As was Princess Direeva. What has been happening in this city? Deputy Consul, are you going to send for the Guards or must I rouse the Council of Sorcerers to apprehend Lisutaris?'

At this moment Tilupasis strides confidently into the room.

'I have sent for Consul Kalius. He will be here shortly. Until then, this news must not be allowed to spread.'

'And why not?' demands Lasat.

'It may prejudice Lisutaris's chances in the final test.'

'The final test? Lisutaris will not be entering any final test. As Senior Sorcerer I am disqualifying her immediately.'

If Tilupasis has a reply to this, she saves it for now, but she motions for Hansius to shut the door.

'Consul Kalius will take care of the matter.'

Lasat, Axe of Gold, reluctantly agrees to await the arrival of Turai's highest official, but I can't see it doing anything but buying us a few minutes' grace. Axe of Gold is not the sort of person to be pushed around by city officials. As Senior Sorcerer of the Guild, and one of the most powerful people in the west, he's not about to take orders from Tilupasis or Cicerius. He'd bring down the city wall before buckling under to a mere government official.

Beside me Makri still looks unwell. I wonder if she might be sick again. On one memorable occasion she threw up over the Crown Prince's sandals. Taking aim at the Consul's feet would certainly lighten things up. Vomiting over Lasat, Axe of Gold, would be even more sensational.

The noise of celebrating Sorcerers drifts into the room, but we wait, quiet and grim, for Kalius to arrive.

CHAPTER
SIXTEEN

Consul Kalius is the city's highest official. Praetor Samilius is head of the Civil Guard. Old Hasius the Brilliant is Chief Investigating Sorcerer at the Abode of Justice. Rittius is in charge of Palace Security and Orius Fire Tamer is his Senior Investigating Sorcerer. Along with Lasat, Axe of Gold, Charius the Wise and Sunstorm Ramius, it makes for an impressive gathering. I don't like the way they're all looking at me.

'I firmly believe Lisutaris to be innocent.'

'We would like to believe you,' says Kalius.

'But we don't,' adds Ramius.

'What grounds do you have for thinking her to be innocent?'

Consul Kalius looks at me hopefully. I've got most of Turai's officialdom on my side. A rare occurrence. Unfortunately, it comes at a time when I'm faced with an almost impossible task. Now that Old Hasius the Brilliant and Lasat, Axe of Gold, have pierced the hiding spell, the pictures are very clear, and they never change. Lisutaris stabs Darius, every time. Praetor Samilius has enquired repeatedly of the Sorcerers if there could be trickery involved, but they're adamant there could not be.

'No one possesses such power.'

'I told you, I discovered a spell that could do it.'

'You discovered it?' Ramius is cynical. But Sorcerers never like to admit there might be spells they don't know.

'A spell to project false events into the past? It can't be done.'

'Well, not exactly project spells into the past. But a spell for erasing past events.'

Once more, I've had to explain my theory of a spell of erasement and a spell of making. To the non-Sorcerers present it's confusing, and to the Sorcerers it's unbelievable.

'I have checked repeatedly,' insists Old Hasius. 'And I firmly believe these to be the real events. Were it not so, I would have located the true reality.'

'Not if it was erased.'

'Even if such an erasement spell was used success-fully, how was the new reality created?'

'I don't know. But anyone who's good enough to do the first part might pull off the second. We can't be sure that Lisutaris did the murder.'

I look round at the doubtful faces. The Turanian offi-cials are desperate for Lisutaris to be innocent. Even against their better judgment they'd be willing to believe me, but I'm not making any impression on Lasat or Ramius. They're insisting that Lisutaris be arrested.

It's a bitter blow. Cicerius, the most patriotic of Turanians, has hardly said a word. He's sitting in the corner looking as miserable as a Niojan whore, though that's not an expression I'd use to him right now, as Nioj is a sore point. Almalas came third in the ballot. If Lisutaris is disqualified, he'll go into the final contest in her place. Not only will Turai suffer the monumental disgrace of having our candidate arrested for murder, we'll face the prospect of a hostile new head of the Sorcerers Guild. Niojan or Simnian, neither one is going to rush to the aid of Turai.

'I feel you are not telling us everything,' says Samilius. The Praetor was appointed to the post of head of the Civil Guard as a political reward and is not an experienced Investigator, but he's shrewd enough. He suspects I've been involved in all this more than I'm saying. So far no one realises that the murder took place in my rooms at the Avenging Axe, and I'm not about to enlighten them.

'I know no more than you. But I've been keeping close to Lisutaris since the Assemblage started and I'm sure she did not commit the crime. She had no reason to.'

'We saw her do it! In the presence of Princess Direeva and the other woman.'

'Both women of Orcish blood,' notes Sunstorm Ramius. 'I insist that you inform the King and arrest Lisutaris.'

He looks to Lasat, Golden Axe. The Senior Sorcerer nods his head.

'I agree.'

'We must at least wait till we hear what Lisutaris has to say,' says Cicerius.

'Where is she?'

'I believe she usually meditates at this time. My assistant is looking for her now.'

At this moment Lisutaris arrives, accompanied by Hansius. Despite the gravity of the situation, the Mistress of the Sky remains calm. This might be due to thazis, but maybe not. Back in the war, she never panicked under pressure. Before she can be questioned, Consul Kalius orders that those not directly involved be removed from the room. This seems to mean me, Makri and Tilupasis.

'Take them to a secure place and do not let them speak to anyone,' commands Kalius. We're led away by a sergeant of the Guard, through the main hall and along a short corridor to another room.

I don't know if this performance fools anyone else, but it's obvious to me that the procedure has been worked out by Tilupasis and Kalius to give us some freedom to act. So it proves. Once secure in a private room, Tilupasis starts issuing orders.

'Makri. Go back and wait for Lisutaris. If they take her anywhere, follow them and make sure she's safe.'

Makri nods, aware that it's time to be performing her bodyguard duties. Now that there's action afoot, Makri has ceased to look ill. She departs. Tilupasis dismisses the sergeant.

'Did you get it?' she enquires briskly.

'You know a good Sorcerer can eavesdrop on a conversation,' I point out.

'Not here. We had this room lined with Red Elvish Cloth precisely for an occasion like this.'

Red Elvish Cloth forms a barrier to magic. No Sorcerer can pry through it. It's fabulously expensive, and lining the room with it must have cost a fortune. If Lisutaris ever gets elected, the citizens of Turai will be paying for it for a long time.

I nod, and hand over a thick document. Tilupasis glances at it, and seems satisfied. The document contains confidential details of an agreement between

Lasat, Axe of Gold, and one wealthy Juvalian merchant named Berisat who's been defrauding the King of Samsarina for the past three years by providing the royal mint with slightly impure gold. It's Lasat's job to test the purity of the metal used for Samsarina's coinage, and he's been illicitly letting the substandard gold through, and taking a healthy share of the profits. Getting my hands on the details cost me a great deal of effort, and Tilupasis a great deal of money.

'Is everything here?'

'I believe so.'

I pumped Irith Victorious for information when he was drunk. I passed the information on to a thief, who stealthily robbed the Juvalian delegation while they slept in their stupor. A successful operation, though what Samanatius the philosopher would say about the ethics of arranging for my own friends to be robbed, I don't like to think. I know what Gurd would say. He'd be disgusted.

'This should be sufficient to make Lasat, Golden Axe, cooperate,' says Tilupasis.

'Risky, don't you think? Blackmailing the Senior Sorcerer in the west?'

'I'll worry about the risk.'

'You won't be around to worry for long if Lasat decides to kill you. Which he could do by waving his little finger.'

'Unlikely,' replies Tilupasis. 'Far easier just to go along with Turai's natural desire to suppress the affair until it has been fully investigated.'

'What if Lasat, Axe of Gold, tells you to go to hell?'

'Then he's going to need all his sorcerous power to

keep him from the scaffold once the King of Samsarina learns he's been defrauding the royal mint for the past three years.'

'I never figured Lasat as an embezzler.'

'He has a very bad dwa habit.'

'Really?'

'He keeps it quiet. This information will buy us time. Lasat, Axe of Gold, will order Sunstorm Ramius not to reveal any details of the murder. Lisutaris will go forward into the final test tomorrow.'

I'm not especially happy at any of this. Though I generally leave ethics and morals to Makri, I can't help noticing I'm participating in blackmail to avoid the arrest of a murderer.

'Even if you can keep Lasat quiet, you won't silence Sunstorm Ramius for ever. If Lisutaris beats him in the final test he'll squeal out loud that she's a murderer, no matter what Lasat says. Unless you have some way of blackmailing him too?'

Tilupasis shakes her head.

'Sunstorm Ramius is unfortunately free of any dark secrets. Don't think I haven't looked. You're right, it only buys us a little time. If Ramius loses the test he'll tell what he knows and every Sorcerer in the west will have access to the pictures. Which means you have one more day to sort it out.'

'I'll do my best.'

'It's time to do better. So far all you've come up with is the possibility of an erasement spell. That's not enough. We need the whole story and we need it quickly.'

I don't like the fact that I'm being lectured. I get enough of that from Cicerius.

'If you don't like my investigating, why didn't you ask someone else?'

'We did. You're not the only man currently trying to clear up this mess. None of you have come up with anything. It's time to get results.'

Tilupasis smiles. She's really well bred.

'So what have you got worked out for the final test?' I ask, as she makes to leave.

'Pardon?'

'The final test. Don't tell me you're going to leave it as a fair contest between Lisutaris and Ramius?'

'Lisutaris would stand an excellent chance of winning such a contest.'

'Maybe. But she'd stand more chance if Turai was planning to cheat on her behalf.'

'The nature of the test is still secret. It is to be set by Charius the Wise. So far he has proved to be annoyingly incorruptible. We're still working on it,' says Tilupasis before departing to blackmail the Senior Sorcerer in the west. I hope he never learns that I was involved. Lasat, Axe of Gold, could blast me to hell without blinking an eye. He wouldn't even have to be in the same city. Just mutter a few words and off I'd go.

I shake my head. I've sobered up. I don't like it. I don't like anything. It's pretty clear why I was recruited for this job. No one would expect me to refuse to do anything shady provided I was paid well enough. A real Sorcerer with loyalty to the Guild wouldn't have been any use. The man they required had to know something about magic but never have been good enough to be admitted to the Guild. He needed to be keen enough for money to not mind much what he did to earn it. He needed to be run down, and not above using people for his own ends. I sigh. I'm the ideal man for the job.

I walk all the way home through the terrible winter. Back at the Avenging Axe I sit morosely in my room in front of the fire, staring at the shapes in the flames. After a while I get out my niarit board and play through a game. I drink some beer and stare out of the window. The sky is dull and overcast, same as it has been for weeks. It's getting me down.

There's a knock at the door. I wrench it open. If it's the Brotherhood or Praetor Capatius's men come looking for trouble, that's fine with me. It's Samanatius the philosopher. That's not so fine. He asks if he can come in.

Samanatius is around sixty, fairly well preserved. His white hair and beard are well trimmed. He's dressed in a cheap cloak and his tunic has seen better days. Neither are suitable for the fierce weather but he doesn't appear to be suffering. He politely refuses my offer of beer.

'Forgive me for intruding. I wished to thank you for your help. Many people would have suffered had the eviction been allowed to happen.'

I'm not in any mood for taking credit. I tell Samanatius in the plainest terms that I only helped out because Senator Lodius blackmailed me into it.

'He needed the poor people's votes.'

'I know this already,' says Samanatius. 'But we still owe you thanks. I have no doubt that if you wished you could have found a way to avoid coming to our aid. I am now in your debt. Please do not hesitate to ask if I can ever do you a favour.'

The philosopher bows, and departs as abruptly as he

arrived. I don't quite know what to make of it. Or what to make of the man. I'm not feeling any sudden urge to join his philosophy school but I didn't dislike him as much as I thought I would.

The stain of blood is still visible on my rug. Darius Cloud Walker was killed right here in my room. So far I've done nothing about it. I should have made more progress. I should have spent more time investigating and less time drinking at the Assemblage. I have to find out the truth of the matter. It's what I was hired to do. I banish all distractions from my mind, then I sit down and think, for a long time.

CHAPTER SEVENTEEN

I wake up in my chair with a bottle in my lap and a pain in my neck. It's morning. The fire has gone out and my room is freezing. Princess Direeva is sitting on the couch, reading my book of spells.

'Very out of date,' she says. 'Sorcery has moved on since this was printed.'

'I haven't.'

'You never qualified. Why not?'

'I was never good at studying. Why are you here?'

My doors are secured with a locking spell, but a Sorcerer like Direeva can walk right through any of my minor incantations.

'Are you cold?' she asks, as she sees me shiver.

'I'm cold.'

Direeva waves her hand. My fire bursts into life.

'Very clever. You got a spell for tidying my room?'

'I have,' says Direeva. 'But you wouldn't like it.'

'I take it you didn't come to Twelve Seas just to demonstrate your power?'

'Lighting a fire requires very little power. I really wonder why you didn't pursue your apprenticeship.'

'Change the subject. First thing in the morning, I hate talking about me failing.'

'As you wish.'

The Princess has never shown any signs of liking me. Sitting in my office she still has something of a disdainful air, as if she'd rather be elsewhere. It's annoying. It's not like I insisted on her visiting. She's welcome to go and disdain somewhere else.

I ask her if news of Lisutaris's detection as a murderer has reached the ears of the Assemblage. It hasn't. Apparently Tilupasis has succeeded in silencing Lasat, Axe of Gold. You have to admire that woman. It takes nerve to blackmail a Sorcerer who could stop your heart beating with one of his lesser spells.

'As far as the Assemblage knows, Lisutaris is in the happy position of coming second in the election and is now about to face the final test. Which is why I am here. I'm concerned for her safety. It occurs to me that Covinius may decide that the magic space is a very good place in which to kill her.'

I don't get this. Lisutaris and Sunstorm Ramius will have to enter the magic space to carry out the final test, whatever that may be, but the magic space in question will not be open to the public.

'How? Charius the Wise will create the magic space when he sets the test. Lisutaris and Ramius will walk into it. No one else will be there.'

'Is Covinius not the master Assassin?' says Direeva. 'May he not have means of following them? A person can die in the magic space just as well as anywhere else. The unpredictability of the dimension could make even a strong Sorcerer like Lisutaris vulnerable to his attack.'

There's something in what the Princess says. Out in the street, Covinius couldn't fire a dart into Lisutaris. Her protection spells would deflect it. But in the peculiar realm which is the magic space, they might not. Nothing is ever certain there. It's not a good place to visit.

I pile a few more logs into the hearth. I'll miss it when these Sorcerers are no longer around to light my fire.

'I intend to follow Lisutaris into the magic space,' says Direeva. 'That way I can watch over her.'

'Since when are you so concerned about Lisutaris? Only yesterday you weren't even sure who you were going to vote for.'

'Makri won me over with her strong arguments,' says Direeva, and almost smiles.

I doubt this is the whole truth. Direeva's father, ruler of the Southern Hills, probably isn't going to last much longer. Quite possibly Turai has secretly offered the Princess aid if she decides to dispute the succession with her brother. Even so, I wouldn't be surprised if Makri's demonstration of strength did influence the Princess. It certainly made Troverus look less impressive.

'I never really cared for the Simnian,' says Direeva. 'Lisutaris will be a better head of the Guild.'

'Charius and Lasat won't allow anyone else into the magic space.'

'I believe I can secretly open a portal which will allow access. Before Lisutaris starts the test I will use a spell to connect us.'

'How difficult is that? Could other Sorcerers do it?'

'Possibly.'

'Then we might have company.'

I've wondered for a while why Sunstorm Ramius and his Simnian delegation haven't been doing more in the way of bribery. They've seemed content to let Turai do its worst. Almost as if they were confident of winning the final test no matter what. Direeva's notion makes me wonder if they might be planning to send some help of their own into the magic space.

'If you're going in I want to come with you.'

'You do? I was thinking more of Makri.'

'No doubt she'll insist on coming.'

The dragon scales in Direeva's hair glint in the fire-light, casting small flashes of reflected colour on to the walls.

'You ever work a spell with those dragon scales?'

Direeva shakes her head.

'No. I just buy them to decorate my hair. Where is Makri?'

'I don't know. Last time I saw her she was going to watch Lisutaris's back. If Lisutaris hasn't been denounced as a murderer she should be with her in her villa.'

'Then we should go there,' suggests Direeva. 'And make preparations.'

I stretch. My neck hurts. I shouldn't fall asleep in chairs. I wonder if Direeva could fix it with a spell. I'm not going to ask. I'm hungry. I'd go and buy pastry from Minarixa's bakery if Minarixa wasn't dead from dwa. I get my cloak. It's cold. I don't heat it up. I don't want to show my poor magical skills in front of a major Sorcerer. I take a quick beer from downstairs and ask Tanrose to throw some salted venison in a bag for me.

Direeva has a carriage outside, driven by two of her attendants, each bearing the insignia of the royal house of the Southern Hills. They're grim men, and remain silent on the journey. I poke around in my bag and take out a hunk of venison. Direeva looks startled.

'I did not invite you to eat in my carriage.'

'I didn't invite you to visit me and interrupt my break-fast.'

'I do not allow people to speak to me like that in the Southern Hills.'

'Since you got drunk and collapsed on my floor, I figure I don't have to worry about etiquette.'

I'm angry. Angry that I'm making no progress. And angry at Direeva for thinking she can waltz into my rooms without an invitation. Direeva is displeased at my lack of civility and we ride in silence to the villa. There we find various servants, but no sign of Lisutaris or Makri.

'Copro is attending to the Mistress of the Sky.'

We wait in silence. It's the day of the final test and I can already feel some tension. I don't trust the Simnians. And Covinius will finally show his face, I'm sure.

Cicerius is expecting me to come up with something to clear Lisutaris. I haven't. It's a long time since I failed so badly on an important case. Makri arrives downstairs after ten minutes or so. Although her nails are freshly painted, she's frowning. Makri knows that she's in for a hard time if it all goes wrong and she finds herself being interrogated by the Civil Guard. The guards are not going to go easy on an alien woman with Orc blood who can't come up with a good explanation as to why her knife was sticking in the corpse.

'I'll kill them all and leave the city,' she mutters. 'I don't suppose you've achieved a fantastic break-through?'

'Not yet. But I have some good news. We're sneaking into the magic space to help Lisutaris in the test.'

'Good,' says Makri. 'Will it clear her name?'

'No. I'm still working on that.'

Direeva expresses some contempt for my powers of investigation.

'A woman could die waiting for you to help. What have you done so far?'

'A lot of thinking.'

'And?'

'And now I need a beer. How long till Lisutaris is ready?'

Makri isn't sure.

'She had a new outfit planned for the final test but Copro was doubtful about the whole concept. They're still discussing shoes.'

'I liked the gold ones she wore yesterday,' says Direeva.

'Me too,' says Makri. 'but they clash with the new necklace.'

I take a goblet of wine and wonder about the final test. Last time the Sorcerers elected a new leader, the two candidates were given fifteen minutes to sorcerously dam a magical river which doubled in volume every two minutes. The winner brought down a mountain to act as a barrier, but some say it was lucky that the mountain just happened to appear in the magic space at the right time.

'Lisutaris will need her wits about her. Is she staying off the water pipe?'

'No.'

'She should be.'

'Well, she isn't.'

'Couldn't you encourage her?'

'Why me?' says Makri, getting belligerent.

'You're her bodyguard.'

'She's still alive, isn't she?'

'Just about. No thanks to you.'

'What do you mean by that?'

'I mean as a bodyguard you're as much use as a eunuch in a brothel. When the Brotherhood knocked on my door you were unconscious, and when Capatius's thugs attacked us you collapsed in a heap.'

Makri is irate.

'Stop bringing that up. Who saved you last year when we were attacked by Orcs? And who defeated Kirith-ar-Yell? He was about to chop your head off till I tossed him off that balcony.'

'I'd have managed.'

'Only if Kirith had stopped for a beer.'

'Do you have to argue all the time?' says Direeva, angrily.

'Who asked you to get involved?' I retort, aggressively

'Who is it that is going to take us into the magic space?'

'I'd have found a way in anyway.'

'The only thing you'd find would be Lisutaris's wine cellar.'

Our nerves are beginning to fray. Fortunately Lisutaris arrives downstairs in time to prevent us from becoming violent. We're not the only ones whose nerves are frayed. At the Assemblage the atmosphere is unusually tense. The Sorcerers are quieter. Whether this is because they've heard some ugly rumours or just because on this day they are required to tone down the celebrating, I don't know, but even Irith Victorious looks subdued. Cicerius practically bites my head off when I'm forced to report no progress on the murder.

'You think this is easy? I'm trying to unravel some sorcerous plot the like of which no one has ever encountered before. Someone very smart entered my office to kill Darius and no one even knows why. And don't forget everything else I've had on my plate, like helping your friend Tilupasis bribe our way to victory. And guarding Lisutaris, Mistress of the Sky, against Covinius, whoever the hell Covinius is. When you gave me the job you didn't mention the Simnians had hired an Assassin to kill our candidate.'

'I am still not certain that is the case,' says the Deputy Consul.

'Well, I am. Lisutaris knows that Sunstorm Ramius hired an Assassin, and that's good enough for me.'

Sulinius hurries into the private room, looking harassed.

'How dare you arrive late on such an important day,' declares the Deputy Consul, and starts giving him a lecture.

'Visus is dead,' gasps Sulinius.

'Dead?'

'A dwa overdose. Last night.'

Sulinius seems on the verge of tears at the death of his young companion. Cicerius is speechless.

'I'll see that it's kept quiet,' says Tilupasis, and leaves the room in a hurry. Cicerius recovers swiftly and tells Sulinius to pull himself together.

'It is time for all Turanians to do their duty.'

All the Turanians who appear in the Deputy Consul's room are already stressed from doing their duty. Praetor

Samilius sullenly admits that none of his Investigators have found out anything about anything. Samilius is resentful that as head of the Civil Guard he wasn't informed of events earlier. Old Hasius the Brilliant, briefly visiting before going to help with the final test, informs us sharply that he still believes Lisutaris to be guilty.

'I do not know why Lasat, Axe of Gold, is allowing her to continue,' he says. 'But I do know that it is pointless.'

'The King's administration does not believe it to be pointless,' says Cicerius.

'Then the King's administration is acting more foolishly than usual.'

The Deputy Consul glares at Hasius, but the Sorcerer is far too old and venerable to be intimidated by anyone. Consul Kalius arrives and Hasius reminds him that he said all along that Lisutaris was not a suitable candidate for head of the Sorcerers Guild. From the look on Kalius's face, he probably agrees, but he's stuck with it now.

The test is due to start in one hour. No one has any idea what it will consist of. Charius will call Lisutaris and Ramius and the three of them will step into the mouth of the magic space. Charius will then give them their task.

I draw Cicerius aside for a private word and inform him that Direeva believes she can penetrate the magic space. Cicerius is pleased, though he expresses some concern.

'If Turai is found to have interfered with the test, Lisutaris will be disqualified.'

'We'll be discreet. Direeva thinks she can get us in unobserved.'

Tilupasis returns from hushing up the death of Tribune Visus.

'An unfortunate occurrence.'

'Very,' agrees Cicerius. 'Young men should stay clear of dwa.'

I find this hard to take.

'Stay clear of it? He was practically ordered to take it. You ought to give him a medal, he died in the line of duty.'

'So you will enter the magic space with Direeva and Makri?' says Tilupasis, briskly ignoring my barb.

'That's the plan. If Covinius arrives Direeva will distract him. Meanwhile Makri protects Lisutaris and I do whatever I can to help. If Sunstorm Ramius looks like he's winning, he's going to find me in his face. Have you managed to find out anything about the test?'

Tilupasis shakes her head. Charius has continued to be incorruptible.

'It might not matter,' I point out. 'Lisutaris could probably dam a magic river as well as Ramius, providing she isn't too stoned.'

'And is she?'

'She's coming round.'

In the main hall the Sorcerers are gathered in their delegations. Sobriety prevails, as is traditional. Even the most hardened hedonist – Irith, for example – is strongly discouraged from enjoying himself while the test is in progress. I notice Irith and his large companions sitting bored at a table at the far side of the room. I'd like to greet them but I hesitate. I was discreet when

I pumped them for information, and even more discreet when I passed the information on to Tilupasis. There's nothing really to connect me with the robbery. But Sorcerers usually have finely developed intuition. I'd be surprised if they don't work out what I was about, eventually.

So far at the Assemblage there has been little ceremony since the King's speech of welcoming. Today is rather different, and once again all non-Sorcerers are banished from the main hall as the two candidates approach the tall robed figures of Lasat, Axe of Gold, and Charius the Wise. Charius has a small globe in his hand, the artefact which he will use to create the magic space. The last thing I see is Lisutaris laying her hand on the globe while the entire Guild looks on in silence. In a way, it's a sacred moment. I hurry to Cicerius's private room to get on with the business of corrupting it.

Princess Direeva and Makri are already there. Makri reports that Lisutaris left her with a clear mind.

'I managed to get her focused.'

Direeva waves her hand to silence us.

'We must enter now.'

'Shouldn't we give them a start?'

'Not if you want to find out what the test is. Now be silent.'

Cicerius steps well out of the way. Direeva takes a small fragment of dragon scale from her hair and holds it in the palm of her hand. She stares at it for a few seconds then mutters a sentence in one of the arcane Sorcerers' languages. The room goes cool. An aura of green light forms round the dragon scale, growing in size till it's the height of a man.

'Let us go,' says the Princess, and steps into the light.

Makri walks quickly in behind her. I hesitate for a second. The magic space isn't a place I really want to visit again. I turn to Cicerius.

'I'm adding this to my bill,' I say, then tramp forward into a place where the sun is a vile shade of purple and we are surrounded on all sides by a tall hedge.

'Where's the talking pig?' asks Makri, looking around.

The last time we were in the magic space we met a pig which was, as I remember, a fairly intelligent creature.

'It won't be here. We're in a different part of the magic space.'

I'm suddenly doubtful.

'Or are we? Or is all magic space the same big dimension?'

'Sort of,' replies Direeva, unhelpfully. 'This is the Maze of Acro. Do not separate or you will become lost. Remain silent while I bring us close to the entry point of the others.'

Direeva leads us through the maze. It's hard to keep our bearings as we're surrounded on all sides by the huge hedge. Everywhere looks the same but Direeva seems to know where she's going. Finally, after some twisting and turning, she leads us to a clearing wherein there is a small pool. On the other side of the pool a green light is beginning to glow. Direeva motions for us to withdraw behind the foliage.

So far this magic space seems to be behaving itself reasonably well. The sun is a horrible colour but the hedge isn't doing anything weird. Not turning into giant mushrooms, for instance. You can't trust this place, though. If we get out without encountering an erupting volcano I'll count myself lucky.

From behind the hedge I hear voices, first that of Charius the Wise.

'You are now in the Maze of Acro. Here is your test.'

'What is this?' enquires Lisutaris.

'A sequence of numbers,' replies Charius. 'Your task is to find the next number in the sequence and bring it to me. The first person to do so will be the next head of the Sorcerers Guild.'

'What sort of test is that?' demands Lisutaris, sounding displeased.

'It is the test I have set you.'

'I'm not a mathematician,' declares Lisutaris. 'I do not count this as a proper test.'

There is no sound of protest from Sunstorm Ramius. Maybe he's a mathematician. Or maybe he's about to cheat. Already I'm highly suspicious. I peer round the hedge. Charius is disappearing into the green light and Ramius is exiting through the opposite gap in the hedge. Lisutaris, Mistress of the Sky, is dragging a large water pipe out of her personal magic pocket.

'That's not going to help,' I say, stepping forward.

Lisutaris looks round.

'Nothing's going to help. Look at this.'

She hands over a sheet of parchment. On it are written the numbers 391, 551, 713.

'Anyone know what the next number might be?'

No one knows.

'It seems like an odd sort of test,' says Direeva.

'Don't you know, Makri? You study mathematics.'

'I'll try and work it out,' says Makri, but she looks puzzled.

'You do that,' says Lisutaris, and takes hold of the water pipe.

'For God's sake, you can't just give up,' I shout. 'Not after all the effort we went to to get you here. Do something.'

'What? I'm no good at numbers. Never was.'

'Summon up a mathematical spirit or something.'

'There's no such thing.'

'There must be some magical way of finding the next number. Otherwise Charius wouldn't have set it as a test.'

Direeva wonders, like me, if this might have been arranged in some way for Ramius to win. Perhaps the Simnians didn't bother bribing the Sorcerers because they'd already bribed Charius.

'If he walks back in here in thirty seconds with the right number, I'm going to be pretty suspicious.'

A unicorn walks by. We ignore it.

'Maybe they have mathematical spirits in Simnia.'

'Maybe,' says Lisutaris. 'But not in Turai. I'm stumped.'

She lights the water pipe. I can't believe she's giving up so easily. Direeva suddenly makes a warning sound. Close to us, a green light is starting to glow. We all hurry behind the hedge, and peer round the edge just in time to see a dark shape disappearing into the forest.

'Covinius!' whispers Princess Direeva. 'He's come, as I thought he would.'

'Are you sure that was Covinius? I couldn't see his face.'

'Who else would it be?'

Direeva steps forward.

'I will take care of him. Lisutaris, you must do what you can with the test.'

With that Direeva strides off, her long hair swinging in the light breeze.

I turn to Makri.

'Stay here with Lisutaris.'

'Where are you going?'

'I'm going to see what I can find.'

'You'll get lost.'

'No I won't. I know all about sorcerous mazes. Maybe if I can rustle up a talking pig he'll know the next number in the sequence.'

'The next number,' grumbles Lisutaris. 'The whole thing is ridiculous. Who knows anything about mathematics?'

'Simnian Sorcerers, maybe.'

Lisutaris sits down with her pipe.

'It's not a fair test,' she mutters, sounding irritatingly like a schoolchild. 'I was expecting to be damming a river. Or building a mountain. I could have done that.'

'Fair or not, we have to find it quick, before Ramius. I'm damned if I've come this far just to let a Simnian win.'

Lisutaris doesn't seem to care. She's given up. Her hair is still beautifully styled. At a reception at the Imperial Palace, other women would be eyeing her with envy.

CHAPTER EIGHTEEN

I set off through the Maze of Acro, leaving Makri to guard Lisutaris. I'm guessing that despite her firm intentions of remaining sober Makri will soon join in on the water pipe. It's a deficiency in her character, brought about by having pointed ears. It will serve them right if Covinius kills Direeva and then chops their heads off. Some bodyguard. Ever since Makri started blubbering about that damned Elf See-ath she's been as much use as a one-legged gladiator.

Was that really Covinius? Direeva seemed certain, but so what? I don't trust her. I don't trust anyone. Lisutaris is a disaster. Makri's unreliable. Cicerius is hopeless. Tilupasis is a joke. Praetor Samilius couldn't investigate the theft of a baby's rattle. Everyone in Turai is useless. If it wasn't for me the city would have fallen long ago. I get out my sword and march through the maze. I dislike mazes, magical or not. They're irritating and pointless. Trust Charius the Wise to send us here.

I turn a corner and almost bump into a small figure I recognise. It's Hanama, garbed in black, with a knife in her hand.

'You're not supposed to be here,' I tell her.

'Neither are you,' she replies.

'I've got more right than you.'

'No you haven't.'

'I'm a Tribune of the People. You're just an Assassin.'

'Since when could a Tribune of the People – an honorary title at best – interfere with the sacred final test of the Sorcerers Guild?'

'Since I decided it was my duty.'

'Your duty? Very amusing. Step aside, Investigator.'

'How did you get in here? And what are you doing here anyway?'

'Protecting Lisutaris. So I have no time to talk,' says Hanama, and walks past. I stare at her retreating figure.

'I've got more right to be here than you!' I roar. 'I'm a Tribune!'

Hanama is now out of sight. Damn these Assassins. Always turning up when you don't want them.

I walk on. By Hanama's standards that was quite talkative. Maybe she's warming to me. Another unicorn appears. Or maybe it's the one I saw earlier. They all look much the same. It trots in my direction. Perhaps it can help. In the magic space, anything is possible. The sun's just gone green, and the daisies are up to my waist.

'Greetings, unicorn. Have you seen a Simnian Sorcerer called Sunstorm Ramius?'

The unicorn regards me in silence.

'About so high,' I say, waving my hand. 'Probably scowling.'

Behind me there's a burst of raucous laughter.

'He's trying to question a unicorn!'

I spin round. Quite a large squirrel is laughing at me.

'Don't you know unicorns can't talk?'

'I figured it was worth a try. I don't suppose you've seen Ramius?'

'The Simnian Sorcerer? Ex-soldier type? Certainly I've seen him.'

The squirrel looks at me keenly.

'You have any thazis?'

'Yes, as it happens.'

I take out a stick and hand it over.

'Take the next right then keep to the left,' says the squirrel, then bounds off, thazis clutched tightly in one claw.

I walk on. I've just bribed a large squirrel with thazis. It's fine, if you don't think about it too much. The breeze is picking up and the daisies are still growing. It's getting colder. I think I hear voices so I creep forward quietly. When the voices grow louder I halt. Sunstorm Ramius is round the next corner.

'You have the question?'

'I do.'

The sound of paper passing from one hand to another. I risk a glance. Ramius is conferring with a tall man in a toga who talks with a Simnian accent. It's the mathematician Makri encountered at the Assemblage. This is outrageous behaviour. The final test is meant to be sacred. Like I always say, you can't trust a Simnian.

The scholar studies Ramius's paper. Quill in hand, he makes some calculations.

'Hurry,' hisses Ramius. 'Lisutaris is working on the problem at this moment.'

The scholar looks rather coldly at the Sorcerer.

'I am the finest mathematician in the west. No one will find the answer faster than I.'

He carries on scribbling. I'm tempted to advance and confront them with their perfidy. Without doubt Charius the Wise was bribed to set some numerical test, and the Simnians had their man ready to enter the field. If Ramius wins I'm denouncing him as the fraud I've always known him to be.

Finally the mathematician seems satisfied.

'The answer is—'

Ramius silences him.

'Don't say it. Lisutaris may be listening in. You can't trust these Turanian dogs. Write it down and show it to me quickly.'

The scholar does as he's told. Ramius glances briefly at the answer then instructs him to take the paper away with him. The Sorcerer pulls a small globe from a pocket in his cloak, waves his hand over it, and the familiar green light grows till it's large enough for his companion to step into, back to the real world. As Ramius turns round I withdraw quickly out of sight. Next second he marches round the corner and bumps into me. I beat him on the head with the pommel of my sword and he collapses in a heap.

'I'm appalled,' I say, staring at his prone figure. 'You Simnians, you're all cheats. And you were no use in the war.'

I hurry off as fast as I can. The air goes suddenly icy and snow starts to fall. Winter has arrived in the magic space. That's all I need. A fierce wind blows the snow into my eyes. I curse. Ramius won't be out for long. If only the mathematician had written down the answer, I'd have stolen it. Maybe back in Turai there's someone who could work it out. That means getting out of here quickly. I need to find Direeva.

The icy wind hinders my progress. Not imagining

that it would be winter here, I'm not wearing my magic warm cloak and am soon as cold as the ice queen's grave and cursing all places magical where you can't depend on the weather to be consistent for two minutes.

The hedges have been flickering, threatening to disappear but never quite going. I'm concentrating on following my path back to Lisutaris and it doesn't immediately register that the hedge on my left has shrunk to just two feet tall. As I glance round, I catch sight of a figure walking along the next path. The snow is flying in my eyes, visibility is poor and I can't be certain, but I'd swear that the person I see is Copro, beautician to the aristocracy. He's carrying a crossbow. Immediately I attempt to leap the hedge. Unfortunately it chooses that moment to grow back to normal size and I bounce off with a face full of prickly leaves.

'Copro?' I mutter. 'With a crossbow?'

By dint of some fine navigational skills I bring myself back to where Lisutaris, Mistress of the Sky, and Makri are sitting beside the water pipe. I tell them what just happened.

'They brought in the mathematician?' says Makri. 'That's really unfair.'

'Didn't I say you can't trust a Simnian?'

'Yes, you said it hundreds of times.'

'What's this about Copro?' asks Lisutaris.

'He's walking around the maze with a crossbow.'

'You imagined it.'

'Why would I do that?'

'Because we're in the magic space, where nothing is certain, and also there's a heavy snowstorm affecting visibility.'

Lisutaris is annoying me so much these days. I can't believe I ever liked her.

'I tell you it was Copro. Where's Direeva? I need to get out of here to find someone back in Turai who can answer the question.'

'Like who?'

'I don't know. I'll go to the university and look for a professor.'

'That'll take too long,' points out Makri. 'How about Samanatius?'

'Could he do it?'

'He's the finest philosopher in the west.'

'But can he do sums?'

Makri thinks so.

'I've been trying to work it out myself,' she adds. 'But I haven't got anywhere.'

'Where is Direeva? I have to get out.'

'Use salt,' says Makri, who remembers that on a previous occasion I brought us out of the magic space by sprinkling salt on the ground. I'm dubious about trying this again.

'It might collapse the magic space, and then what would happen to the test?'

'Wouldn't work anyway,' says Lisutaris, looking up from her pipe. 'Charius's magic space is different. Stronger.'

'Can you send me back to Twelve Seas?'

'Yes. But it'll create a large disruption in the magic field. Charius the Wise will know something has happened. If we want to be discreet, we need Direeva.'

The snow starts coming down more heavily. Lisutaris waves her hand and a fire grows up beside her. Direeva walks into the clearing and collapses. Blood spurts out of a bad wound in her shoulder, caused by a crossbow bolt which is deeply embedded in the flesh.

'Who did it?'

Direeva didn't see her assailant's face.

'It was Copro!' I yell.

'Why did they hire this Investigator?' says Princess Direeva. 'He gets more foolish every day.'

'You never liked Copro,' says Makri. 'But that's no reason to start accusing him of assassination attempts.'

I ignore this.

'Can you get me back to Twelve Seas?' I ask Direeva, as Lisutaris tends to her wound. The Princess regards me with distaste but, ignoring her injury, concentrates briefly and opens a breach in the magic space.

'You've got five minutes,' she says, as I step through, emerging at the corner of Quintessence Street.

I step over the rubble into Samanatius's academy. Inside the dingy hall Samanatius is lecturing a group of students. I march through their midst and take a firm grip on the philosopher's arm, drawing him to one side.

'Samanatius, about that favour you owe me. I need to find the next number in this sequence and I need it right now. It's to help Lisutaris.'

Samanatius grasps my meaning immediately. He excuses himself from his students and examines the paper I've thrust under his nose. After thirty seconds or so he nods.

'A sequence of products of prime numbers, I believe.'

I'm expecting him to start scribbling some notes, but apparently Samanatius has the mental capacity to work it out in his head.

'One zero seven three.'

'Are you sure?'

'Quite certain. The sequence is—'

'No time for that. Thanks for your help.'

I hurry out of the academy, impressed by Samanatius's mental powers. Maybe he deserves his reputation as philosophy's number one chariot. I'm almost glad I saved him from eviction. I wonder what he's like at working out odds on the races.

The green portal of light is still visible in the street, now wavering slightly. I throw myself through it, arriving back in the magic space some way from the clearing. Copro the beautician is advancing towards me, crossbow in his hand.

'So it's you!' I roar. 'You're Covinius. I've suspected this all along. It's a fine disguise, Assassin, but not fine enough to fool Thraxas the Investigator.'

The maze alters again and I find myself on my own, surrounded on every side by vegetation. I swing my sword desperately in an effort to cut my way through to Lisutaris before Covinius can reach her. The hedge in front of me bursts apart and Makri appears, axe in hand.

'What's going on? The hedge just started growing all over us.'

'Did you see Copro?'

'Are you still on about that?' says Makri.

'I tell you, he's the Assassin.'

'Why would he be? He's such a fine hair stylist.'

'I've had my eye on him for a long time. He didn't fool me with his deft make-up and effeminate ways. The man is a deadly killer. Where's Lisutaris?'

'I don't know.'

'Then keep chopping.'

'This is more like the magic space I remember,' says Makri, as penguins start to wander through the snow. 'Do you have the answer?'

'Yes.'

'So have I,' says Makri.

I pause for a moment.

'What?'

'I have the answer. I worked it out.'

Makri looks pleased with herself. I'm irritated.

'It took you long enough. Couldn't you have done that before I went beating Ramius over the head?'

'You beat Ramius over the head?'

'Yes. Before I visited Samanatius. It was all a lot of trouble. Which could have been avoided if you'd come up with the answer before I set off.'

'Well, I didn't,' says Makri.

We start chopping through the maze again, calling for Lisutaris.

'You might give me some credit anyway,' says Makri.

'What for?'

'For solving the puzzle.'

'I solved it first.'

'You didn't solve it at all,' contests Makri. 'You just asked Samanatius.'

'I got the answer, didn't I?'

Makri rests her axe.

'You know you're really getting on my nerves these days, Thraxas. Everything is always about you: "I did this, I did that". Do you have any idea how tedious it is having to listen to your lousy stories all the time? And if it's not that, it's some stupid criticism of me for getting on with my life. I tell you, it's about time—'

'Will you stop acting like a pointy-eared Orc freak and keep chopping?'

The hedge beside us splits apart in a sheet of yellow flame and we find ourselves confronted by an angry-looking Sunstorm Ramius.

'Thraxas hit you on the head,' says Makri. 'I had nothing to do with it.'

Ramius hurls a spell at me. My protection charm saves my life but I'm tossed to the ground and lie in a heap. Seeing that I'm still alive, Ramius draws a sword and charges forward. He's almost upon me when Makri leaps forward and pounds him on the head with the flat of her axe.

'Apologise for calling me a pointy-eared Orc freak,' demands Makri.

I struggle to my feet.

'Are you crazy? There's no time.'

Suddenly Hanama appears.

'Hanama,' says Makri. 'Do you think it's right that this fat drunk can just go around insulting me all the time?'

'What are you asking her for?' I scream. 'She's an Assassin, she doesn't care.'

'I resent the way you always imply I have no feelings,' says Hanama.

'Oh for God's sake, what's going on here? Who's responsible for this? Is the Association of Gentlewomen driving you all insane?'

'I'm not familiar with them,' says Hanama.

'Never been to a meeting,' claims Makri.

We start hewing our way through the still-growing vegetation.

'I need a new place to live,' says Makri to Hanama. 'It's hell in the Avenging Axe with Thraxas rolling around drunk all the time. It's putting me off my food.'

The hedge in front of us once more erupts in flame. I get ready to fight, but rather than Ramius it's Lisutaris who appears, with her water pipe in one hand and Princess Direeva leaning on her shoulder.

'I still don't believe that Copro is Covinius,' says the Sorcerer.

'Copro?' exclaims Hanama. 'Copro the beautician is Covinius?'

'According to Thraxas,' says Makri. 'But you know how trustworthy he is.'

Makri asks Direeva if it could have been Copro who shot her but as the Princess did not see her assailant's face, she can't say for sure.

'The bolt caught me unawares. My protection charm deflected it enough to save my life.'

'If he's the Assassin, why didn't he try and kill me when he was doing my hair?' asks Lisutaris.

'Maybe professional ethics forbade it. And we should discuss this later. Right now we have to get out of here. Ramius is unconscious and I have the answer, so if we can get back to Charius, you win the test.'

Seeing the sense in this, Lisutaris starts burning away the huge hedge that surrounds us and we make progress back towards the clearing. The snow has now stopped but the ground is frozen, and we slip and slide as we go. High in the sky the sun has gone blue and shrunk to a fraction of its normal size, as if mocking us.

By this time Direeva is looking less than healthy. Blood is still seeping from her shoulder. I ask her if she has enough power left to get us discreetly home without alerting Charius. She thinks so.

'It's the clearing,' cries Makri.

'It's Ramius,' cries Lisutaris.

He's dead. The Simnian Sorcerer is lying in the clearing with a great gash in his neck.

I turn to Lisutaris and demand to know if she killed him. She denies it. I shake my head. Just like she didn't kill Darius.

'It would have made my job a lot simpler if they'd told me you were going to butcher all your opponents. I'd have planned accordingly.'

'I have not killed anyone,' insists the Mistress of the Sky. 'Although this is going to be hard to explain to the Sorcerers Guild. They get suspicious if someone dies in the final test.'

'Don't worry,' I say. 'If things look bad for you, I'll just tell them you were too stoned to walk, let alone kill Ramius.'

'Is that a criticism?'

'You're damned right it's a criticism. When this is over I never want to see you and your water pipe again. And that includes Makri, Hanama and Direeva.'

I'm still annoyed that no one believes me about Copro. To hell with them all.

'I don't understand this,' says Makri. 'I thought it was Ramius that hired the Assassin?'

'It was,' asserts Lisutaris.

'So why did he kill Ramius?'

'We don't know an Assassin killed Ramius,' I point

out, and incline my head towards Lisutaris.

Direeva starts preparing our exit. Lisutaris glares at me.

'You have to tell me the answer to the final test now,' she says, stiffly.

'Of course. Yet another thing I've sorted out for you.'

'So what is it?'

I open my mouth, then close it again. I've forgotten. The excitement has driven the answer out of my head. I stare at Lisutaris helplessly.

Makri guffaws with laughter.

'He's forgotten it. Ha ha ha! The big Investigator forgot the answer. Thraxas, you're as much use as a one-legged gladiator. The talking pig was smarter than you.'

Makri turns to Lisutaris.

'Fortunately I worked out the solution. In my head. Using my mathematical skills. I didn't have to cheat like Thraxas, going to see Samanatius. I worked it out myself. I'm far smarter than he is. I worked it out by—'

'Perhaps you could tell me now?' suggests Lisutaris. 'I think Princess Direeva is about to faint.'

'It's 1073.'

With the last of her strength Direeva creates a portal for us to leave the magic space while Lisutaris makes a door of her own to take her back to the Assemblage. We take a last look at the body of Sunstorm Ramius, then depart.

'I still don't believe Copro is Covinius,' says Hanama, as we materialise back in Cicerius's private room.

Cicerius is startled to see us arriving looking like we've been in a battle.

'Princess Direeva needs a doctor, and quick. We found

the answer. Lisutaris will win the final test.'

'Excellent,' says Cicerius, meanwhile sending Hansius off for medical aid.

'Ramius is dead. His throat was cut.'

'That is not good.'

No one else was meant to be in the magic space, which leaves Lisutaris, Mistress of the Sky, as the only suspect.

'Tell me the details,' says Tilupasis, who's already thinking of the best way to deal with the situation.

M y second meeting with Turai's leading officials is
even more uncomfortable than the first.

'In brief, the situation is as follows,' says Consul Kalius.
'Lisutaris, Mistress of the Sky, has won the final test and
is now due to be confirmed as head of the Sorcerers Guild.
Unfortunately she remains the main suspect for the
murder of Darius Cloud Walker. Additionally, Sunstorm
Ramius, one of the best-known Sorcerers in the west,
was killed during the test. Although you report that various other people had infiltrated the magic space, as far
as the Sorcerers Guild is concerned there were only two
people there – Ramius and Lisutaris. Naturally Lisutaris
is now suspected of this murder.'

Kalius is worried. As Consul, he has a gold rim running round his toga. It's the only gold-rimmed toga in
the whole city state and he doesn't want to lose it.

'So what are we going to do about this?'

'Deflect criticism from Lisutaris,' replies Tilupasis
promptly. 'There is no certainty that Ramius was murdered. People can die of natural causes in the magic
space.'

'His throat was slit,' points out Kalius. 'It doesn't look
natural. No one is going to believe he was attacked by
a rogue unicorn. Who did kill him?'

'We believe that the Simnian Assassin Covinius may be involved,' answers Tilupasis. 'I've already put this out as a rumour.'

'Why would a Simnian Assassin kill the Simnian Sorcerer?'

'Internal politics?' suggests Cicerius, hopefully. 'Whatever the reason, we must certainly spread the story that Covinius killed Ramius.'

Everyone agrees it's very unfortunate that Covinius chose this moment to attack Sunstorm Ramius. Had he but killed him earlier in the week at the Assemblage, it would not have looked so bad for Turai. With plenty of foreign Sorcerers around we could have blamed anyone. Personally, I don't know what to think. Since learning that Simnia had hired an Assassin I've been working on the assumption that he was here to kill Lisutaris. Which doesn't seem to fit the facts, with Ramius being the victim. Unless Lisutaris really did kill Ramius, and the Assassin felt unable to attack her in the magic space because of the presence of Direeva and Makri. Is Copro Covinius? I'm no longer sure, though he can't have been up to any good wandering around in the magic space with a crossbow. It has to have been him who shot Direeva.

I'd like to ask Hanama what she got up to after we parted, but Hanama has disappeared. Disappearing is a speciality of hers.

'How long do we have to sort this out?' asks Praetor Samilius.

'Six hours,' replies Tilupasis. 'Lisutaris is due to be confirmed as Chief Sorcerer this evening, but before that happens, Charius the Wise will denounce her as the killer. I have bought us a little time but nothing I can do will prevent him from speaking out at the confirmation.'

'Could we . . . er . . . get to Charius?' suggests Samilius.

'No. He has resisted all our efforts and is now safely in the company of Lasat, Axe of Gold, and all the most powerful Sorcerers in the Guild.'

Kalius asks Samilius if the Civil Guard have come up with anything useful. They haven't. All eyes turn to me.

'I have some leads. I'll get on to it.'

Not wishing to expose myself to further ridicule, I'm not planning on denouncing Copro till I have some proof against him.

'You have six hours.'

'I'll do my best.'

Though Turai's leading politicians aren't about to include me in their discussions of state policy, I'm well aware that there is more riding on this now than Lisutaris's welfare. The city state of Turai is small. We have a lot of gold which other nations crave. If Simnia is looking for an excuse to make war on us, the murder of their Chief Sorcerer isn't a bad one. If the Abelasians decide to join them because of Darius, you don't have to be sharp as an Elf's ear to realise that Turai isn't going to be the safest place for a man to live.

So far all my efforts have come to nothing. Maybe I should have been more determined in questioning the Sorcerers. I might have been if I hadn't been forced to spend time pumping the Juvalians for dirt about Lasat, Axe of Gold. Old Hasius the Brilliant again scans the city, but with so little to go on, even the efforts of such a formidable Sorcerer are futile. I ask him once more if he's had any further thoughts on the matter of a spell for remaking reality.

'There is no such spell,' he repeats.

I'm really sick of hearing that.

Lisutaris is resting at her villa, waiting either to be confirmed as head of the Sorcerers Guild or arraigned as a murderer. Also there is Princess Direeva, recovering from her wound. Makri is with them, or so I thought. I'm surprised when she arrives at the Assemblage just as I'm leaving. I stare at her suspiciously. Last time I called her a pointy-eared Orc freak she attacked me with her axe.

'I've come to help,' she says. 'Providing you give me a fulsome apology.'

'You think I need your help?'

'You always need my help.'

I apologise. It'll only make life hell at the Avenging Axe if I don't.

'Any insult was purely accidental. Your pointed ears are just one of your numerous excellent features. Many people speak highly of them. Now why are you really here?'

'Lisutaris wanted me to make sure you didn't kill Copro. She thinks my duties as bodyguard should extend to protecting her favourite hairdresser.'

Cicerius provides us with an official carriage and we set off to visit Copro at his home in Thamlin. I tell Makri that no matter what Lisutaris thinks, Copro is up to something.

'I saw him in the magic space.'

Makri nods. She knows me well enough to realise I don't suffer from hallucinations.

'It wouldn't really surprise me if there was more to

him than he's saying. He was amazingly skilful with his scissors. And for a beautician, he did have a surprising grasp of world politics.'

Makri wonders why Covinius, whoever he actually is, suddenly ended up killing Sunstorm Ramius instead of Lisutaris.

'I'm wondering that myself. Damned unreasonable, seeing as we've spent the week protecting Lisutaris. If he'd just got in touch beforehand and said he was here to assassinate Ramius it would have been simpler all round.'

'Is it a crime you have to solve?'

'Definitely not. The Simnians can look after their own Sorcerers. All I have to do is show that Lisutaris didn't do it.'

Copro lives in an impressive villa. Not quite as large as those belonging to our wealthy Senators, but big enough. Few tradespeople of any sort live in Thamlin. The average working Turanian dwells in far more humble surroundings, and even those whose skill or good fortune have made them rich – some of our goldsmiths, for instance – wouldn't really be welcome here. But Copro seems to have attracted a higher status to himself. The grounds at the front of his house, now covered in snow, are in summer a marvel of exuberant good taste, with plants, trees and bushes arranged in glorious harmony according to his own design. As with hair, make-up and dress, Copro's gardens have had a profound effect on the fashions of the city.

Inside the gate I trample on a frozen bush so it breaks.

'You don't like the man, do you?' says Makri.

'I don't. Where was he when I was defending the city against the Orcs? Sitting comfortably in the Palace. Now he lives in a villa and I've got two rooms above the Avenging Axe.'

'You really should address your self-loathing some time,' says Makri, brightly. I scowl at her, and march up the long path.

Copro isn't in. A servant tells me so at the door, and after I bundle her out the way and search the house, it seems to be true. Other servants run around threatening to call the Civil Guard. I grab one of them and demand to know where Copro is. He claims not to know. I slap him. He falls down but when I drag him up he still doesn't know.

'I don't have time for this. Tell me where he is or I'll throw you downstairs.'

The servant starts wailing. I drag him to the top of the stairs, then halt, and let him go.

'I smell sorcery.'

Makri looks interested.

'What sort?'

'Not sure. But I can always sense it. Someone has worked a spell in this house, not long ago.'

We start hunting again, straining to find the source of the magic. Finally I stop in front of a bookcase. I drag it out of the way. Behind it the wall looks much as it should do. I put my shoulder to it and it creaks. I throw my full weight at it and the wall gives way. It's thin wood, a panel hiding a secret room. Inside are books, charts, phials, an astrolab and various other things normally to be found only in the workroom of a Sorcerer. At the back of the room is a particularly ugly statue of some sort of demon with four arms.

'How interesting.'

'So he's a Sorcerer as well as an Assassin?'

'Will you stop calling me an Assassin?' says Copro, materialising in the centre of the room.

Makri takes her twin swords from her magic purse.

Copro laughs.

'Do you imagine those can hurt me?'

Makri, not one for banter while she fights, waits silently, swords at the ready. Copro ignores her and speaks to me, telling me of the great enjoyment he has obtained from monitoring the incompetence of my investigation.

'Do people hire you for your amusement value, fat man?'

'All the time. I crack them up at the Palace.'

'Well, I am not an Assassin. I find myself baffled that you could think me to be Covinius.'

'I don't think you're Covinius. I used to, but it just occurred to me that you're Rosin-kar. Once the disgruntled apprentice of Darius Cloud Walker.'

Copro looks less pleased.

'And what do you base that on?'

'Summer Lightning. An Abelasian hair-styling term, I believe.'

'That is hardly proof,' retorts Copro.

'Maybe not. But it was enough to get my intuition working. And it will be enough to get the Sorcerers Guild to investigate your past and link you with Darius's murder.'

'Darius's murder? Lisutaris has been shown to be guilty, I believe.'

'You faked the evidence,' I say.

Copro smiles.

'You don't know how I did that, do you? I've spied on you, Thraxas, as you've toiled round the city, asking questions. Every Sorcerer you came to, you asked the same question. Is there a spell for remaking reality? Everyone said no. No one knows how to do it, except me. I am the greatest Sorcerer in the west, and the world will soon know it.'

By this time I'm starting to worry. From the tone of Copro's voice and the glint in his eye, I'd say I was dealing with a fairly insane beautician. Probably he never really got over being booted out by Darius.

'So why did you kill Darius?'

'I owed it to him.'

'Maybe. But why bother to frame Lisutaris for the murder?'

'I was well paid by Sunstorm Ramius. The Simnians were just as keen as the Turanians to eliminate the opposition.'

'But why get involved?' exclaims Makri. 'You're such a great beautician. Weren't you happy doing that?'

'Moderately happy,' replies Copro. 'But in truth, I was finding it wearing. And I loath Lisutaris. Eternally sucking on that water pipe. The woman is a disgrace to Sorcerers everywhere. While she and her kind have stagnated in the west, I have travelled the world in an effort to hone my skill. I have learned sorcery unheard of in these lands. Now I'll show the Guild who it was they refused to allow to finish his apprenticeship.'

Copro is looking madder all the time.

'I offered my services to Simnia. When Ramius was elected head of the Guild my reward was to be Chief Sorcerer of the conquered lands.'

'What conquered lands?'

'Turai and Abelasi.'

'Tough on you it's all gone wrong. Ramius is dead and Lisutaris won.'

Copro's eye starts to twitch.

'I intended to kill her in the magic space. I didn't understand why she had not been arraigned for the murder. Despite the excellent job I did in framing her, Turai had somehow managed to keep her name clear. I found that most annoying.'

Copro shrugs.

'No matter. She will be tried for the murder eventually. No one will find the secret of my spell for remaking reality. And no one apart from you will ever realise I am Rosin-kar. I see that you are wearing spell protection charms. It may take a while for me to wear them down. Rather than waste time I will now introduce you to one of my favourite creations.'

Copro claps his hands. The statue behind him opens its eyes, and steps forward. It raises its four arms, each one carrying a sword. I raise my own weapons to defend myself. Makri does the same. The statue advances a few steps then topples over with a terrific crash and lies motionless on the ground. Makri looks puzzled.

'Is that it?'

Copro is furious.

'Don't feel bad,' I tell him. 'Animating a statue is a really difficult thing to do.'

Copro claps his hands again and tigers appear from nowhere, rending at us with their claws. Makri starts fighting but I remain calm. I know these are illusions. I walk straight through a tiger and they all vanish.

Immediately serpents slither down the walls and slide towards us. I feel them twining round my legs as I walk forward. It takes all my concentration to keep going. Illusionary or not, I hate to be covered with snakes. Dragonfire erupts from the walls, covering me in golden light, and a nameless demon jabs at my eyes with a spear. I ignore it all and keep walking. Finally I back Copro up against the far wall. The illusions fade away.

'You have a stronger will than one would suspect,' says Copro.

'Cheap illusions never bother me.'

'Speak for yourself,' says Makri. 'Those snakes were really disgusting.'

'The Sword of Aracasan is no illusion,' says Copro, suddenly pulling a short blade from beneath his tunic.

I stare at the blade, rather worried by this turn of events. The Sword of Aracasan, a fabulous item long thought lost to the world, has the property of making its bearer invincible in combat. Armed with such a blade, a novice could hew his way through an army.

'That's not really the sword of—'

Copro swings it at me. The blade travels faster than the eye can see, and were I not already protecting myself with my sword it would have taken my head off. As it is, the flat of my own blade slams into my face and I fly back across the room and bang my head on the four-armed statue. I try to rise but my legs no longer seem to be functioning. Copro smiles. The sword flickers in the air, again faster than the eye can see.

'A remarkable weapon,' he says, and advances towards me. He isn't paying much attention to Makri. Possibly Copro doesn't feel threatened by any woman whose hair he's styled. Makri leaps at him and engages him in combat, but even her gladiatorial skills can't overcome the Sword of Aracasan. They fight furiously for a minute or so, but each time Makri attempts to land a blow the magical sword parries it, and she's hard pushed to avoid the answering strokes. Finally she leaps backwards and yells.

'Get him, Thraxas!'

Copro turns towards me. Makri stabs him in the back. He slumps to the floor with a surprised look in his eye.

I struggle to my feet. Makri is looking sadly at the body.

'You should've stuck to the beauty trade. You were good at it.'

She sighs.

'Lisutaris isn't going to be pleased.'

She looks more cheerful.

'On the other hand, I suppose this ends the case? I mean, we've killed the bad guy. That usually does it.'

'We've killed one bad guy. Covinius is still around and we don't have any proof it was he and not Lisutaris who killed Ramius.'

I'm bleeding. I rip a length of cloth from a towel and wrap it round my head. The villa is in chaos, with servants running around and screaming.

'Furthermore, I don't have any proof that Copro killed Darius. He confessed to us, but who's going to believe it?'

'When Samilius and the Sorcerers come down to investigate, won't they find things? You know, auras and such like?'

'Maybe. Quite probably Old Hasius and Lasat might

find enough here to link Copro to the Avenging Axe and the death of Darius. There's still the matter of this re-making spell, though. If I knew how that was done, life would be easy.'

'Let's take the sword,' suggests Makri.

I reach down, but before I can grasp the hilt it vanishes.

'I guess we weren't worthy.'

I tell the servants that the head of the Civil Guard will be here soon to take care of the crime scene and if they touch anything they'll all be in big trouble. Having no more time to waste, we depart into the cold and make our way back to the Assemblage.

'Do you have any thazis?' asks Makri.

'You need to calm down?'

'No, I just want some.'

We light some sticks as we ride back to the Royal Hall.

'Lisutaris has better thazis,' says Makri.

'Is she planning on cutting down when she's Chief Sorcerer?'

Makri doesn't think so.

'She did say she might be able to get some excellent plants imported from the south once she had better contacts in the Guild.'

'You're far too keen on thazis these days, Makri. And dwa. You used to be a pain in the butt when you were studying and working all the time, but at least you got things done. What happened to you?'

'I got sad about See-ath,' she says.

'Any chance of cheering up?'

'I'm feeling a bit better after the fight.'

CHAPTER
TWENTY

Though the main room at the Royal Hall is crowded with Sorcerers awaiting the confirmation, there is little sign of celebration. Fatigue has set in, and dismay at the death of Sunstorm Ramius has sobered them up. Losing one Sorcerer was bad enough, but the death of a second makes this the most unfortunate Assemblage since the infamous episode in Samsarina twenty years ago when three drunken apprentices burned down a tavern in a dispute over a game of cards, killing themselves in the process.

They huddle in their delegations, discussing the various rumours that circulate through the building. As Lisutaris is about to become the new head of the Guild, few Sorcerers want to come right out and accuse her of killing Sunstorm Ramius. That might be a very bad career move. But there are plenty of whispered comments, and much talk about foul tactics by the Turanians.

My report to Cicerius and Direeva is brief and to the point.

'Copro the beautician turned out to be Rosin-kar, one-time apprentice to Darius Cloud Walker and now secretly transformed into a powerful Sorcerer. He's dead in his villa. If Praetor Samilius gets some of his people down there quickly enough they can probably find evidence linking him to the murder of Darius. As for Ramius, I'm nowhere, and since his body was hauled out of the magic space the Sorcerers are starting to talk. I still think that Covinius was the most probable killer, but I don't have any proof.'

'We have proof,' says Cicerius.

I'm stunned.

'What do you mean, you have proof?'

'A witness saw Covinius emerge from the magic space.'

'What witness?'

'A man called Direxan, who's here with the Matteshan delegation. Not a Sorcerer, he's Matteshan Tribune.'

I don't understand this at all. Cicerius explains that Direxan was minding his own business outside the Royal Hall when a green portal of light suddenly opened and the notorious Covinius appeared. He dropped a knife, and disappeared into the snow. The knife had a fragment of cloth on it, which has been matched with Ramius's cloak.

'Is this true?' I demand.

'Absolutely. Direxan has already made a sworn statement in front of Kalius and Lasat, Axe of Gold. It will shortly be announced to the Assemblage that the notorious Assassin Covinius was the killer of Sunstorm Ramius. Lisutaris is in the clear.'

'But how did this Direxan identify Covinius? No one knows what he looks like.'

'Direxan does. He was present three years ago when Covinius assassinated his superior, the Deputy Consul of Mattesh.'

'It's extremely fortunate that such a good witness was available,' adds Tilupasis.

'More than fortunate,' I say.

'Presumably it was an internal affair involving Simnian politics,' says Cicerius. 'It was my opinion all along, you will recall, that we did not have to worry about Covinius. Our concern is Lisutaris, who is now close to triumph. Have we enough evidence to now clear her name with regard to Darius?'

'No.'

'Why did you kill Copro before gaining such evidence?'

'He attacked me with a vicious magical sword.'

'You must find evidence. The confirmation is in one hour.'

Two apprentices knock and enter, with Charius the Wise in their wake. He regards Cicerius and Tilupasis with cold anger and struggles to control his manners.

'Are you still planning to have Lisutaris put forward as head of the Guild?'

'Certainly,' says Cicerius, in his friendliest manner. 'After all, she won the test.'

Charius's long moustache sways slightly as he draws himself to his full height to stare down at the Deputy Consul.

'I am well aware of the tactics employed by Turai to gain this post. In my twenty years as master of the final test, I have never witnessed such a shameless display of illegal behaviour by any nation. You have used every underhand means at your disposal to unfairly influence the outcome of the election.'

Cicerius and Tilupasis, being politicians, are taking

this calmly enough, but I can't resist butting in. After all, it was me that had to struggle round the magic space in a snowstorm.

'Come on, Charius. Are you trying to say that other nations weren't doing exactly the same? And as for that final test, whose novel idea was it to set some mathematical problem? Lisutaris could have beaten Ramius in any test of sorcery. Smart idea, setting a problem she couldn't do, then sending in a Simnian mathematician. Whoever thought that up was sharp as an Elf's ear.'

Charius looks like he'd like to say a lot more on the subject of Turai's infamous behaviour.

'You went too far with murder, Deputy Consul. You may have cleared Lisutaris of the death of Ramius – though I am not the only one with doubts about the veracity of your witness – but she still stands accused of killing Darius Cloud Walker. I will not allow her to be confirmed. Unless she immediately withdraws I will expose her to the Assemblage. The pictures of her stabbing Darius will be made available to all.'

'It's a fake reality,' I say.

'There is no spell for faking such a reality,' retorts Charius the Wise, then sweeps out, his dark rainbow cloak trailing behind him.

'If there was, you wouldn't tell me about it,' I mutter.

Kalius walks in briskly, his scribe and assistant behind him.

'Is Lisutaris ready to leave?'

'She is being prepared,' replies Cicerius. 'Though we are still hoping to avoid that eventuality.'

Once again I'm obliged to muscle into the conversation.

'Leave? Leave for where?'

'Lisutaris must go into exile immediately,' says the Consul. 'There is no other option. Once Charius denounces her to the Sorcerers Assemblage there is no telling what may happen.'

'At least this way she may yet become head of the Guild,' adds Cicerius. 'If we can find evidence to clear her, she may be able to return some time in the future.'

Poor woman. She loses her favourite hairdresser then gets sent into exile, all in the same day. I curse myself. I've failed my client. No one rushes to reassure me that I did my best. When you fail a client, you just fail.

'Can't you buy us any more time?'

They can't. Even Tilupasis has come to the end of her resources. Time has now run out. We've failed. Damn it.

In the Room of Saints, Makri is sitting on her own in a corner. She's heard the news.

'It's not fair. She didn't kill Darius.'

'I know.'

Makri wonders if Lisutaris gets to be head of the Guild.

'I think that's a moot point. She won't be confirmed in the post. But I don't think the Sorcerers' rules allow them to elect anyone else till she's dead.'

'From what I've seen of Sorcerers' politics, that might not be too long,' says Makri.

It's true. If Turai's enemies in the Guild decide that they want a clear run at electing a new leader, Lisutaris will be vulnerable to attack in exile. We fall silent. There's around thirty minutes to the confirmation, an event which is not now going to happen. Sorcerers drift in and out. From their ugly mood I'd say that Charius was already showing the pictures of Lisutaris wielding the knife. I drink a beer, and another, and another.

'I like Lisutaris,' says Makri, bleakly.

I drink more beer. It's been a strange couple of weeks. Started off looking for a dragon-scale thief and finished off in the Maze of Acro. In between there was a lot of drinking and two murdered Sorcerers. Most of the time I've been cold as the ice queen's grave and at the end of it I've accomplished nothing. I should stick to simple cases, like tailing ex-actresses for their suspicious husbands. I wonder how that couple are getting on now. Strange that I first encountered Copro giving the wife beauty treatment when he called at her house.

'Very strange really,' I say out loud.

Makri looks up from her beer.

'What's strange?'

'Copro. Visiting that actress. The one I was watching. He was giving her beauty treatment.'

'So?'

'So Copro was booked up with Senators' wives, Princesses, Lisutaris and her like. Why did he visit a merchant's wife? They were rich, but his other clients were richer. You might have thought it beneath him to take on the wife of a merchant as a client.'

Dragon scales went through that house. It was on the list. I presumed they were for purposes of decoration. Maybe there was more to it. I haul myself to my feet and shake my head to clear it.

'Makri. Go outside and find some fast horses. Steal them if necessary.'

I hurry into the main hall and burst into Cicerius's

private room. I need documents and I need them fast. Minutes later I'm running through the hall and out into the entrance, where Almalas is still lecturing apprentices on the right way for a Sorcerer to conduct himself. Makri has two horses ready. Their owners aren't happy about it but Makri holds them off with the point of her sword.

'Official government business,' I cry. 'You will be fully compensated.'

I leap into the saddle and we set off through the driving snow.

CHAPTER
TWENTY-ONE

I arrive back at the Assemblage with a very tired horse and an unwilling companion. There I find that Lisutaris is refusing to leave the city.

'Why should I? I didn't kill anyone.'

'Even if you didn't, Charius can prove that you did. The authorities will have no choice but to put you on trial if you stay.'

'What do you mean, authorities?' demands Lisutaris, facing right up to the Consul. 'You're the authorities. And I'm head of the Sorcerers Guild. No one is running me out of Turai.'

I've arrived back at the Assemblage with Habali, wife of Rixad, the woman I spent so much uncomfortable time watching in the freezing cold. Though I have important news I'm having trouble getting a word in. Faced with an uncomfortable exile, Lisutaris is mad as a mad dragon.

'You expect me to just set off through the winter and find a new place to live?'

'We will provide you with funds,' says Cicerius.

'And work towards your eventual recall,' adds Kalius.

'It's for the good of the city,' says Tilupasis. 'And your own. No one benefits if the Sorcerers Guild produces their pictures and demands you stand trial.'

'I'm getting sick of those pictures,' says Lisutaris, her voice rising. 'How about if I just blast anyone that tries to show them again? If anyone tries to chase me out of Turai I'll be down on them like a bad spell and that's that.'

Hardly rational, but Lisutaris is angrier than I've ever seen her. She should take up thazis. Might calm her down.

'If I could make a suggestion,' I say, barging my way forward through the assorted assistants and guards who ring the room. Since I became Tribune, it's proved a lot easier to get places. A few weeks ago I'd have been about as welcome as an Orc at an Elvish wedding at a meeting of the Consul, Deputy Consul and head of the Civil Guard. Now they're almost pleased to see me, even though I'm aware I smell of beer. I wouldn't normally notice, but it clashes with Lisutaris's perfume.

Beside me Habali is nervous. When I persuaded – or threatened – her to accompany me, she wasn't expecting to have to face a roomful of arguing politicians. Before I can speak further the room starts filling up with Sorcerers.

'Didn't I say there were to be no interruptions?' snaps Cicerius.

'I insisted,' retorts Charius the Wise. Filing in behind him is a large delegation. He's brought the Chief Sorcerer from each country with him. Even Princess Direeva is here, her shoulder heavily bandaged.

'It's time,' says Charius.

Cicerius looks helplessly at Kalius. Kalius looks helplessly at Tilupasis.

'We require a little longer,' says Tilupasis. She's still

unruffled, but it's a hopeless task. Charius isn't going to wait any longer. Beside Charius, Lasat, Axe of Gold, is looking on with grim satisfaction. He may have been blackmailed into silence but he's not going to be sorry to see the Turanian disgraced.

'It's time—' repeats Charius.

'—for some explanations,' I say, using my weight to break through the throng.

'Explanations?'

'About the remaking of reality.'

A general groan issues from the Sorcerers present, all of whom know of my fruitless search for such a spell. I must have approached every delegation, and everyone has told me to forget it.

'I take it you've all now seen the pictures of Lisutaris, Mistress of the Sky, killing Darius Cloud Walker. And you've probably all heard my theory that someone erased what really happened. And just about all of you have told me there's no way a Sorcerer could make some phony pictures to replace it—'

Charius the Wise interrupts me.

'Must we listen to this man? He is already known to us as one of the principal troublemakers at the Assemblage. I insist that Lisutaris, Mistress of the Sky, is arrested immediately.'

Strong sounds of approval come from all round the room. I'm losing my audience. I hold up my hand.

'You can insist all you want, Charius the Wise. But in Turai, no citizen can be arrested on a capital charge without the approval of the Tribunes. And I, Tribune Thraxas, withhold my approval until you hear me out.'

This sounds impressive. It isn't true, but it silences the room. I thrust Habali forward.

'You've all seen Lisutaris stabbing Darius. You say no spell could create the illusion. And you're right. There is no remaking spell. The pictures as conjured by Old Hasius are entirely accurate. A woman did walk into the Avenging Axe and stab Darius. But it wasn't Lisutaris. It was Habali, dressed to resemble her. Meet Habali, once one of Turai's most promising actresses.'

My revelation is met by silence and a lot of puzzled looks.

'An actress? Impossible!' says someone, eventually.

'Not impossible at all. That room was dark. The only light came from the fire. In a wig and wearing the proper clothes, Habali was good enough to fool anyone. It fooled all of you. And me, which is more impressive, because I make my living by not being fooled. For all the world it looked as though Lisutaris murdered Darius, but she didn't. She wasn't in the room at the time. Copro entered my office and killed him, then used his sorcery to erase all trace of events. Then he sent Habali in dressed as Lisutaris and she pretended to stab Darius with one of those fake knives they use in the theatre with a retracting blade. All the time he was already dead.'

I turn to Habali.

'Isn't it so?'

For a moment I think Habali is going to let me down. Not surprisingly, she's not keen on confessing to conniving in a murder in the presence of these people. However, she is already carrying a written pardon signed and sealed by Cicerius and a promise of enough gold to leave the city and set up in another state where she won't be bothered by her tiresome husband. All in all, it's not a bad deal from her point of view.

'It's true,' she says. 'I did it. Copro paid me. I impersonated Lisutaris to make the illusion. I also helped in the first part of the plan. He obtained the dragon scales he needed for the erasure from me.'

The controversy that follows is long and loud. Figuring I've done my part, I mostly stay out of it. Using the authority of the Tribunate, I send an assistant off to the Room of Saints to bring me beer while the Sorcerers once more conjure up the pictures of the murder.

'Look,' says Habali. 'I'm wearing the same earrings I have on now.'

'But you look so much like Lisutaris.'

'That's because Copro styled my wig and did my make-up.'

'He was such a great beautician,' sighs Tirini Snake Smiter, making her only contribution to the debate. The arguments continue. I take a seat. Makri sits down beside me.

'I think that was a good piece of investigative work,' she says.

'Thank you.'

'It sounds like we're winning the argument. Of course, I deserve a lot of the credit.'

'You do?'

'Certainly. You'd never have got the answer to the final test. Do you want to know how I did it?'

I pretend to be interested. Makri launches into an explanation.

'The sequence was 391, 551, 713. I wasted some

time trying to see if the difference between each pair of numbers was significant, but it didn't seem to be. Then I thought about prime numbers.'

'What's a prime number?'

'It doesn't divide by anything except itself and one. Three is a prime number, for instance, or seven. So I broke each of the numbers into their factors. It took a while but eventually I found that 391 was 17 times 23. Five five one was the product of 19 and 29. Of course by then it was becoming clear. The third number, 713, turned out to be 23 times 31, which I knew it would. So by then anyone could see that the answer to the test, the next number in the sequence, would be 1073, which is the product of 29 and 37. Do you want me to write out the sequence of prime numbers to make it clearer?'

'No, you've explained it all very clearly already. It was brilliant of you to find the answer.'

Makri sips her beer.

'Easy really, but I was under a lot of pressure. Time was limited, the magic space was misbehaving and there were Assassins and unicorns wandering about.'

I haven't understood a word Makri has said. I congratulate her again on a fine piece of work anyway.

'Make sure you tell Cicerius to remember that when I need his help getting in to the university.'

'You're still going?'

'Of course I'm still going. Why wouldn't I?'

'I thought you might be taking up a career as a useless drug user instead.'

'Stop bringing that up,' says Makri. 'I was sad about See-ath.'

I get a final boost for the magic warm cloak from Irith and let Makri wear it on the way home. She does deserve some reward.

CHAPTER
TWENTY-TWO

T hree days later I'm sitting comfortably in front of the fire at the Avenging Axe. It's early evening and the tavern is not yet crowded. I'm moderately satisfied. Lisutaris, Mistress of the Sky, is now head of the Sorcerers Guild and I have been well paid for my efforts on her behalf.

'Fine efforts, though I say it myself.'

'Many times,' says Makri.

Makri is taking a break before the evening rush. Since the end of the Assemblage she's been in a fairly benevolent mood. She struggles to manage on the money she gets at the Avenging Axe, so payment for her duties as bodyguard will make her life easier for a while.

'I got paid for fighting. Like being a gladiator really. Except when I was a gladiator I didn't get my hair done. Well, I did, in fact, but that Orc woman wasn't really up to the job. A shame about Copro.'

'I understand our female aristocracy is devastated.'

'Tirini Snake Smiter has sent to Pargada for their best man.'

'Why would she do that?' I ask. 'Doesn't everyone say she's already the most beautiful Sorcerer in the world?'

'So?'

'So why does she need an expert beautician?'

Makri looks at me.

'I doubt you'd understand even if I explained it to you.'

She frowns.

'Now I'll be an outcast. Which is unfair. I had to kill Copro.'

'Don't worry about it, Makri. You were already an outcast.'

Makri has cleaned her armour and carefully stored it away. Back at work and needing to earn tips, she's reverted to the chainmail bikini. The firelight glints on her skin. Sailors and workmen are pleased enough at the sight to hand over a little extra.

My winnings on the election were very modest. I picked up a little on Lisutaris, but I was so busy I missed out on the opportunity to increase them.

'I hate to miss out on a bet. I'd have got more down if Honest Mox's son hadn't gone and killed himself with dwa.'

Minarixa the baker. Mox's son. And young Tribune Visus. The city's going to hell.

'Don't involve me in any gambling,' states Makri. 'I'm saving my money. I have fees to pay when the Guild College opens. I need to get back to studying. I'm way behind with rhetoric. Four days on the water pipe and I forgot all the best-known speeches from last century.'

I refrain from commenting.

'I'm still puzzled by the witness,' says Makri.

'What witness?'

'Direxan. The Matteshan who saw Covinius emerge from the magic space after killing Ramius. You said no one had ever seen Covinius.'

I sip my beer. Gurd really knows how to serve his beer. And Tanrose really knows how to cook a venison pie. They should get together. They'd be the ideal couple.

'It was all arranged, I imagine.'

'Who by?'

'Cicerius. Or more probably Tilupasis and her boyfriend the Consul.'

'You're losing me here.'

'Covinius was hired to kill Sunstorm Ramius. Turai hired him. I wasn't meant to know about him. I wouldn't have if Hanama hadn't accidentally learned about it.'

'You mean this city actually hired an Assassin to kill Lisutaris's main opponent?'

'So I believe. No wonder Cicerius kept telling me to ignore Covinius. He knew all along he wasn't a danger to Lisutaris.'

Simnia hired Copro. Turai hired Covinius. It was hard to sort it out. I wasn't really meant to. Makri muses on this for a while.

'Doesn't Cicerius make a big thing about being the most honest politician in Turai?'

'He does. And he's right, mostly. He never takes bribes and he never allows the prosecution of opponents on trumped-up charges. When it comes to foreign policy I suppose he has to be pragmatic.'

I drink my beer, and try and calculate the cost of winning the position of head of the Guild. Two murders, several accidental deaths, and gold and dwa beyond count.

'An expensive victory. But worth it to the government. Especially as the city's masses will end up paying for it in taxes.'

'Are you still in trouble with Praetor Capatius?'

'No, Cicerius is keeping him off my back provided I don't do any more Tribune-like actions. Which I won't. Anyone looking for help in an eviction can go elsewhere.'

Senator Lodius sent me a payment for my services. I still don't like Lodius. I kept the payment.

'Am I still in trouble with the Brotherhood?'

I shake my head. The Traditionals have influence with the Brotherhood and Cicerius has smoothed that one out for us as well.

'Great,' says Makri. 'Everything worked out well.'

Lisutaris has been confirmed as head of the Guild. The foreign Sorcerers are already leaving the city. In a week they'll all be gone, apart from those few still receiving treatment by the city's doctors after the excesses of the Assemblage.

'How is Sareepa Lightning-Strikes-the-Mountain?' asks Makri.

'Still sick. One of the worst cases of alcoholic poisoning the apothecaries have ever had to deal with, apparently. She'll thank me in the end.'

As the tavern begins to fill, Makri returns to work. I spend the evening drinking beer, and playing a game of rak with Captain Rallee and a few others.

'Damned Sorcerers,' says Rallee. 'You know they were all immune to prosecution for dwa? City's going to hell.'

Captain Rallee is in a foul temper due to being out on patrol on one of the coldest nights of the year. I'm not planning on leaving the comfort of the tavern for the rest of the winter. Now I've been paid, I don't have to. Come the spring, business should pick up. I just did some sterling service for the city and I'm expecting the city to be grateful. Between them, Cicerius and Lisutaris should be able to put a few wealthy clients my way.

It's deep into the night by the time I make it upstairs to my rooms. My office is surprisingly warm. A fine fire is lit and an illuminated staff casts a warm glow over the shabby furnishings. Lisutaris, Mistress of the Sky, Makri and Princess Direeva are all unconscious on the floor. I sigh. Makri's good intentions haven't lasted for long.

Direeva opens her eyes.

'For a woman who doesn't like me, you spend a lot of time in my room.'

Direeva shrugs, drunkenly.

'What really happened in the magic space?' I ask her.

Direeva doesn't look quite so drunk any more.

'You don't get on well with your brother. He controls the army and you control the Sorcerers. Pretty soon the Southern Hills is going to erupt in a civil war. Turai would much rather have an alliance with Lisutaris's friend Princess Direeva than your brother.'

'What are you talking about, Investigator?'

'Was Covinius even in Turai? No one ever saw him, apart from you and a phony witness Tilupasis bribed with gold.'

'Of course Covinius was in Turai. He killed Ramius.'

I look at her.

'Maybe he did. But an intelligent man might think it was you.'

'No one would mistake you for an intelligent man,' says Direeva.

'If Turai paid you to kill Ramius, I wouldn't be

surprised. And I won't be surprised if Turai comes to your aid when you're deposing the King.'

The Princess laughs.

'A foolish theory. Was not Hanama the Turanian Assassin also in the magic space?'

'She was. Protecting her friend Lisutaris, I imagine. She might have killed Ramius. But I think you're a more likely candidate.'

I don't really care one way or the other.

'You expend a lot of effort in your work,' says Direeva.

'Is that a compliment?'

'No. Your work is pointless.'

'It's better than rowing a slave galley.'

I haul Makri to her feet and drag her along the corridor. Restricted space or not, she can entertain her friends in her own room. Direeva takes Lisutaris.

'Poor Copro,' mutters Lisutaris, coming briefly back to consciousness.

'Don't worry. There will be another brilliant young beautician emerging next season. Now you're head of the Guild, you'll be number one client.'

'Sharp as an Elf's ear,' says Lisutaris, but whether she means herself, Copro or me, I'm not sure.

Now my room is clear of intoxicated Sorcerers and barmaids, I have a final beer before going to bed. I wonder how long my term of office as Tribune is supposed to last. However long it is, I'm withdrawing from politics. A man should never get involved with these people. It's far too dangerous.

Orbit titles available by post:

❏ Thraxas	Martin Scott	£5.99
❏ Thraxas and the Warrior Monks	Martin Scott	£5.99
❏ Thraxas at the Races	Martin Scott	£5.99
❏ Thraxas and the Elvish Isles	Martin Scott	£5.99

The prices shown above are correct at time of going to press. However the publishers reserve the right to increase prices on covers from these previously advertised, without further notice.

ORBIT BOOKS

Cash Sales Department, P.O. Box 11, Falmouth, Cornwall, TR10 9EN
Tel: +44 (0) 1326 569777, Fax: +44 (0) 1326 569555
Email: books@barni.avel.co.uk.

POST AND PACKING:

Payments can be made as follows: cheque, postal order (payable to Orbit Books) or by credit cards. Do not send cash or currency.

U.K. Orders under £10	£1.50
U.K. Orders over £10	**FREE OF CHARGE**
E.E.C. & Overseas	25% of order value

Name (Block Letters) _____

Address _____

_____

Post/zip code: _____

❏ Please keep me in touch with future Orbit publications

❏ I enclose my remittance £_____

❏ I wish to pay Visa/Access/Mastercard/Eurocard

Card Expiry Date

